Something—the flashlight—crashed into the side of Patrick's head. He shook it off and bored in again, behind a barrage of short lefts and rights. The big man had his back to a bulkhead, trying to fend off the punishing blows with the jagged wreck of the flash.

The cabin lights came up. Patrick caught a glimpse of pale-faced Gillian standing by the switch. With a crazed bellow, the man hurled himself at Patrick, swinging the stub of the light in a vicious downward arc. Patrick stepped inside it, feeling a burning sensation, like a red-hot wire, across his shoulder. He drove a quick left-right-left just under the man's heart, and followed it up with a savage upward jerk of his knees.

This time he did not miss. His opponent jack-knifed forward, his hands going to his crotch. . . .

DEAD RUN

Tony Gibbs

IVY BOOKS • NEW YORK

For the family:
Elaine, Eric, Bill, and now Michelle

TRAFFIC SEPARATION SCHEME

One-way traffic lanes overprinted on this chart are RECOM-MENDED for use by all vessels traveling between the points involved. They have been designed to aid in the prevention of collisions at the approaches to New York Harbor but are not intended in any way to supersede or alter the applicable Rules of the Road. Separation zones are intended to separate inbound and outbound traffic and to be free of ship traffic. Separation zones should not be used except for crossing purposes. When crossing traffic lanes and separation zones use extreme caution.

The Nantucket to Ambrose Traffic Lane coincides with the route normally followed by westbound traffic, including passenger vessels. The Ambrose to Nantucket Traffic Lane passes 12.8 miles north of the departure point for passenger vessels and other vessels adhering to the North Atlantic Track Line Agreement; this lane is not intended to alter the practice of those vessels.

PRECAUTIONARY AREA

Traffic within the Precautionary Area may consist of vessels making the transition between operating in Ambrose or Sandy Hook Channels and one of the traffic lanes. Mariners are advised to exercise extreme care in navigating within this area. The normal Pilot Cruising Area is outlined.

Norwalk

LONG ISLAND SOUND

Throgs Neck

Hudson River

City Island

Oyster Bay

NEW YORK

East River

LONG ISLAND

JERSEY CITY

Babylon

BROOKLYN

GREAT SOUTH BAY

JAMAICA BAY

Coney Island

Lighted Tower

Fire I. Inlet

Fire Island

STATEN I.

Verrazano Bridge

E Rockaway Inlet

Jones Inlet

(A) GONG DANGER
Explosives Jettisoned

RARITAN BAY

Sandy Hook

LORAN TR.

PRECAUTIONARY AREA

CAUTION DANGER AREA

Cholera Bank

Shrewsbury Rks

Eric Elias

1

❧❧❧

CITY ISLAND
WEDNESDAY, MAY 8
TEN-THIRTY P.M.

Gillian swung the RX-7 off the bridge onto City Island
Avenue, and the knot that had been forming in her
stomach suddenly cinched up tight.

I can't do it. Not tonight. It's just too goddamn much.

But the little car glided down the empty street as if it
knew the way. A momentary reprieve at the first traffic
light; the steering wheel was wet and slippery where her
hands clamped on it. The light turned green, and the RX-
7 moved off, past a bus coming in the other direction. She
slowed approaching the next light, slowed until the car
behind gave an irritated honk, but the light stayed green.
Up ahead, the sign: *TREMAINE'S*, in boldly Gothic print,
flaking here and there. And beneath, in smaller lettering,
Boat Works, nearly obscured by time and weather.

*Maybe the gate's locked. Maybe, for once, they've
locked it.*

Her eyes searched the gloom, and then headlights flickered on, back behind the chain link fence. A sedan lurched
out the yawning gate and slid past her, picking up speed.
Someone working late, she told herself, beating the spring-
time weekend rush that clogged the parking spaces and
strangled the power in the few electrical outlets. She drove
through, turned and braked with a spatter of gravel in her
usual parking space. The car's headlights lit up the huge,
canvas-shrouded shapes that stretched away into the dark,
shapes jammed so tightly that even a person as slight as

1

she had to slip sideways between some of them. *Glory* was way down by the water, out of sight from where she sat. She turned off the ignition, killed the lights.

Come on, get out—you're late already. It's not fair, making Barr wait; Dennis isn't *his* uncle.

She shivered, but it wasn't cold. She knew what would be waiting for her. Uncle Dennis would be in bed, of course—it was two weeks since he had last been able to leave it. His big, semicircular bunk occupied most of what had once been the ladies' cabin aft, smelling of mildew and bilge and sick old man. Dying old man, if you could bear to look at the truth of it.

Her hands had locked on the steering wheel so hard her fingers ached. If she didn't hurry, Uncle Dennis would be unconscious. Barr gave him the pills almost continuously now, to keep the pain at a bearable level, but Uncle Dennis insisted on being coherent when his grandniece came back from work, no matter what it cost him. It was a gallantry that, last year, might have charmed her. Now she just wished desperately that he wouldn't make the effort, especially tonight. Her life was collapsing around her, and Uncle Dennis's fairy-tales couldn't help.

The day had begun badly at Constable's, the sail loft she had spent five years building into a small but profitable operation. Not that she had pretensions as a sailmaker. The Boy—Thomas Constable, her boss and sometime lover—was an authentic genius in his field, but he had been going broke when Gillian, fresh out of college, bounced into his life and turned his business around. For a while, she and The Boy really seemed to have something going, and then he decided to sell out, making Constable Sails just one loft in a chain. Fewer risks, he had told her. A nice, regular flow of business, fueled by national advertising.

National drivel. Her palm slammed the wheel. Boring corporate slime. It wasn't bad enough to be losing something that was her own creation, or mostly her own, but she had to assist at the dismemberment. And on top of it, Uncle Dennis, who had been looking worse and worse over the past summer, came back one day from Sloan-Kettering with death on his face. He had refused to tell her, but she wormed the truth out of Barr. Bone cancer: she still could not say the words aloud, but they hovered in her mind.

He had seemed immortal. Big as a door and strong,

despite the more than seventy years he carried. For two summers, she and Uncle Dennis had been able to sail *Glory*, all sixty-five feet of her, by themselves. It was therapy for her, after her father's death, and she hadn't noticed how much it was taking out of the old man. Then one day Barr materialized, and Uncle Dennis, in one of his patented strokes of impulsiveness, had taken him on as *Glory*'s skipper. She wondered if Barr had imagined, when he accepted the job, that it would wind up like this.

One thing you had to say for Barr: he had stuck. Even when the money ran out and his salary would go unpaid from week to week, he stayed on, silent and unobtrusive. Gillian thought they would lose him when Uncle Dennis, to save *Glory* from his creditors, had sold the boat to her for a derisory sum, but by then Barr was more nurse than captain, and his presence more necessary than ever. Gillian had nerved herself up to beg him to stay, but when he sensed the drift of her request he just said "of course," and that was that.

Now the boat might be going, too. Gillian's teeth gritted at the thought of it. The conversation that afternoon was etched on her memory from the moment she had picked up the phone: "Miss Verdean?" The woman's drawl was pure finishing-school lockjaw, and Gillian felt herself bristle. "One moment please for Mr. Visconti."

Visconti. It rang a muffled bell, but before she could begin to place it, the man himself was on the line, a deep, polished voice, the English just too precise to be natural. No preliminaries, either: "I understand Dennis has sold you *Glory*."

It took her completely aback, as, of course, he had intended. "How . . . ?"

"The Coast Guard. Transfers of documented yachts are on file at the Battery. But I have some bad news for you."

Already she smelled creditor in the air—being around Uncle Dennis gave you a nose for them. "What?" she said, keeping her voice flat.

"I'm afraid I can't let the sale stand. It's a fraud, to avoid Dennis's debts, and Dennis owes me a great deal of money."

"It's a legitimate sale, Mr. Visconti," she replied. "If you have any problems, you'd better talk to our . . . to Mr. Falk's lawyer."

"Winfield Hitchcock, isn't it?" She could hear the patronizing, male amusement in his voice, and it made her boil. "I shall, if you insist. But I think we can settle this more easily, just you and I. And your great-uncle, of course." He paused, and she waited, refusing to be drawn. "Think it over, Miss Verdean. Better still, ask Dennis. Tell him I'll come by tomorrow afternoon—no, evening: you should be present, of course. Seven o'clock, Miss Verdean." And the line was dead.

There was, she supposed, no other way. She would have to ask Uncle Dennis about this Visconti—she was sure he'd mentioned the name; if only she had listened more closely to those interminable anecdotes of his.

And if I'm going to ask him, I'd better press on with it.

Press on with it: the phrase broke her fingers from the steering wheel. She slipped out, locked the driver's side door and picked her way over the gravelly cinders. For the tenth time she reminded herself to bring a flashlight on her next visit. At least she wasn't as clumsy as Barr— it was strange that a man who could move like smoke when he was on a pitching deck couldn't cross a room ashore without knocking something over.

Ahead, down a slot between two powerboats, *Glory* towered alone, propped on her immense keel. It made Gillian's heart stop to look at her, to realize that this work of art belonged to her, though only on paper. But if Uncle Dennis still dominated his boat, Gillian paid the bills, and they were slowly crushing her. It was all very well for him to insist that everything would be all right, that he would get her the money—she had heard it too often, including the stories, when the old man was drunk or, more recently, half doped, about what he called his nest egg. In his day, back in the fifties, Dennis must have been a big-league wheeler dealer, really rich. Now he was lower than broke, but with a new loony project twice a week. Barr, who never commented on his employer, had astonished Gillian one day by remarking that Dennis's finances reminded him of the old line about Viennese politics—desperate but never serious.

Serious enough now. She forced herself forward. The ladder she had left propped against *Glory*'s side was lying in the dirt, and she heaved it up into place, then climbed the fifteen feet to *Glory*'s gunwale. Up on deck she had a clear view over the peaked canvas covers, south across the Sound to where the lights of the Throgs Neck Bridge flashed and glittered, a sight she found intoxicating. She had made the mistake of mentioning its beauty to Barr, one evening when the two of them were sitting on deck and half a bottle of rum had seemed to be thawing him. "Well, it's just a traffic jam," he had said.

She kicked off her shoes and crept aft over the teak deck that she had spent the whole weekend bleaching and oiling—as an excuse for staying out of Uncle Dennis's cabin. The companionway hatch was open, and a faint red light shone up the almost vertical ladder. She would have to speak to Barr about the hatch: Uncle Dennis felt the cold more and more, and the slightest draft was torture for him. But Barr was nowhere to be seen; either he was attending to Uncle Dennis (a pang of guilt) or he had gone forward to his own cabin in the fo'c'sle to drink himself blind again. Not that she could blame him.

At the base of the companionway ladder the red safety light faintly illuminated the high, deep chart table on one side of the passage, but left the shelves of books above in shadow. Across from the table was the closed door of the aft guest cabin, and what looked like a smear of something on the wood. Wet. She wiped her fingertips absently on her jeans. The door to Dennis's cabin was shut, a line of light under it. She paused a moment: no sound—he was probably asleep, then. She felt a surge of relief, followed instantly by another stab of guilt, and opened the door as quietly as she could.

Her own explosive gasp seemed to come from someone else, and for a moment her mind froze and she could take in every detail without emotion. The blood was everywhere—great Rorschach smears on the violently crumpled sheets, spattered arcs on the mahogany bulkheads, a congealing pool on the deck at her feet. Uncle Dennis was on his back, half out of the bed, his pajama jacket ripped open to bare his bony, bloodied chest. One leg was tangled in a fold of blanket, dragging the pajama pants down across his belly. His head was hanging nearly to the deck, and his arms were flung wide, bloody hands clutched in the sheet.

She grabbed him by the shoulders, pulled him up on the bed with a strength she did not know she had. His mouth was open, his eyes closed, and she knew he was dead. Then an eyelid flickered. "Uncle Dennis!" she cried. "What happened?"

His big, gaunt head—hairless, ever since the radiation treatments—rolled slowly back and forth, and he made a gargling noise deep in his throat. She let him go, her sole idea to summon help, but one bloody claw of a hand closed like a vise on her wrist. Slowly his eyes opened, at first seeing nothing and then, with agonized concentration, focusing on her face. The grimace he forced might have been intended for a reassuring smile. His lips moved, but no sound came.

"Please," she said, her voice cracking. "I have to get you a doctor."

He shook his head again. He was trying to say something, and she bent forward. Her eyes dropped to the hand that clutched her wrist: three of his fingernails were gone—had been ripped out. Her head spun, but now she could hear his voice, faint and dreadfully urgent. It sounded like "down sail," but as she bent closer she realized it was "Don't sell her." Over and over: "Don't sell her."

"I won't, Uncle Dennis," she managed. "I promise. Now let—"

He heard her, but he would not be stopped. She propped him with her free arm as he went on, every word a gasp of pain. "I didn't tell them. I saved it for you."

She tried to mumble something, choked on it.

"It'll pay you back," he said, his eyes boring into hers. "Like I always said."

His grasping hand fell away, and she thought he was gone, but he was shaking his head again, as if in irritation. She bent over, heard him say, "Not the first place . . ." He stiffened and his big yellowed eyes opened wide and he gave a liquid cough that brought a rush of thick blood from his gaping mouth. Gillian cried out in anguish.

Behind her, she heard uncertain footsteps in the passageway. She turned, saw Barr, in khakis and a T-shirt, standing in the doorway. He was holding a broken bottle in one big hand. His thin, angular face was blank, but white as paper under the tan. Without a word, Gillian sprang to her feet, knocked him aside and sprinted up the companionway ladder three steps at a time.

2

CITY ISLAND
ELEVEN-THIRTY
P . M .

Surreptitiously, Patrick O'Mara eyed the nude body that lay against his on the opened sofa bed. Bobbie, he decided, had finally slipped over the line, gone from cuddly to just plain fat. She was lying on her side, her head on his chest and her soft breasts and belly damp against his flank. Her breathing was just coming back to normal; in about a minute, as he knew all too well, she would squirm around and look up at him, and say something like "God, that was great, soldier. Let's do it again!" She'd made up the godawful nickname and insisted on it, although—maybe because—she knew he hated it. She used it like a signal, when she wanted more. And she never got enough: Patrick had had her two hours ago, standing up, in the cramped engine room of her father's yacht. And just now. And in a half hour or so he would have to perform again. Bobbie wasn't just predictable, she was insatiable, and he was fiercely bored with her and her demands.

The trouble was, he couldn't see how to get rid of her. His job, as Senator Herman Cardegan's professional skipper, beat hell out of soldiering, the only other work he knew, but there was no way he could keep it without the collateral duty of satisfying the senator's daughter—or at least keeping her from running wild through the bedrooms

7

of Nassau County. Senator Cardegan, owner of one of
Long Island's biggest Cadillac dealerships and a state leg-
islator of great seniority and clout, knew perfectly well
what was going on between his daughter and Patrick, and
had (without actually saying so) let Patrick know he did
not object; it kept Bobbie out of singles' bars and news-
paper columns. Marriage—another marriage—for her was
out of the question; no one man could handle Bobbie's
remarkable needs, and anyway, Patrick knew, only his
own offbeat background had held Bobbie's interest this
long. If he'd been a doctor or a lawyer instead of an ex-
mercenary soldier turned boat driver, she would never
have done more than sample him, the way she sampled
everything male that came along. As it was, she enjoyed
dangling her stud in front of her more uptight friends. If
he looked twice at one of those friends, of course, Bobbie
could be counted on for an explosion that was usually
public and always physical. She had been exciting at first—
as well as thinner. In his twenty-five years he had never
met anyone like her. But after a while even the frequent
and fancy sex couldn't make up for her jealous tantrums.
All Patrick asked of life was to float free—why did women
always want to pin you down?

Bobbie shifted herself against him. He felt her head
move, and looked down. "God, soldier, that was great,"
she said. "Let's—" And was interrupted by the telephone
on a table at the head of the sofa bed.

Patrick jumped. His phone almost never rang, except
when the senator was calling. And the senator never called
when he knew Patrick was with his daughter. Almost gratefully, he reached out and picked up the receiver, as Bobbie
muttered, "Oh, shit."

"Patrick O'Mara," he said.

The voice at the other end came from his blackest night-
mares—from deeper than that, even, since Patrick had
truly never expected to hear it again.

"Good evening, Mister O'Mara," it said, a slight emphasis on the Mister. "Am I interrupting something?"

"No," said Patrick automatically; then: "What do you
want?"

From that other life, the one he had stuffed far down
in his mind and covered up, he heard the braying, high-
pitched laugh. The sweat sprang out on him, though the

air was cold on his skin. "It rather hurt our feelings, the way you left without saying good-bye," said the voice. "But we always stay in touch with our former employees. And with their relatives," it added, after a deliberate pause.

"What do you mean?" Patrick demanded, feeling his stomach turn over.

"Still keeping up with your responsibilities, Mr. O'Mara? Still sending money to—what was the name of that dreary town? Bay Shore, wasn't it? One-twenty Lake Street, as I recall. I do hope they're both well. We do want them to stay well, don't we?"

To come this far, building a new life—and then this. He felt as if the floor had dropped from under his feet. "What do you want?" he asked dully.

"Do you know a man—a colleague of yours, actually— named Jeremy Barr?"

"No."

"A yacht, then. A large, rather elderly yacht, named *Glory*?"

"No." What in hell would they want with a yacht?

"It belongs—belonged until recently to a man named Dennis Falk." The speaker paused, as if unwilling to give more information than necessary. "Barr's her captain. But he's not important, really—just thought you might know him. It's the boat that matters."

"So what do you want me to do?"

"For the moment, you're to get a place in her crew. There'll be a further assignment later."

"Hey, wait a minute . . ."

"Starting immediately. Repeat: immediately."

"But I've got a job," Patrick objected, and felt Bobbie stir next to him. Silence at the other end of the telephone line.

They had him, and they knew it. His next question was surrender: "This yacht. Is she here at City Island? Is she in the water?"

"Right down the street from you, in an establishment called Tremaine's. And not yet afloat."

"What kind of a boat is she?"

"A yacht," said the voice impatiently. "What you Americans call a sailboat. Fairly large—large enough to sail across the Atlantic. And, as I said, quite elderly." Another pause; Patrick could hear the rumble of a second voice in the background. "Yes," said his inquisitor, "forty years at least."

"That's crazy!" Patrick snapped. "I don't know anything about sailboats. And I told you . . ." Bobbie was motionless, rigid, and Patrick caught himself. "It's just crazy, that's all."

"Mister O'Mara"—there was the emphasis on Mister again—"as a family man, though an unmarried one, you must know how fragile small children are . . . how easily things can happen to them." The voice turned silky: "Remember whom you're talking to, O'Mara."

How could he forget? "All right," said Patrick, but he felt a tiny spark of rage in the back of his brain.

"That's better. Now, I shall give you some names to write down."

"Wait one." He pulled himself up and found a pencil and a pad on the telephone table. Bobbie was trying to look over his shoulder, but he no longer cared.

"The yacht's name, as I said, is *Glory*. The captain is Jeremy Barr, spelt the way it sounds. The new owner is named . . . one moment. Yes: Gillian Verdean. V-E-R-D-E-A-N. She's the grandniece of Dennis Falk, the previous owner, and she's only had the yacht for a month or so. A pushy little piece, but not unattractive, if you like hoydens. Perhaps that's your avenue of attack. She might even take to you. Like the one in Entrura, if you recall."

Patrick tried and failed to keep the impotent fury out of his voice. "I remember."

"See that you do. We shall reach you when necessary. Now get down there immediately." There was a click, and the line went dead. Patrick picked up the paper from the small table.

"I've got to go," he said to Bobbie, and got up. He felt light-headed. Dazed.

"Where?" she demanded, her voice rising. "What in hell are you up to?" Heaving herself up from the sofa bed, her body jiggling, she lunged for the paper in Patrick's hand. He fended her off without thinking, and she grappled with him, soft and sweaty. "Bastard!" she snarled. He pushed her away, holding her at arm's length with one hand while he carefully tucked the paper under the telephone. Then he turned to Bobbie and hit her across the face with his open hand. It rocked her head back but, as he had intended, never broke the skin. Slowly, she put her hand to her mouth, inspected it for blood.

"Sorry," he said, after a silent moment. "It was someone I knew, from a long time ago . . ." His voice petered out. Pulling himself together, he began again: "I have to do something, Bobbie. Right now."

She was staring at him in a way she never had before. "By God, you're scared," she said. "I wouldn't have believed it—Patrick O'Mara frightened." There was amazement in her tone, and, he thought, contempt.

"Look," he said. "Just get out of here. Please."

She started to say something, then silently began pulling on her clothes. "Will I see you tomorrow?" she asked.

"No. I don't know," he said. "I'll call you in the morning."

At the door to his apartment, she held her face up for the obligatory kiss. "Be good," she said, as she always did: half farewell, half admonition. "And don't think you're getting rid of me."

He mumbled something—just a noise, not words—and shut the door hastily behind her. He stood with his back to it for a long minute before he realized that he was shivering and sweating at the same time. Blankly, he stared around the small room, neat and bleak as a barracks, except for the rumpled sofa bed. Still numb, he went over, straightened the covers to military precision, folded the bed back into a couch, and replaced the cushions.

That son of a bitch. That black-hearted son of a bitch. He's got my number—he's had it from the beginning.

Without warning, Patrick's overloaded memory took charge, threw him back to the last time he'd heard the voice: a year-and-a-half ago and five thousand miles away. A dusty, dirt-floored shack, lit by an oil lamp on one corner of the scarred desk. Patrick was standing between two other men, and his clothes, like theirs, were gritty and acrid from two days' fighting. In Patrick's memory, even the smell of sweat and kerosene was still sharp. The man behind the desk was thin, immaculate, his battledress neatly creased. He looked up, his tight smile expectant, and a warning light flashed in the back of Patrick's head. "Captain Shaw. Sergeant O'Mara. Sergeant Boeren," the man said thoughtfully, looking them over. The thickly built, blond-headed man at Patrick's side stiffened to attention. "As I recall, Captain Shaw, the order was to stand and hold—no more retreating." The seated man's tone was honeyed, but Shaw, the Rhodesian, took a belligerent half step forward. "Listen, man," he began, "we've been holding your bloody line . . ." His eyes widened as the thin man's hand appeared from beneath the desk, holding a revolver and pointing it at Shaw. "What . . ." the Rhodesian began, his hands in front of him like a shield. The pistol roared and bucked—the noise was deafening in the confined space—and Shaw was flung backward, crashing off the hut's flimsy wall and then sliding to the dirt floor. Rigid, Patrick saw from the corner of his eye the gaping wound just below the Rhodesian's breastbone as his clawing hand fell away. On the packed dirt Shaw's heels had scored two troughs, and in one of them lay his severed thumb, oozing blood. The thin man, still smiling, laid down the pistol. "You gentlemen will split the late Captain Shaw's company," he said. "What's left of it. I trust you'll follow orders more precisely than he did. You may send the sentry in as you leave."

Patrick returned to the present with a shudder. His eye caught the paper under the telephone, and he picked it up. The three names on it were in a straggling, uneven hand completely unlike his normal precise printing.

Setting the paper down cautiously, as if it might burst into flame, he went into the tiny kitchenette. In the cupboard were three bottles—an expensive rye, a cheap brandy and an awful sweet liqueur, orange-flavored chocolate, that was favored by Bobbie after exertion. Patrick took the brandy bottle out, looked at it thoughtfully, and then exchanged it for the whiskey. He poured a triple shot into a wineglass and drank it off in a gulp, like medicine. He rinsed out the glass and set it in the dish drain to dry, then returned to the living room.

He was out of practice for raw whiskey, and it cut a path all the way to his stomach, but in a matter of seconds he felt the unreasoning panic begin to ebb. Dutch courage. A fair name for it, he thought; I'll take any kind I can get. He picked up his khaki trousers from the armchair, where they had been hurled earlier in the evening—for some reason Bobbie always insisted on tearing his clothes off and throwing them around. He guessed that it was supposed to indicate uncontrolled passion, and it never failed to annoy him. He pulled on the trousers, and his wallet fell out of the hip pocket. He retrieved it and, without quite knowing why, flipped it open. Wedged behind the driver's license was a photograph of a six-year-old girl. Not a studio picture, but a grainy black-and-white telephoto shot. She was swaddled in a furry parka, sitting on scrubby grass and looking up at someone who was out of the frame, except for a pair of hands. Woman's hands, with a wedding ring.

Patrick shook himself, and slid the photograph back behind the license. *I should have known. I thought I'd lost them for sure, bugging out like that. That skinny bastard adjutant—he must have been tracking my mail right along. He knew where I'd come back to. Someday . . .*

He forced himself to concentrate on the mess at hand. *The best way to get out of it was to do what they wanted. Get it over with. Yessir, nossir, three bags full, sir.* It was like going up against hostile fire: the only way to do it was to put your head down and go. He marched over to the end table, picked up the piece of paper, smoothed it and looked again at the three names.

I need to scope this out before I jump in. He turned to the small bookshelf that hung on the wall above the even smaller TV set. The idea of reading for fun had never occurred to him, and the few books he owned were strictly professional, bought in the course of studying for the motorboat operator's ticket that hung, in a dime-store frame, over the old-fashioned radiator. The bookshelf held a worn, secondhand copy of Bowditch's *American Practical Navigator*, a new *Chapman's Piloting, Seamanship and Small Boat Handling*, the American Red Cross's first-aid textbook, a much-thumbed text of the U.S. Coast Guard Navigation Rules, a grubby paperback entitled *Marine Diesel Engines*, and—bought at a church bazaar down the street, more out of curiosity than anything else—the 1977 edition of *Lloyd's Register of American Yachts*. He took down the fat red volume and found the Gs.

Glory . . . there were two, one a schooner and the other a ketch. His eye hit on the name of the ketch's owner: Dennis Falk. *Bingo.* He sat down on the edge of the armchair to consider the information before him. The pages of Lloyd's were wider than they were high, and the information about each yacht was compressed into eleven ruled columns across the two-page spread. Even abbreviated, it told a lot. The left-hand column assigned each yacht a reference number. The second listed her present and all previous names, if any, and he saw that at unspecified times in the past, *Glory* had been known as *Titania* and then as *La Pasionaria*.

The third column contained what he had been looking for—data about her hull, rig and sails. Unfamiliar with sailing vessels as he was, Patrick still knew enough to be reasonably sure that "K FD Aux Kch" meant that she was a keel boat with a flush deck instead of a raised cabin, and that in addition to being ketch-rigged she carried an auxiliary engine. Her sails had been made by Ratsey, in the mid-1960s, and totaled some seventeen hundred square feet, a figure that made him whistle under his breath. The following columns gave her Coast Guard documentation number and her radiotelephone call letters. Her gross tonnage was listed at twenty-seven, her net at twenty-five, meaningless figures until he knew her better.

Her physical dimensions, in the adjoining column, were more useful—the kind of tangible information Patrick preferred. Sixty-five feet six inches overall. Fifty feet on the waterline, with a fourteen-foot beam—a narrow vessel, then, compared to modern boats—and a draft of nine-and-a-half feet. That seemed a lot, but he supposed it might be normal for big sailboats. Designer: N.G. Herreshoff. Builder: Herreshoff Mfg. Co. of Bristol, R.I.; date of construction, 1922—more than sixty years old, then. Under the heading "Machinery" was the entry "Gas Eng. 4 Cyc. 4 Cyl. Gray 1946." "Jesus," he muttered, not without reverence. A gasoline power plant of that age would need a magician, not a mechanic. Owner, as of 1977, of course, was Dennis Falk. Port of registry, Bridgeport, Conn., and her home port—where she could presumably be found during the sailing season—South Norwalk, maybe twenty-five miles from where he was sitting.

He put the book back on the shelf, and picked a clean khaki shirt from the row lined up on hangers. As he buttoned it, he caught himself humming "Legion of the Rearguard" under his breath. His mind had made itself up, and the prospect of action—any action—was better than sitting and worrying. He had no idea how he was going to get himself onto *Glory*'s crew, but the first step was to reconnoiter the ground. Whatever happened, he reminded himself, it was for the kid. For Tracy. He wondered what she was doing right now—asleep, probably, in that tiny room in back of the shabby house. He hadn't seen her in three months, and then only from two hundred yards' distance, through binoculars. She was big, like him—not like her weedy stepfather at all. He wondered if she was bright, like her mother. He might never have the chance to find out, but even if he had no part in his daughter's life, he was determined she would never be hurt because of him. Quite calm now, Patrick knew that one of these days he was going to have to kill Major Leslie Giles St. John fucking Bellairs, late of Her Majesty's Scots Guards. But not until Tracy and her mother were safe.

The thought of Bellairs made Patrick look down at his watch. Tremaine's was just up the street, and when Bellairs said immediately, that was what he meant. Patrick slipped his single-cell miniature flashlight into one hip pocket and his Swiss army knife into the other, and shut the door quietly as he left.

He was a block and a half from Tremaine's when he realized that something was going on there. Two police cruisers were nose to nose on the sidewalk outside the gate, with their flashing lights cycling and scraps of radio transmission crackling on the cool night air. A handful of frowzy bystanders huddled in a knot, peering past the patrol cars. A couple of cops were leaning on the hood of one car, ostentatiously ignoring the people who were watching them. Patrick changed direction without breaking stride, into the narrow side street that flanked Tremaine's, and followed it down to the water's edge. The boatyard's chain link fence ran right into the cold, dirty water, but he was able to swing himself around its end without getting wet.

He eased his way past a shrouded hull, staying well back out of the glare of floodlights that lit the draped canvas covers like a stage set. In the open space in front of him someone had set up a bright worklight that illuminated the high side of an uncovered sailboat hull, dirty red from keel to waterline and above it a deep, dusty green that faded up into shadow. A long, decrepit ladder was propped against the hull. Yellow tapes marked off areas of the gravelly ground, and to one side, from behind another hull, the reflection of a red light flickered steadily. Half a dozen men in civilian clothes, wearing badges, stood looking up at the big sailing yacht's hull, their shadows distorted and immense. As Patrick watched, one of them called, "Okay, bring it down slow." From above, a folding metal stretcher began thumping and scraping its way down the side of the hull at the end of a couple of ropes. As the light picked it up, Patrick could make out a large, limp bundle swathed in reddish-brown plastic and strapped into place. After two wars, Patrick had not an instant's doubt what was under the plastic.

A couple of men in rumpled white clambered down the ladder and began to untie the lines that secured the stretcher. Several other figures descended behind them, but only one caught Patrick's eye: She was about five-three, maybe a hundred and ten wringing wet, with short brown hair and a face that might be reasonably good looking when it wasn't gray and haggard. She was wearing a navy-blue sweater as thick and shapeless as a sleeping bag, and blue jeans with dark stains down the right thigh.

For a moment, she stood staring at the stretcher and its bundle, which had sagged to one side during the descent. A middle-aged man in a sport coat came clumsily down the ladder. A badge was pinned to his lapel and his tie was slightly askew. He turned to the young woman. "We're just about done here, Miss Verdean," he said, and then, "Miss Verdean?"

She turned slowly, and Patrick was just as glad he couldn't see her shadowed eyes. "Yes, Lieutenant. I heard you."

"You got a car someplace, right?" the cop said. "You okay to drive? I'd ask Mr. Barr to take you home, but I don't think he's up to it."

Her head snapped around. "That rummy's not taking me anyplace." Uh-oh, thought Patrick. A few sparks left in that one. "I'm surprised you're not hauling him in."

"Arresting him?" the cop asked. He was in his forties, running to fat around the middle. A family man, from the way he looked down at the young woman. "Arrest him for what? For being passed out when your uncle was killed?"

"And you're sure he's innocent?" she demanded. Anger had brought some color back into her face, but Patrick sensed she was running with the needle on empty.

"We're a ways away from being sure about anything," the cop said. He was humoring her, but his tone told Patrick he was not about to be pushed around by young women.

A thin, bony-faced man with tousled, straw-colored hair came out of the shadows behind Gillian Verdean. His T-shirt was stippled with ugly brownish stains and his khaki pants had been slept in. He held a rumpled sheet of paper in his left hand. He paused just long enough to hear Gillian say: "Well, maybe you won't arrest him, but you can't stop me from firing him. As of now, Jeremy Barr doesn't work here anymore."

The cop, looking past the girl at the thin man, said, "Maybe you better tell him yourself."

"I got it the first time," the man said. His voice, quiet and detached, matched his appearance.

Gillian had turned quickly. Even from where he stood, Patrick could feel her willing self-control. "I'll say it again, Barr. You're through. You can stay the night, but I want you off *Glory* in the morning." She turned to the cop. "If that's all right with you, Lieutenant."

He shrugged. "Just so I know where everybody is. You're going home now, Miss? Back to Connecticut?"

"I guess so. Yes," she said. Then she softened. "Is there anything more I need . . ."

"Call me in the morning," the cop said, handing her a card. "Try and get some sleep."

Her eyes were suddenly very bright. Her voice wavered slightly. "Thank you. I . . ." She shook her head, unable to continue, and turned on her heel.

The cop turned to Barr, who said, "Here's that list of drugs you wanted. As much as I could remember." Not waiting to hear more, Patrick dropped back into the shadows. Moving as silently as he could over the gritty surface, he ghosted around two boat hulls until he saw the young woman standing by the side of a not-quite-new fire engine-red sports car. She was holding a key ring, and it glinted as her hand trembled. After a moment she put it back in her purse. "I need a drink," she said unsteadily, and looked around to see if anyone had heard her. The only people in sight, however, were a couple of bored ambulance attendants. Closing the purse, she jammed it under her arm, squared her shoulders, and strode off through the gate.

The cops were still there, and Patrick slipped quickly back to the fence. Once around its end, he sprinted up the side street to City Island Avenue, just in time to see Gillian step into the Running Light, a neighborhood bar where Patrick had spent more than one evening hiding from Bobbie. The place was a tourist hangout on weekends, jammed wall to wall with flushed, loud-talking New York City sailors who came there for the pitchers of beer and cheap, ice-cold red wine. Late on a weeknight, though, the only occupants were a dozen or so sullenly stewed boatyard workers, most of whom had obviously been there for hours. Against the reality of paint-splotched coveralls and out-of-focus television, the decor of fiber glass figureheads and plastic harpoons looked even more fake than usual.

Those customers still capable of turning without falling off their barstools were watching Gillian with interest. She was saying something to McDonough, the bartender—a sour, fat woman-hater from Galway who was shaking his head at her. Patrick eased up to the bar in time to hear her say, "If you can't do a sandwich, for God's sake give me some peanuts or potato chips or something."

McDonough opened his mouth to speak, gloomy righteousness on his flat, broken-veined face, when Patrick slid in beside Gillian and said, "Jesus, Charlie, a ham sandwich won't break your back." Her attention was fixed on the bartender, and she started as if Patrick had pinched her. Her face was barely level with his shoulder, and she looked up at him warily, her brown eyes tired and angry.

The bartender's mouth worked, wanting to say no, but Patrick was a good customer—a drinker whose company other drinkers enjoyed. At last McDonough spoke, as if to himself: "I guess I could do a sandwich. Only ham on white, though."

"Ham on white's fine," Gillian said, forcing a smile.

McDonough would not smile back, but at least he was looking at her. "Mustard and lettuce?" he said.

"Both, please," she said.

"Coming up," he replied. "Something for you, Patrick?"

"I'll have a beer with the lady. And with you, too, Charlie." McDonough, mollified, swung away to the dented refrigerator at the end of the bar, and Patrick risked a quick wink at Gillian, who had turned to size him up. For several moments she looked at him without blinking, until he said "Pass inspection?" and smiled down at her.

She smiled back, barely forcing it this time. She had one of those faces that lit up when she smiled. "I didn't mean to stare," she said. "It's been a hell of a day."

"No fear," he said. McDonough arrived with a pair of beers and one, slightly larger, for himself. Patrick picked one of them up and raised it to her and then to Charlie. "*Slainte*," he said.

She took a long, long swallow that ended in a choked gulp. Setting the glass down, she looked back at Patrick. "You're Irish?"

"With a face like mine, you have to ask?" he replied. "Patrick O'Mara. Not Pat, and never Paddy. Patrick." He put his hand out, as to a man, and she took it. Her hand was small enough to disappear in his grasp, but callused, with broken nails like a laborer's.

"My name's Gillian Verdean," she said. "You're not in the army, are you? The uniform threw me for a moment."

He glanced down at his knife-edge khakis and gleaming shoes. "I was, once," he said. "But not any more. I'm a skipper. A captain, if you please."

Charlie returned with the sandwich and set it down in front of her. It was huge, the thickness of a double-decker, and she rewarded him with a brilliant smile. To Patrick's surprise, he seemed to thaw slightly. "I hope it's okay," he said. "I didn't know you were a friend of Patrick's."

"Looks great," she said. "Thanks." And to Patrick: "You come here a lot, then."

"It passes an evening. I have a room down the Avenue—when I'm not aboard, that is."

"Do you suppose we could sit at one of the tables?" she asked. "I'm feeling a little wobbly."

She did look paler than when she'd come in. He took her plate in one hand and her elbow in the other, pulled a chair out with his foot. "Here."

She sank into the hard seat with a grateful sigh. He put her beer in front of her, and turned back to the bar. "I think we might have a couple more, Charlie."

When he turned to sit down, she was watching him intently. "What kind of boat?" she asked, through a mouthful of sandwich.

"Sixty-five-foot Pace," he said; then, seeing her blank look, added, "a powerboat."

"Oh."

"What's 'oh'?"

"I was just thinking," she said. "If you'd said a ketch or a schooner, it would've started a conversation. But when you said a powerboat, that killed it."

He laughed aloud, and her lips twitched in response. "Sailboat people," he said. "You can always tell them."

"But you can't tell us much," she agreed.

She seemed composed enough now, but shock was a tricky thing. She might go on like this for hours, or fall apart any minute. Patrick decided to push it, felt a surprising reluctance as he spoke: "That looks like blood on your jeans. You been in an accident?"

Her eyes widened, and he knew instantly he had taken her to the edge of her self-control. She shook her head. "My uncle," she began. She took a deep breath and tried again, speaking fast and precisely. "My uncle was killed tonight. Murdered. Just up the street, at Tremaine's. On his boat. I found him."

He held her reddened eyes with his. "Tell me."

"Somebody . . . They cut him. I've never seen anything like that." Her shoulders heaved, and she plunged her face in her hands.

"Hey, baby," said a harsh voice from the bar, "if O'Mara can't show you a good time, why don't you let us try?"

Patrick's chair shot back. In two steps he was facing the speaker, a solidly built bearded man in filthy coveralls. The man's guffaw had crinkled his paint-spattered face until his bloodshot eyes were slits—slits that abruptly widened as the barstool was kicked from under him. He was halfway down, clutching at the bar with one hand, when Patrick stepped inside his flailing free arm and drove a right like a piston into his belly, six inches under the ribcage. The heavyset man's wind went out of him with a noise somewhere between a grunt and a whoop, and he slid the rest of the way to the floor, where he lay doubled up in a pool of beer, wheezing in agony. The men on either

side of him were on their feet, but one look at Patrick's
face brought them up short. "I think," said Patrick softly,
"it's time for your friend to go home. I'll take care of his
tab—and yours, if you'll help him get there."

One of the men, whose mouth was open, shut it like a
trap. The other shrugged: "'S not my fight. Gimme a hand,
Paulie."

Patrick laid a twenty on the bar and McDonough, who
had been hovering a few feet back, stepped forward to
scoop it up. Patrick turned back to Gillian. Her face was
wet, but she had stopped crying and was looking at him
with surprise and interest. "Sorry," he said. "Best thing
with a clown like that is to cut him off quick."

"Quick?" Her eyes were wide. "I didn't even see you
hit him. You did hit him, didn't you?"

"Well, he mostly lost his balance," Patrick replied, part
of his attention on the three men lurching toward the door.

"Baloney," she said. "Say, were you ever a prizefighter?"

"In the service, a little." He gave her a grin—what Bobbie called his number-one ladykiller—and went on: "I
don't have enough brains that I can afford to scramble half
of them. Besides, boats are what I grew up with."

She responded to the grin, but a thought's shadow
crossed her face. "A powerboat skipper," she mused
aloud. "You don't happen to know any good sailboat skip-
pers who might be looking for a job . . ."

He nearly went for the opening, but realized he could
spoil everything by moving too quickly. Besides, there
might be a better, surer way. "Sorry," he said, "I don't
know any sailboat people at all. Except you."

Her smile faded, and beads of sweat suddenly appeared
across her hairline. She saw him looking at her hands. "I
can't stop them shaking," she said. "I don't know what it
is."

"Just shock," he replied, quiet and matter-of-fact. "You
feel cold?"

She nodded carefully, as if afraid her head might fall
off. "So why am I sweating?" Her eyes were angry. "God
damn it, anyway," she cried.

Patrick pulled a ten from his wallet and laid it on the
table. "Come on," he said.

"Where?" She allowed him to help her to her feet. She

was shivering all over. "Where are you taking me, Patrick?"

"Don't worry," he murmured. "It's all right. I know what to do." As he eased her toward the door, he could tell it was his tone she was responding to, not the words.

Outside, the chill spring air almost leveled her. "Oh, Christ," she gasped. "This never happened to me before."

He scooped her up easily, feeling the slender, sinewy young body shuddering uncontrollably in his arms. By the time they reached his door she was sobbing quietly, hopelessly, her face buried in his chest.

3

❧❧❧❧❧❧

CITY ISLAND
MIDNIGHT

Barr sat chainsmoking Camels, his legs dangling over *Glory*'s gunwale. His head was throbbing, and even the cigarettes could not blanket the birdcage taste in his mouth. The cops had gone at last, and the ambulance. The yellow plastic tape they had strung around the area was gone, too. The gravel far below him was still wet where he had dumped the buckets of water with which he had sluiced the horror from *Glory*'s after cabin. The police had taken the bedding, and he hoped never to see it again.

"Damn," he said, under his breath. At least the cops seemed to believe him, though he was not sure Gillian did. He had tried to force his memory of the early evening, but close to an hour of it remained obstinately blank. Dennis had been in more pain than usual, obviously worried about something, but not worried enough to confide in Barr. Three of the big brown pills had barely slowed the old man down, though every time he changed position a moan of torment escaped him. Barr had washed him as gently as he could, and they had not had to go through the ritual of the bedpan—Dennis was barely eating at all, and Barr was guiltily grateful.

Gillian had been late, which was unlike her. When the old man at last slid reluctantly into a muttering, groaning semiconsciousness, Barr retreated forward to his quarters in the austerely empty triangle of the fo'c'sle. The first bottle, with about three fingers of Mount Gay in it, had

23

gone in a single, breathless swallow. He should have stopped there, knowing that when he broke the seal on the second fifth he would drink himself straight into what passed for sleep these days—into the same inescapable nightmare: He was coming on deck for the dogwatch, as *Windhover* bashed her way through the warm Caribbean. Finding Ann and the two others in a single tangled embrace, and then the awful, rending crash as the yacht—his life—impaled itself on Horse Shoe Reef. The dream never changed. Why should it? Everything in it was the literal truth.

This time, though, the dream had been different; desperate cries of pain, someone calling his name, over the solid crash of the seas and the tearing of wood. Had it been Dennis, calling for help? He shivered and threw the cigarette down into the blackness, heard it hiss out on the wet ground.

The fact of Dennis's death was beginning to break through. It was hard to accept, though Barr had prayed for it over the past weeks, as the cancer ate into Dennis's bones. Still, the old man had had so much life in him; it was hard to believe he was gone.

Barr found himself recalling the breezy April day a little more than a year before, when he had met Dennis Falk, and had first seen *Glory*. He had only been back from the Caribbean a few weeks, and was still dazed from the cataclysm that had laid his life in ruins. He was standing at the office window of Carey & Willard, the East Norwalk boatyard, when he saw the big ketch slipping into the anchorage under working sail. Mrs. Mulvey, Carey & Willard's bookkeeper and resident oracle, was standing beside him. "*Glory*," she said, not waiting for Barr's question. "Mr. Falk's old Herreshoff. He must've had her forty years, and she wasn't new when he bought her. She comes in every spring for hull work, and takes an outside mooring for the summer. Wasn't she around when you worked here before, Jeremy? When was that, anyway—seventy-two?"

"Seventy-three, Mrs. M. I was just out of the service."

"Well then, I guess Mr. Falk must have started coming here after you moved down to Florida. Seventy-five, seventy-six—like that."

"I guess," Barr replied absently, his attention on *Glory* as she short-tacked her way neatly among the early-spring speckling of vacant mooring buoys. Long and low—she'd be a wet boat—and fast; she was transparently a thoroughbred, a classic beauty that made him, boatless as he was, ache just to watch her move. She rounded up in a clear patch of water, and her staysail and main fluttered down together. Only two crew were on deck: a boy forward, muzzling the staysail, and the skipper, a bulky man who carried himself in an oddly awkward way as he stood at the wheel, behind the luffing mizzen. The maneuver was not badly done, Barr reflected, as the boy—or could it be a girl?—finished with the jib and darted aft to guide the massive main boom into its crutch and furl the heavy sail. That done, the slim figure moved back to the cockpit, and across the water Barr heard a high, clear laugh. So it was a girl. A puff of oily smoke emerged from under the starboard quarter, followed a half second later by a wheezing mechanical cough.

"Maybe this year he'll replace that engine," said Mrs. Mulvey. "Every year he says he's going to." It sounded terrible to Barr, who—unlike most sailors he knew—understood small boat engines as thoroughly as the Army Transportation Corps could teach them. His diagnosis was immediate: one dead cylinder out of four, and water in the gas. Last year's gas, more than likely, half turned to gummy varnish over the winter. "You'd better go help them tie her up, Jeremy," Mrs. Mulvey added. "He's a good sailor, Mr. Falk, but his landings aren't so hot."

Said by Mrs. Mulvey of a longtime customer, this was a searing indictment, and Barr was out the office door almost before the words had left her mouth. As he sprinted across the parking lot toward the pier, he could hear that *Glory*'s engine was racing but just waiting to stall. A blustery spring breeze urging thirty tons of yacht down onto a rickety floating pier had the makings of a very public disaster. On the dead run, Barr caromed off the yard's parked pickup, staggered, snatched a couple of oversize fenders from the workboat, and managed to position himself on the landing float as *Glory* crabbed helplessly down toward him. Barr could see the man Falk—a face the pale yellow of Swiss cheese, shiny with sweat despite the chill air.

At the last possible moment, Falk jammed the racing engine into reverse and it stalled out, as Barr had known it would. *Glory* lurched slightly to the final thrust of the propeller and took the pier broad on her starboard bow, but instead of the tearing crash of wood against wood, there was the squeal of wood on rubber, then a loud explosion from one of the air-filled fenders Barr had jammed between boat and pier. The echoing silence that followed was broken by a woman's voice from above Barr's head: "Take a line?"

He looked up and felt his heart pause between beats; for a moment it was Ann, lithe and youthful as she had been in life, and then the image shifted and he was staring up at an ordinary young woman—pretty enough, in a thin, boyish way, but not Ann even in her coloring. She was holding the line out to him, as to an idiot, and, feeling like an idiot, he took it and dropped an automatic clove hitch over the nearest piling. Took the other lines that were passed to him—his heart was pounding now—and set up the stern and spring lines. It was not the first time memory had tricked him, but never before had the sense of Ann alive again been so clear or so convincing. The young woman jumped gracefully down to the pier, despite her seaboots, and held out her hand. "That was fast thinking," she said.

"Thank you." His mind, released, was spinning on ahead. The girl turned to the skipper, who was climbing painfully over the lifelines. "Easy, Uncle Dennis. Give me your hand."

"God damn it, Gillian," said the old man, between clenched teeth, "I'm still ambulatory." His broad smile took any sting from the words, and he turned to Barr, who tried not to show his surprise at being confronted by a face that was entirely hairless—no eyebrows, or even lashes. He was bigger than Barr had thought: six feet and two or three inches. What must once have been a solid, powerful frame was now gaunt, though padded by an ancient army field jacket over what appeared to be at least two sweaters; a fiercely checked scarf was wound twice around his throat, and a navy-blue wool watch cap was pulled down around his ears. Close to, his skin looked smooth as wax and shiny wet, but his grip was powerful, and he pumped Barr's hand in the European manner. "Dennis Falk," he announced. "I think you just saved me a paint job. At least. How would you like to be my skipper?"

Barr had put him off with a grin and a mutter, but had finally given in two weeks later, when he realized Falk meant what he had said. After a while, it dawned on him that Falk always meant what he said—at least when he was saying it. A man who was predictably impulsive, who would bet everything in his pocket on which of two circling flies would land in the sugarbowl first. "A charmer," as Mrs. Mulvey put it, "but a total nut." All the same, that hard-faced lady would turn herself inside out for Falk; it amused Barr, who, silent and omnipresent, soon became invisibly indispensable to *Glory*'s extroverted owner. As the weeks went by, Barr gradually realized that a second, quite different man was living in the same body with the cheerful lunatic. A second man who kept his life in watertight compartments; who had most of his mail delivered to him at the boatyard, but walked with obvious pain the full mile to the post office for the rest; who never got phone calls at the yard office like every other owner, but made occasional, cryptic transmissions on a portable cellular telephone.

In Barr's private life incuriosity had become a religion, a fact that his employer obviously valued. As the old man's illness became more and more consuming, Barr found himself pressed into service as sick berth attendant, messenger, secretary, and—to his intense discomfort—confidant. In Falk's last days, when only incessant talk seemed to keep the old man's pain at bay, his conversation became an embarrassing mixture of romantic reminiscence and elliptical anecdote that always teetered on the verge of something important. Barr had shut his ears to the first and ignored the second.

And now all the old man's talk was done. Barr needed another drink, to ease the headache and take the awful taste from his mouth. The second bottle of rum had apparently slipped from his unconscious hand and shattered on the floorboards, but there was one more, as he recalled, tucked behind his berth mattress. As he heaved himself to his feet, he heard the crackle of gravel from the ground, fifteen feet below.

The woman who stepped out from behind the next boat was tall, even seen from directly above, and her slenderness was emphasized by her perfectly fitting slacks and blouse. Her face was largely masked by a pair of huge glasses with reflecting lenses and a Bowery Boys cap, under which her hair had been tucked. Even in the semidarkness, the translucent whiteness of her skin glowed as if lit from within. She stood with her face held up toward him, the light caught on the strong planes of her cheekbones. "Hello, Barr," she said. Her voice was low and carrying. Whatever else people called her, she was also a trained actress. "Well?" she said, and he realized that he had been gaping at her.

"Hi, Emerald," he said. "What brings you to City Island? You and your . . . friend." He had not immediately noticed the squat figure—a fire hydrant in a pin-striped suit—standing off to one side. The heavy-set man moved forward a step or two and stopped. He was wearing brown leather gloves, and he held his hands stiffly out from his sides.

"I heard about Dennis," said the woman. "What happened?"

"He was murdered. I don't know why—the police seem to think it was some druggie, after his painkillers."

"And you don't think so? Where were you?" She seemed wholly unmoved, but he remembered that violence was no stranger in her life.

He made himself look her in the eye. "Forward. Passed out. I didn't hear a thing." Unless those had been real screams. "I'm not so sure—somebody really worked him over before he died." He paused. "How come you're here?"

"I have to talk to you, Barr. Alone."

"I guess you want to come aboard."

"Unless you feel safer with me down here," she said.

"Come on up, then," Barr replied, steadying the ladder for her.

Halfway up, she felt the heavy-set man put his weight on the bottom rung. "No," she said, before Barr could speak. "Go back and keep an eye on the gate, Johnny." The man muttered something under his breath, and she added, "I want a pair of eyes out there. Knock on the side if anybody turns up."

Johnny, his sullen face turned up toward her, backed off. He might have been attractive once, if your taste ran to the fleshily sensual, but now there was too much flesh, and the sensuality was overripe: too-thick lips, black hair elaborately combed to hide the bald spot, the once-soulful eyes slightly pouched. But there was muscle beneath, and a simmering resentfulness that could be felt ten yards away. A dangerous man, Barr sensed; unpredictable as well as brutal.

Emerald lifted herself easily over the gunwale and looked back. Johnny had disappeared. She turned to Barr: "I want to be private. Let's go downstairs."

He winced, before he realized she was teasing him, and led the way down the steep companionway to the unlit cabin below. His extended fingers knocked over the mason jar on the shelf just inside the saloon doorway, where the wooden matches were kept; he found one and struck it, lit the polished brass oil lamp on the bulkhead and watched the golden light wash over Emerald's perfect skin. She dropped gracefully to the settee, took off her glasses and cap and placed them on the scarred surface of the big gimbaled table. Her huge green eyes were in shadow, but her incredible copper hair rippled down like a waterfall. "So, Barr. It's been a while."

Gingerly, he sat down across from her. "A month, anyway," he agreed. "He talked about you. Thought you might come."

"I don't go out much. My public"—she grimaced—"sometimes reacts funny if they recognize me in the street. And what if I'd run into the girl? How would she take the idea of her precious uncle's one-time mistress being a porno-movie actress?"

"She'd have been fascinated," said Barr. "Gillian's one of your fans."

She looked surprised and amused. "Honest? Does she know about me and Dennis?"

"He told her himself," Barr said. "Blurted it out—I don't think he meant to—after Gillian saw that movie of yours, the one that made you so famous, with you and the five—"

"*King's Mistress*," Emerald supplied. "And it was four guys and a girl."

"I trust your friend Johnny wasn't one of them."

She laughed. "Troiano? Johnny naked isn't exactly a box-office smash," she said. "Besides, he's too shy. No, he's just my partner."

"Partner?"

She shrugged. "And bodyguard. In my business, you need a little applied muscle sometimes."

"So he wasn't Dennis's replacement, then," Barr said evenly.

"Who could ever replace Dennis?" Her affectionate tone seemed quite genuine. "No, I picked Johnny up long after I left."

"Well, he certainly looks menacing enough," Barr said. "I was impressed by that Quick-draw McGraw pose."

"The hands, you mean?"

"And the gloves. It seems a little warm for gloves."

The shadow of a smile came and vanished. "They hide his thumbs," she said equably. "Or what's left of them, after he got greedy. His previous boss had the tips removed—you might say I got him at a discount. But he can pull a trigger."

"I'm glad for him. But he's a limited topic for conversation."

"That's for sure," she said. "Let's talk about money. Let's talk about us getting rich." She drew the word out into a caress.

"Rich," Barr said, his voice flat. He took out a cigarette and lit it.

"You and me."

"And Mr. Troiano."

"He comes out of my half."

"Your half of what?" Barr said.

"Don't be a dork, Barr," she said. "It's not your style. Your half of the old man's stash."

"So he tried that fantasy out on you? Don't tell me you believed him."

"Let me tell you something, Barr," she said, leaning forward. "Men give you a lot of lies in bed, but they say a lot of true things, too—things they don't mean to say, sometimes. The trick to being a woman is knowing which is which." She smiled, and her perfect teeth flashed in the lamplight. "Sure, Dennis was full of crap most of the time. But he was rich, too. More than once. And he had deals going right to the end. He wasn't going to die broke: that I do believe."

He eyed her thoughtfully. "You seem to have this all figured out."

"No," she said. "There's lots of things I don't know yet.

But I'll tell you what makes me sure I'm right. Two guys have been in touch with me lately. They're very interested in Dennis."

"Who?"

"Maybe you know them," she replied. "One's named Visconti—I met him a couple of years ago, when he was running some kind of scam with Dennis. The other's a Kraut, calls himself Hals. General Hals. Dennis used to talk about him a lot. They go back a long ways. They each say Dennis owed them a fortune, and they're the kind of vultures who sure wouldn't take time to console the dying, unless there was something in it for them."

If only I'd listened, Barr thought, suddenly furious with himself. It seemed like eavesdropping, though, even when he was talking to me. "How'd they know where to find you?" he asked. "I thought you'd pretty well vanished, after you and Dennis broke up."

"Some people I let find me. When I want them to."

"I see," Barr said slowly. "And you decided to come to me. Why?"

"Fifty-fifty seems fair," she said. "For old employees."

"And what about creditors? Or the owner of the boat, for that matter—you heard Dennis sold her to Gillian?"

The half smile had widened, but it did not reach her eyes. "Listen, Dennis flimflammed half the world at one time or another. You could say he owes everybody a fortune. But there's only one fortune, and I figure our claim is as good as anybody else's. And I think we could make a team."

He felt himself warm under her approval, and appreciated the performance. "Quite a team," he said. "A clapped-out sailor and a . . ."

" 'Whore' is a good, all-purpose word," she said. The smile was as fine as it had been, the trained voice as silky, but he could sense under the surface a layer of steel. "Why don't we think of it as a partnership of two survivors," she offered.

"And besides, we both need the money."

At last the smile lit up her magnificent eyes, and she tilted her head to make sure he got the full force. "Everybody needs money," she said. "Look, we can be philosophical all night, but why don't we cut the crap and get down to it? Dennis had some kind of nest egg, and it's stashed in here someplace. You know this old boat better than anybody else alive, and I—well, I've got the connections to unload whatever we find."

"You don't know what it might be, then," he said.

"If I knew what, I could guess where," she replied. "But I want a deal before this conversation gets any more specific."

"And I—I'm sorry—need more . . ."

"Reassurance?" She was watching him closely, her expression unreadable.

"Maybe." He felt foolish and angry—at himself, at the old man for leaving this unresolved mess. "Look," he persisted, "I ain't much, but I'm all I've got."

"Wait a minute," she broke in. "What about this Gillian Verdean?" She weighed the look on his face. "You don't like her. Are you working for her?"

"I was till tonight. She fired me, for being drunk when Dennis was killed."

"You figure you still owe her? Some kind of guilt trip?"

He shook his head. "Not really. It's hard to explain . . ." Only a little earlier, he had been on the verge of taking whatever might be hidden aboard. Now, encouraged, why did he find himself resisting?

"Let me tell you where I'm coming from," Emerald said. "Maybe that'll help you sort yourself out. In my business, you get a very short life-span, and I'm almost at the end of mine."

"But you're beautiful," he objected.

"Thanks. Really: I wasn't fishing for compliments. And I know what I'm talking about. Look . . . have you ever seen one of my movies? I didn't think so." She paused, as if about to embark on a difficult translation. "At first they come to see a new body, one they haven't seen before. If the body is good, like mine is, so much the better. Straight fucking is enough. After a couple of flicks, it's got to be more—with another woman, or maybe with two guys at once. And then more, and more. And after a while, there isn't any more. You're down to screwing dogs. . . . You follow me?" Her tone was matter of fact, a mechanic talking shop, but her eyes were coldly serious.

"Most of it," Barr said. "Enough."

"You ever see a woman making it with a dog? No, of

course not. Well, don't bother: the dog doesn't like it much, and the woman is dead, only she may not know it." She looked down momentarily at her hands, clenched in her lap. "That's never going to happen to me. Never. I've come too far."

"Where are you going?" he asked.

"Up and out," she replied, with a wry smile. "Though it might not seem that way to you. I've bought me a house—of ill-fame, that is. Out on Long Island."

He was disappointed. "You're a madam? That's up?"

"Honey, from where I am, most ways are up. It's a first step, that's all. But I need money, a lot of it, to get going right. You know what's the biggest problem starting a cathouse? Undercapitalization. Don't laugh—I mean it. Getting the right girls is expensive, and so is decorating. And the payoffs, you wouldn't believe. But if you're going to make it go, you've got to have cash, otherwise you start off owing too many people too much."

"And after that?"

Her face lit up, and for a second she looked like a teenager. "I'm going to cash in and get out. Buy myself a little place in the Caribbean and fill it full of books. Top to bottom. Then I'm going to get a refrigerator full of fattening food, and I'm going to spend the rest of my life filling me, reading and eating."

He laughed aloud, and she did, too. "Eating?" he asked. "But you're so thin."

"That's because I haven't had a square meal in years," she said. "My exercise schedule would terrify an Olympic athlete. At heart, I'm a *saftiges Mädchen*."

He eyed her openly, for the first time. "What a tragedy that would be."

"Don't worry," she replied. "I can take responsibility for my own life." She stood up. Even without high heels, she was eye to eye with him. "So have we got a deal?"

"Yes" was almost out of his mouth, but he heard it change to "I don't know." Then to, "I have to think it over."

"Till tomorrow," she said. "There isn't much time: the vultures are in a hurry." She picked up the cap and glasses, and gave the tabletop an experimental push with her fingertips; it swayed silently forward and back, and she watched it with distaste. "God, how I hated this boat," she said, giving the counterweighted surface another push. "This wouldn't be so ugly if you resurfaced it."

"I've been working on *Glory* all winter," said Barr defensively. "There's a limit to what you can do without money."

"Exactly." She climbed the steep companionway stairs as easily as any sailor.

They were in the cockpit. Spread below them, the yard was black as ink, but there was a glow of streetlamps and moving headlights from the street. From the foot of the ladder, Troiano's hoarse, grating whisper floated up. "You finished?"

"For now," she said. "Hold the ladder." She slipped over the side and started down. "One thing, Barr."

"Yes?"

"Don't think you can take your business elsewhere." She laughed softly. "Sleep tight. Sweet dreams."

4

CITY ISLAND
MAY 9
TWO A.M.

Gillian awoke in the unfamiliar bed and made herself lie still while she allowed the day's memories to seep upward, under tight control. She was lying with her head on Patrick's shoulder, his arm cradling her against him. He was breathing quietly, and she found herself marveling at how his smooth skin modulated the raw power of muscle and bone beneath, like silk over chain.

The moment he had opened the bed and laid her on it she knew what was going to happen—knew she would hurl herself eagerly toward the flame. He began with a practiced gentleness that she immediately rejected: "Come on!" she remembered demanding. "I won't break. Come on!" He responded cautiously at first, then with a gathering eagerness that matched her own, and proved her wrong. But she reveled at tearing off his shield of expertise, knew that he was right alongside her on the last, uncontrollable ride. She shivered, remembering, and felt him shift next to her.

There was a light next to the bed, and she reached out to turn it on. Looking up, she saw uncertainty in his face. "Sorry," he said. "My arm was asleep."

"That's all right." She realized that her grief, while still very much there, had become supportable.

"I hope you don't think . . ." he began, clearly unsure of her mood.

"Don't apologize," she cut him off. "If that's what you were going to do. It was what I needed. Uncle Dennis would've approved." He looked distinctly startled, and she felt a surprising urge to giggle. "You know, you look kind of dumb with your mouth open like that. But you were great."

He recovered his composure quickly. "Isn't that supposed to be my line? Anyway, you were great, too—you must've done this before."

"Don't push it, big boy," she said, icing her tone a shade. "Anything worth doing is worth overdoing." Before he could answer, she added: "Why'd you mess up the tattoo?"

"What?" He glanced down uneasily at a diffuse blue smear that half covered his right bicep. "Oh, that. We weren't friends any more."

She took his big arm in her small callused hands. "Doesn't look like just a girl's name," she said. "More like a fancy X with a couple of words underneath."

He pulled free. "It was a design," he said. She didn't care about the answer. He was where she wanted him, off balance. She pushed the covers back and jumped quickly out. This was always the hardest moment, when you were naked in front of him, in the clammy chill of afterward. She forced herself to look him in the eye, but he seemed only concerned.

"You sure you're okay? You don't have to go," he said, sitting up.

In the light he was even more of a hunk than she'd thought. "Yes, I do," she said, pulling on her jeans. There was a stiff stain on one leg, but she made herself ignore it. "I don't want to ruin your reputation," she went on, pulling the sweater over her head. "And besides, what if your sweetie came back while I was here?"

Touché. His face went a dusty red under its tan. "What . . ."

"Come off it, Patrick." She picked up the pillow from what had been her side of the sofabed and sniffed at it. "Your friend must swim in that stuff. What do they call it—Raw Lust? I hope she didn't leave you any other souvenirs." His face went blank. "Listen," she said, changing the subject with her tone. "I want a favor from you."

"If I can," he replied, wary.

"Your job's just in the daytime, right? . . . What's so funny?" She followed his meaningful look, and tossed the pillow on the bed. "Oh, I get it: boss's wife?"

His lips were quivering as he shook his head. "I'll never tell."

"And they said chivalry was dead," she laughed, thinking: not wife—maybe daughter. "Anyway, I want you to do something for me."

"If I can," he repeated.

"It's just for the next few days, till I get things sorted out," she said. "I own this sailboat, that my uncle was living on. I need somebody to keep an eye on her at night. There's people around the yard all day, but the place is deserted after about six." He seemed to be wavering, and she almost said something about keeping him company, but instinct told her it would be a mistake. "I can't pay much, but it's very important to me."

"I guess you must have a lot of valuable stuff aboard," he said. "Electronics. Like that."

She thought of the ancient two-way radio and the broken speedometer. "Not exactly. But there's personal things." He still hesitated, and she added, "Or maybe you have a friend who'd like to make a couple of bucks . . ."

"That's okay," he said quickly. "I'll be glad to do it. And don't worry about the money. But it's just for a few days, right?"

At Tremaine's, Gillian was about to start up the RX-7 when she saw, between the shrouded yachts, the wink of a cigarette up on *Glory*'s deck. Deliberately suppressing second thoughts, she determined to have it out with Barr then and there. Something inside her expected satisfaction from putting him in his place, and some other part of her was half prepared to relent if he asked to stay, or if he even apologized. But when he responded to her announcement about Patrick with a calm "Right. I'll be off first thing in the morning," it left her feeling shabby, drained of the adrenaline she had been running on. The hour's drive home to Westport looked as long as an ocean passage.

Still, just being behind the little Mazda's wheel again was relaxing. The post-midnight traffic on I-95 was light, mostly big semis, and Gillian dropped the RX-7 neatly between two empty fourteen-wheelers that were pressing along the center lane at sixty-five. By the time she hit the Connecticut line, the car was driving itself. Besides, there

was so much else to think about. It had been a stroke of
luck, talking Patrick into baby-sitting *Glory* for her, at least
until she could move aboard herself. When he'd picked
her up in the bar, Gillian's first thought was that he was
just another pretty face—almost too pretty, except for that
slight break in the bridge of his nose. But he was certainly
handy with his fists . . . and the rest of him wasn't so bad,
either. Too bad he was only a powerboat type. All the
same, he'd be a perfect watchman.

Which brought her back to the thought that had been
struggling to surface since she had held her dying uncle in
her arms: Why would anyone break into a ratty-looking
sixty-year-old ketch? The cops seemed to think it was jun-
kies, and it was true that Uncle Dennis's huge collection
of painkillers was gone, the only things missing. But suppose Uncle Dennis had been telling her the truth? Suppose
that somewhere aboard there really was a hoard of . . .
what? And where was it? That was the problem: Gillian
had sailed *Glory*, cruised her for a week at a time, helped
haul her and winterize her; she knew the old yacht as well
as anybody—except Barr, of course—and she hadn't the
first idea where to start looking.

It could be anything, too. Even assuming that only half
of what Uncle Dennis said was true, his adventures had
taken him everyplace. Running guns across the Atlantic
and in the Mediterranean, spying against the Nazis, getting
out of Cuba one jump ahead of Castro—his life had been
like a movie or something.

Maybe it was gold; she'd read a novel once, about a
sailboat whose ballast keel turned out to be gold. Or jewels; she'd heard of a cruising skipper whose bankroll was
a handful of industrial diamonds, invisible at the bottom
of a bottle full of gin. Or some kind of precious documents
that could be slipped between a couple of planks.

Gillian's interior pilot, having wheeled the RX-7 safely
off the highway at Westport, tugged at her. With a sigh,
she turned her attention back to driving. Down the Post
Road and then left, through silent back streets and up the
long, winding hill to home. The house was dark, of course:
the Bernheims were seldom awake after ten-thirty. But
they had left a light on, outside the converted garage where
Gillian lived. The twenty-foot-square space was far nicer

than most of the town's mildly illegal apartments, Joan
Bernheim being a decorator by profession, and the setup
had been perfect until Gillian dropped the fact that she
was an orphan. From that moment she was faced not only
with a procession of the chinless trolls that Joan called
"nice boys," but also with the serious danger of being
mothered to suffocation. Still, there were worse things than
finding a tin of cookies or a quart of clam chowder on your
doorstep after a day at work.

She slid the Mazda in next to Joan's big diesel
Mercedes—like putting a cheetah alongside an ox, she
always thought—and switched off the engine. When she
got out of the car her knees were rubbery, but her mind
was still racing.

Maybe another beer would slow me down, she was
thinking, as the sedan, its headlights off, coasted down the
driveway and stopped, blocking her in.

She stood motionless, clutching her handbag. Two men
wearing topcoats got out. The driver was as thin as Barr
but taller even than Patrick, and slightly stooped. His face
was oval and flat, with protruding, light-colored eyes, a
small hooked beak of a nose, and a lipless mouth. His
passenger was stocky, with white hair shaved close at the
temples and parted precisely down the middle. He must,
Gillian saw, be nearly seventy. His eyes were surrounded
by a network of sunlines, and his face had been gullied by
time, wind and heat. He stepped forward, brought his heels
together, and inclined his head in a sort of quick bow.
"Miss Verdean," he said. "I apologize if we have alarmed
you."

Gillian's voice came back to her, louder than she intended: "You're from Visconti, is that it?"

The older man's face stiffened with, she could have
sworn, a shadow of dismay. He managed a humorless
smile. "No, no. My name is Hals. A friend of your great-
uncle. A very old friend."

"Is that so?" She could not remember Uncle Dennis
mentioning anyone named Hals, but there had been so
many names.

"Yes. Has something happened to him, please?" He
saw her surprise. "We came to visit him, at the boat, and
saw the ambulance and the police. We took the liberty of

following you." He paused, and Gillian felt her face go hot. But Hals was apparently unconcerned with her behavior. "Was it his illness, then?"

"No," she said. She took a deep breath and blurted it out. "Someone broke into the boat and murdered him."

Hals shot a quick look at his tall companion and turned back to her. "I am sorry to hear it. Was it to rob him?"

"The police think so. Uncle Dennis had a pile of drugs—painkillers and sedatives. They were all gone."

"So," said Hals. "You are sure of this?"

His abruptness brought her anger boiling to the surface. "What do you mean?" she snapped. "And what the hell are you doing here anyway? It's the middle of the night."

"My apologies," said Hals, with a second little bow. "I would not trouble you, young lady, if it were not very important."

"So?" The anger ebbed as quickly as it had risen, and she was suddenly very aware of being by herself, with two strange men who seemed quite unaffected by the idea of murder.

"Miss Verdean," said Hals carefully, delivering a prepared speech, "your great-uncle had something that belonged to me. In his illness, he must have forgotten to return it. Since he lived on his boat, I presume it is there, and my friend and I must look for it."

"What is it?" she said, too quickly. The tall man's eyes, incurious till now, focused on her.

"Not large, I think," said Hals. "Easy to overlook."

Or hide. "But what is it?" she insisted.

"We are not precisely sure of the shape," Hals went on, as if she had not spoken. "Perhaps as small as an envelope. But we will recognize it." He paused, searching for the right words. "I am afraid we must insist." The tall man's mouth turned up at one corner.

"No." She meant to sound firm, immovable, but it came out half an octave too high. "*Glory*'s mine now. Uncle Dennis sold her to me. There's nothing on her that belongs to you, and anyway . . ." She had no idea where the sentence was going, and it trailed off. The tall man took a step forward, and she saw there was something heavy pulling down the right-hand pocket of his coat.

"*Ein Moment*," said Hals, in a peremptory tone, stopping him.

"Look, Mr. Hals," said Gillian, "I think you're just mistaken. My uncle didn't have anything valuable left. He was penniless when he died. That was why he sold *Glory* to me. He may have been rich once, back in Cuba in the fifties, but he hasn't had more than just enough to live on for several years." Her voice vibrated with sincerity; for a moment, she even convinced herself.

"I am sorry to have to disillusion you, Miss Verdean," Hals replied. "Your great-uncle had five million American dollars within the past eighteen months. I myself gave him a check for the money, on behalf of interests I represent." He waited for her to respond, and then added, "It was to be passed on, as part of a business arrangement for which your great-uncle was acting as agent. My principal has not received the merchandise, and he is very impatient."

The tall man sniggered abruptly, a braying noise. Hals's look wiped the smile from his face. "It is only with difficulty," the old man went on, leaning forward to look into Gillian's eyes, "only with the greatest difficulty, that I have convinced my principal to accept something of equivalent value to the money. Something I know your uncle had for a long time, something he would not sell or give away." Gillian opened her mouth, but Hals raised his hand to silence her. "Please. You are a person of intelligence. You must believe that I would not want to injure the niece of my old friend. But there are others involved who are not so sentimental as I."

The tall man reached into his coat pocket, a faint smile now curving both corners of his thin mouth. "Wait," Gillian said. Part of her was terrified—would probably have been more terrified, had she not been so tired; but another part, to her own surprise, was coldly furious. "What do you want me to do?" she asked, trying to sound helpless.

"Come with us," said Hals. "We will merely obtain our property, and then you are free."

"Please, can't it wait till morning?" she begged. "I'm so tired." Tears—real tears—filled her eyes; it would be so easy just to fold up at their feet.

The tall man was eyeing her with what looked like hunger, and Hals shook his head. "Tomorrow is too late," he said firmly. "I will drive, and you will sit with Major . . . with my friend, in the back seat."

That settled it: there was no way under heaven she would

get into a back seat with the tall man. "All right," she said, letting her shoulders sag. The tall man motioned her forward, opening the sedan's back door, and she took an unsteady step toward him. As she did, she sniffed noisily. "Got to get a Kleenex," she said, groping in her purse. Her fingertips found the slender cylinder, groped for the little knurled tab at the side and pulled it back till she felt it seat with a snap. As the tall man's right hand came out to take her left elbow, she let the purse fall. Instinctively, he bent forward, and Gillian pressed the end of the cylinder into his ear. "Don't move!" she snapped. He stiffened, awkwardly half bent. "This thing is called a pen gun," Gillian announced, amazed at the icy precision of her voice. "It can fire a red phosphorus flare two hundred feet straight up. I don't know what it would do to your head."

"Idiot!" said Hals, under his breath. The tall man moved his head slightly, and Gillian jammed the pen gun mercilessly into his ear.

"I'm going to reach into your coat pocket," she said. "Don't move again. Not even a little." She slid her left hand slowly into the side pocket of the tall man's coat and felt the plastic grips of a pistol. She drew it free—her heart almost stopped when its hammer snagged momentarily—and held it gingerly in her left hand. It was a revolver, that much she knew, and amazingly heavy. Did you have to cock it to fire? She had no idea.

"Now you," she said to Hals.

"I am not armed, miss," he said. He seemed quite calm.

She thought for a moment. "You," she said, pressing the pen gun against the tall man's head. "Lie down on the ground. On your stomach, arms out wide."

For a long moment he was motionless, and then Hals said, "Do it."

With the thin man on the ground, Gillian turned to Hals, who silently raised his arms over his head. "No, not like that," she said, bolder now. "Come over here. Stop there." In the moonlight, he seemed to be smiling. "Now lean forward and put your hands on the hood of the car. What's so funny?"

He shook his head. "Nothing, Miss Verdean."

"You just shut up, then," she said. Quickly, she stepped

behind him and patted under his arms and along his hips.
"All right. You can stand up."

At one corner of her vision, the Bernheims' front door
light went on and, a moment later, the door opened. "Is
that you, Gilly?" called Howie Bernheim, looming in the
doorway.

"It's me," and, softly, to Hals: "That's my landlord.
He's a State Police lieutenant, so you'd better watch it."

"Is everything okay?"

"Just fine, Howie. These gentlemen were leaving."

"Indeed," said Hals quietly. "I can see we have under-
estimated you. May my associate get up now?"

"Up and out of here," said Gillian. Howie was standing
in the door, and she willed him to be silent.

Hals and the tall man got into their car. "*Auf Wieder-
sehen*, Miss Verdean," said Hals. "Until we meet again."

Not if I see you first, Gillian thought. The tall man was
silent, refusing to meet her eye. Hals started the car and
backed awkwardly up the driveway. As they turned down
the hill, Gillian's hands began to shake, and she stuffed
the pistol in her coat.

From the front door, Howie eyed her quizzically. "You
really okay?" he asked. "Who were those guys?"

"I'm okay, Howie. Thanks. I just have to get to bed."

"Sure." He started to close the door and paused.

She was almost too lightheaded to stand. "Good-night,
Howie." He shook his head, but shut the door; a second
later the light went off.

Her legs held up just long enough for her to collapse
into her armchair. I ought to call the police, she thought.
I have to call Uncle Hitch—see if there's a will or anything.
Oh God, Uncle Dennis, I wish you were here.

The thought of him released the tears she had promised
herself, and she was still crying when she fell asleep.

5

MANHATTAN
MAY 9
NOON

"**I** do wish Gillian had managed to call me last night,"
Winfield Hitchcock was saying. "I feel sure I could
have calmed her down." Gillian's lawyer was sitting across
from Barr, at a corner table in a midtown restaurant whose
clientele straddled several worlds. Barr, in his working
clothes—a faded navy-blue flannel shirt and jeans—almost
blended with one segment of the chattering crowd. Hitchcock, in his own uniform—a three-piece suit seemingly
designed to replicate the clothing of Calvin Coolidge—
came close to blending with many of the others.

"Can't blame her, I guess," Barr replied quietly.

"I gather that Gillian blames you, though. For Dennis's
death."

"You've talked to her, then?"

"She finally got in touch with me," Hitchcock said, his
old man's mouth pursing with irritation. "About nine this
morning. Beat my office boy with the *Daily News* headline
by about two minutes. I did my best to talk her out of
letting you go. Thought I'd succeeded, in fact. It's pre-
posterous, you having anything to do with Dennis's
death." Was there, Barr wondered, just a slight question
implied in that very flat statement? There was no way to
respond to it, in any case.

"She and I were both pretty edgy last night," Barr said,
trying for a neutral tone. "Probably my fault as much as

hers." Maybe she had been ready to take him back, but her manner told him it would be as her paid hand, not *Glory*'s skipper. It was a difference he could not explain to Hitchcock.

"Don't pay too much attention to what she says, Jeremy." The old man eyed Barr as if deciding how to phrase what he was going to say next. "You know she admires you tremendously."

"It's an odd way of showing it," said Barr.

"To tell the truth," the lawyer continued, "I think she feels she ought to be more broken up about Dennis, and she's taking her guilt out on you." He leaned back in his chair, glancing about the crowded, smoky room. A waiter, misinterpreting his look, hurried up with two menus.

"Let me tell you about our specials today," he began, but Hitchcock waved him off.

"Another round, please. We'll order in a bit. You will have another round, Jeremy?"

"Sure," said Barr absently. He didn't really want the rum—hadn't wanted the first one. It had been a long time, he realized, since he'd been impatient to be up and doing. If only he had a clearer idea of what he was up to.

"What will you do now?" Hitchcock asked. "How are you fixed for money? If you don't mind my asking."

Barr grinned. "I can't afford to mind."

Hitchcock smiled thinly. "You'd be open to other employment, then?"

Barr smiled back, but he was thinking that half his pitifully small bankroll was already gone, for a tiny, boxlike room on a back street in City Island. "It depends," he said cautiously.

"Last night," said Hitchcock, lowering his voice slightly, "our offices were broken into—my own office, to be precise."

"Your office?" Barr repeated, trying to take it in. "Why? What was taken?"

"Nothing, as far as I know," Hitchcock answered. "It's difficult to be certain, but I think someone just went very thoroughly through the files on Dennis Falk and Gillian, and then tore things up generally."

"That must've taken quite a while," said Barr, thinking aloud. "Just to find the right files, I mean, never mind searching them. Don't you have burglar alarms, that kind of thing?"

"Of course," Hitchcock said with a snap. "Obviously, it was someone who knew the office arrangements." Barr opened his mouth to speak, but Hitchcock forestalled him. "An employee, I imagine. That irritates me, I must confess. I'd never presumed our staff was proof against subornation, but this is so . . . so brazen. Almost a gesture."

" 'Here's what we can do?' " said Barr.

"Exactly," Hitchcock replied, something like approval in his voice. "In any case, that's why I called Tremaine's and asked to meet you. None of my colleagues are likely to come here." Hitchcock was clearly waiting for Barr to say something, but the younger man only raised an eyebrow questioningly. "I have a job for you, Jeremy, if you're interested. But I want it to be private, between the two of us."

"I'm not a detective," Barr said.

"It's not to do with the break-in," said Hitchcock. "That's over and done. Finding the culprit would be more disruptive than just ignoring it: it'll turn out to be some office boy or messenger. No, I take the warning, but I'm not about to run around advertising it."

"Then what do you want from me?" Barr lit a cigarette and watched Hitchcock narrowly through the initial cloud of smoke.

"I want you to keep an eye on Gillian," Hitchcock said. "I'm worried about her."

"Presumably you don't think I had anything to do with Dennis's death, then," said Barr slowly.

"Of course not," Hitchcock replied. "And neither do the police; I talked to a friend downtown this morning. They're still entranced with their drug theory."

"And you're not?"

"I told you about Gillian's telephone conversation with this Visconti fellow," said Hitchcock, weighing his words. "And the man Hals, with the German accent. She thinks Dennis left some mysterious treasure on *Glory*—oh, that's not what she says, but it sticks out a mile."

"And you think she might be right, is that it?"

"We-e-ell," said Hitchcock. His hard old eyes watched Barr closely. "I'm concerned that someone else might think so. Someone who might do something dangerous to frighten Gillian off."

"Fat chance," Barr muttered. "Frightening her off, I mean. She's going to keep *Glory*, isn't she?"

"Strictly speaking, she hasn't said. But, yes—she'll certainly keep the boat."

"How can you trust me?" asked Barr suddenly.

Hitchcock smiled, assembling his reply with care. "There are areas where I might hesitate, Jeremy. But I'm confident that you'll keep your word, once you give it."

"It's about all I have left. That's why I'm careful about what I promise."

"The promise I want from you concerns Gillian's physical safety only," Hitchcock said. "I don't want to know about what may or may not be aboard *Glory*. Officially, of course, I take the position that there's nothing there."

"Of course," Barr answered solemnly.

"Tell me, Jeremy—what do you think of this new young man Gillian has hired. Is he so very handsome?"

"Did she say he was?" Barr looked up sharply.

"She went to so much trouble to avoid saying it that I assume he's Adonis, at least," Hitchcock replied.

Barr laughed. "What an old fox you are. I can't say, myself—haven't met him. But he's coming by the yard this afternoon, to take over."

"O'Mara," said Hitchcock reflectively. "Do you know him, Jeremy? Being in the same line, so to speak?"

"No. He works another part of the forest."

"I see." Hitchcock pursed his lips. "It was remarkably fortuitous. The two of them meeting like that."

"I suppose," Barr said. "But he's only filling in as night watchman. It's not as if she was taking him on as skipper."

"Not yet. Anyway, I distrust coincidences of that magnitude."

"Try convincing Gillian," Barr said evenly. "O'Mara's definitely her flavor of the month."

Hitchcock shrugged. "I could be wrong, I suppose— there's nothing certain," he said. "But I think we ought to keep an eye on Captain O'Mara."

"We? When did I say I'd take your job? And what will you tell Gillian?"

Hitchcock picked up the menu. "We shall," the old

lawyer announced with exaggerated care, "connive at a small subterfuge. We won't tell the child what we're up to."

"Then who's paying me?" Barr asked, and to the hovering waiter, who had chosen that moment to pounce, "A double hamburger, please. Fries, no onion. And a cup of coffee."

"The fruit salad," Hitchcock said. "And tea." Turning to Barr, he changed his tone, from magistrate to accomplice: "Your salary—will three hundred a week, plus expenses, do? Good—it'll come from me. Perhaps when all this is over, we shall find some assets of Dennis's we don't know about. If not, we'll call it a bad debt. I have a platoon of bright young men who deal with this sort of thing; don't give it a thought."

"So you want me to keep an eye on Gillian," Barr said. "Protect her from physical danger."

"Yes."

"What about *Glory*? Am I supposed to protect her, too?"

"*Glory*, alas, is a conflict of loyalties. Your brief from me covers Gillian only. What happens to the boat is between the two of you."

"Between more people than that," said Barr. He removed the upper half of his hamburger bun and covered the thin, gray patties of meat with a sea of catsup. "Hard to protect someone you're not on speaking terms with."

"Not necessarily," Hitchcock replied. "This is canned—the fruit. Not necessarily at all. Might be easier that way."

"Considering the protectee," said Barr through a mouthful of hamburger bun, "you may be right." He swallowed. "All right—I'll do it, but on one condition."

Hitchcock delicately removed a chunk of pineapple core from his mouth and laid it on the edge of his plate. "Name it," he said.

"I expect you've got some of your people researching Hals and Visconti. I want to know what they find out."

"Fair enough. You'll use the information only to protect Gillian?" Hitchcock's left eyebrow had risen nearly to his hairline.

Barr laughed. "Never you mind. The promise was about physical danger—that's all."

"Quite. Agreed." He looked about him. "Do you suppose their brandy is as dreadful as their food?"

"Not for me," Barr said. "I have a busy afternoon."

Barr looked sadly around the small, triangular cabin that had been his home for a little under twelve months—the second home he had lost in a year. Unlike the rest of *Glory*'s interior, the white-painted fo'c'sle was spotless. Shabby, but spotless. In the bulkhead forward, where the bows narrowed, was the hatch that led to the anchor-chain locker. Aft to port was the hanging locker, a narrow closet that held Barr's own working clothes, his foul-weather gear, his one ancient suit. Under the berth on which he sat were half a dozen drawers. What was left of his clothing occupied three of them, and the others were empty.

When *Windhover* had gone down, she had taken with her nearly everything Barr owned. He scarcely remembered the loss of his clothes, but he had mourned his books, the small collection of volumes he had been accumulating for fifteen years. Most of them had been paperbacks, because of weight and space, their spines reinforced with silver tape; none had survived the sinking. In the year since, he had made a halfhearted new beginning, picking up a book here and another there at the City Island secondhand shops. There was a split-spined paperback of Peter Heaton's *Cruising*, the first sailing book he had read, way back in boarding school; and Hervey Garrett Smith's *Arts of the Sailor*, with a burnt match marking the place where Barr had been following the instructions for making a canvas mast boot. Slocum, of course—not just *Sailing Alone Around the World*, but also *The Voyage of the Liberdade*, which Barr found less affected, more believable. And Francis Chichester's *Alone Across the Atlantic*. Three collections: *The Portable Mark Twain* and two volumes of Sherlock Holmes stories; a biography of the British explorer Shackleton; and three of Patrick O'Brian's historical novels, which he had borrowed from a British delivery skipper and never returned. One of the Tolkien stories, which he had not been able to finish. The books huddled together in a corner of the bulkhead shelf.

Slowly, he wrapped each of them in a piece of clothing and then thrust it into his laundry bag. When he had finished he sank down again on the starboard berth.

The fo'c'sle had once held a pair of berths, port and starboard, their feet meeting at the bow, with a bare and functional toilet between—the classic, unadorned crew's cabin. The toilet's plumbing had perished by the time of Barr's arrival, and instead of fixing it he'd removed the instrument and sealed off the intake and exhaust pipes. Sometime before Barr had come on the scene, the port berth had been converted to a sail bin by the simple expedient of ripping off its top and taking out the drawers. *Glory*'s mizzen staysail and dubious jib topsail were there now, the only relics of her previous suit of sails. Her new set, made by Gillian's firm at employee discount, lived on the booms when *Glory* was in commission, and currently were bagged and stowed in the forward guest cabin, filling it completely.

Beyond the galley, Barr could hear Patrick O'Mara moving about, settling in. The man had been pretty much what Barr expected: smooth, handsome, self-assured . . . Had he slept with Gillian? There was something in her manner with him that hinted as much. Barr told himself again that it was less than none of his business, that he had no right to let the idea get under his skin. He put the laundry bag down and stepped through the doorway into the galley. Aft, in the center of the main cabin, O'Mara was standing, hands on hips, looking up at that tarpaulin-covered skylight. He turned as Barr came in. "This cabin smells," he said.

He was right, though Barr scarcely noticed it any more. "It won't be so bad once you get the skylight open and some air in here," Barr replied. "Do you want the guided tour now? I don't want to hang around after your new employer gets back."

"I'll let her show me the boat," said O'Mara. "I could use some lunch, though."

"The cupboard is pretty much bare, I'm afraid. I can do instant, and there's most of a coffee cake, but it's a little stale. You're welcome to both."

"No, thanks," O'Mara said. "Listen, there's a place down the street . . ." After a moment he added, "I'll buy for both of us."

I guess poverty shows, Barr thought. Or maybe he's not supposed to let me out of his sight. "I appreciate the thought," he said, "but I'm not hungry. You go to it. I'll pack—don't worry, I won't steal the boat while you're gone."

O'Mara's teeth gleamed in a quick smile. "Okay," he said, after a moment's hesitation. "Be back in a flash."

Barr watched him bound up the steep companionway, felt the vibrations through the hull as he went down the ladder, heard the scrape of his feet on the gravel below. Only then did he walk over to the chart table, in the passageway aft between the main and ladies' cabins. The table's surface was made for serious work—for high-seas navigation—and it was the best such area Barr had ever used. Big enough to take the largest chart fully unrolled, with four deep drawers below that accommodated nearly a hundred more charts—of places Barr knew intimately, like Bermuda and the Bahamas and the Windward and Leeward Islands and Chesapeake Bay; and of places he had only touched at, like the South Coast of England and the Canary Islands. Above the table were racks for the navigator's tools—parallel rules and dividers and pencils—and a padded locker for Falk's sextant, an ancient, beautiful Plath that Barr had coveted since he had first seen it.

Over the racks were bookshelves, stoutly built affairs with removable mahogany bars to hold the contents firmly in place in any seaway. Bowditch was there, of course, and Dutton's; last year's *Nautical Almanac*; the five maroon-bound volumes of the Sight Reduction Tables; American Sailing Directions and British Admiralty Pilots for both sides of the Atlantic and the Caribbean—books that Falk had kept up to date by hand, until illness overwhelmed him. Barr remembered the old man, sitting in his bunk in the ladies' cabin, books piled around him and sheets of the *Notices to Mariners* in drifts over everything, annotating each page as carefully as if he planned to set sail the next day. As long as he could stand for fifteen minutes at a time, he had updated the charts as well, with meticulous care; when he became too weak, he would lie in his berth and call out the corrections to Barr, standing at the chart table. Or to Gillian, who would pretend to make the changes, unable to see the charts for the tears coursing down her face.

Barr shivered in the chill air from the companionway. Time to get the tarps off and let the spring sunshine in . . . Hell, Gillian could do that. It was her problem, now.

Idly, Barr picked up the flashlight that lay on the chart table and flicked it on. Its batteries were nearly gone—he had planned to replace them as soon as he found himself with some cash. He played the fading light over the massed volumes, row upon row. Gillian would save them, he was sure: she could be relied on to do that, anyway. A thought was nagging at the back of his mind, had been picking at his consciousness for several minutes, but he could not isolate it. Something to do with books, and with Falk.

The logbooks—that was it. Falk had kept them all, of course, from the time he had bought *Glory*, back in the thirties. They were bound in red leather, their spines stamped in gold with the yacht's name and the years each book covered. Barr had seen the outsides of them often enough, but had never read them—had only, once or twice, glanced at the pages over Falk's shoulder. The old man always made the entries himself, refusing to let anyone else touch the books. Toward the end, when Barr had been handling *Glory*'s navigation alone, they arrived at an uneasy compromise: Barr penciled out a rough log, in a cardboard-covered, spiral-bound notebook, and Falk would then transfer the information to the permanent log.

"Story of my life," he had remarked, once, his hand caressing the leather spines. "Everything is in here someplace. Everything *Glory*'s done—everything I've done, for that matter."

Of course. The books were kept in a special locker in the ladies' cabin, secured by a formidable-looking combination lock. The police had insisted on forcing it the previous night, but had been uninterested when it was clear the logbooks hadn't been touched in months.

O'Mara would be back any minute, he knew. Without willing it, Barr found himself in the ladies' cabin. The semicircular chamber was dimly illuminated by a dusty skylight, partly covered by a canvas tarp. It looked grim with all the bedding gone, and even in the half light Barr could see reddish-brown speckles he had missed. Above and abaft of the settee was the big U-shaped berth, and built into the settee back under it was a row of lockers with carved mahogany doors. The one he wanted was at the starboard end, its decorated wooden face still open to reveal the steel box within. Barr had never till this moment given much thought to the reasons for such a secure hiding place—had put it down as just one more eccentricity. Now he looked at the black, crackle-finished metal, with the single dial in the center and the handle below it. He heard the thud of O'Mara's weight on the ladder against the hull, and he pulled the box free, closed the locker door and hurried forward to his own cabin.

Barr had gotten the furnished room through a sympathetic friend in the office at Tremaine's; it belonged to a son off at college, and the decor was a little youthful for Barr's taste, running to garish posters stuck to the walls with Scotch tape and empty bottles that had contained exotic brands of beer. Now, as Barr returned after his solitary dinner, the room had a more striking decorative note— Emerald, stretched full-length on the bed, reading *Sailing Alone Around the World.* She was wearing dark slacks and a loose sweater, a combination that, on her, failed to be unobtrusive. Her flaming hair was in a neat bun, and she had exchanged her oversize sunglasses for a more businesslike pair that she was wearing cocked up on top of her head.

Barr closed the door behind him. "Been waiting long? I'd have thought you'd be staking out *Glory.*"

"We are," she replied, closing the book in time to see his eyes go, uncontrollably, to the closet, where he had left the laundry bag that contained his belongings. "Dennis's little box—what do you want with that? Oh, I haven't peeked," she said, answering his expression instead of his words. "But I was tempted. You didn't waste any time."

In the closet, the strongbox had been taken out of the bag and sat waiting for him. He lifted it with an effort and brought it over to the bed. Emerald closed the book and sat up, making room for him. "You recognized this, then?" he said.

"Of course."

"You know what's in it?"

"Those dumb books. The ship's logs, or whatever you call them."

"Right," said Barr.

"I don't see why you want them." Her exquisitely plucked eyebrows suddenly lifted: "Unless you think there's some clue to where the . . . whatever we're looking for is."

"You've got it. A proper log is like an accounting ledger," Barr said. "Just bare facts: dates, places, courses steered, that kind of thing. I never really read Dennis's log, but when I looked over his shoulder—by accident," he added, firmly, "—I could see *Glory*'s was more like a diary. He told me himself that he wrote down everything in those books. And maybe that everything includes some useful hints." He spun the dial irritably. "The police forced this thing open last night, and now it's jammed shut."

She smiled. "I don't think that's a real problem." She picked up the thin, dingy pillow from the head of the bed.

"What do you mean?" Barr asked.

"Watch." She opened her purse, a handsome leather bag nearly the size of a briefcase, and produced a short-barreled revolver. Wadding the pillow around the gun, she set the muzzle against the strongbox dial and pulled the trigger. A muffled *whack!*, like someone hitting a mattress with a board, was instantly followed by a clear, bell-like clang, and a strong smell of burnt feathers. The strongbox's scarred dial spun in little circles on the floor, catching the light at each turn. With a practiced flick of her wrist, Emerald snapped the gun's cylinder out, replaced the spent cartridge, and dropped the weapon and the brass casing into her purse. Barr watched her, grinning, as she fished in the bag and came up with a long, thin nail file. She probed for a moment or two through the hole in the box's door, and then something inside clicked and it opened. "*Voilà*," she said, and then, seeing his expression, "What's so funny?"

"You. Showing off like that," Barr replied. "I was going to go out and get a hacksaw: the sides and back of that thing are so thin you could almost get through them with a can opener."

Her slow smile made Barr feel like a co-conspirator. "That's what I told Dennis," she said. "But you know the way he was—once he saw how neatly that cockamamie little box fitted in the locker, he had to have it."

"Well, let's see what we've got," he said. The six books were wedged so snugly into the strongbox that Emerald had to pry one volume out with her nail file, scarring the leather cover. Barr arranged the books in a row on the bedspread, with their spines up, in chronological order according to the dates gold-stamped on them. The first one, a shade larger than the rest, and bound in a marginally different kind of leather, was labeled "*Titania*: 1922–1930." Barr opened it.

"That's not Dennis's writing," said Emerald, who was looking over his shoulder. Barr was suddenly very aware of the faint odor of her perfume, the clean smell of her hair. She was not touching him, but there seemed no space between them at all.

"No," said Barr, trying to keep his voice steady. "That must be the original owner. Or his paid captain." He riffled through the pages until, near the end, the cautious, constricted printing ended, replaced by a familiar, theatrically swooping hand.

"Now, that's Dennis," Emerald remarked approvingly.

"Look," Barr said, closing the book but marking his place with his finger, "I can't concentrate with you hanging over me like that, and I think that if we're going to find what we're looking for, we've got to go at it systematically."

She sat back, eyeing him thoughtfully. "Partners?" she asked.

"Partners," he agreed. "With a couple of provisos: No matter what, we don't damage *Glory*. And we don't rough anybody up, unless they come at us first."

She looked at him with spurious delight. "I love it," she said. "Listen, Barr, did you ever read a book called *Don Quixote*?"

"No, but I take your point," he said. "All the same, Emerald, that's how it's going to be. And we split three ways—you and your tame hood, Gillian, and me. Agreed?"

"Oh, sure. Of course," she replied. "And how does Miss Verdean feel about this setup? You haven't told her yet, have you?"

"I will," he said, not meeting her eye.

"Just so I'm there when you do," she replied. And then, her voice hardening, "But let me tell you something, Barr: I'm in this for what's coming to me, not to preserve some old boat or for showing up some snippy kid or for any other mixed-up reason. I hope you've got that straight."

"I think I can grasp that much," Barr replied, glaring at her. He saw the corner of her lip curl, and both of them began to laugh.

"By the time we're through," she said, "we'll deserve each other. Now let's get down to it. What are we looking for?"

"I'm not sure," Barr replied. "But Falk hinted to several people, at different times, that he had some kind of nest egg, right?"

"Well, I know he said something to me at least once," she replied cautiously.

"He hinted to you, he hinted to Gillian, he hinted to Mr. Hitchcock," said Barr. "But he never outright told anybody."

"If he did, nobody's admitting it," she replied.

He nodded approvingly: "You're right. But let's assume that if he didn't tell his old friend and attorney or his beloved niece or his mistress, chances are he didn't tell anybody—and that wasn't like him."

"By God, you're right there," she agreed. "Fastest mouth in the east."

"Well, my bet is that he told these books—that he gloated over his own secrets in here."

"Could be," she said, looking at him with a respect that he found oddly pleasing. "Okay: I'll buy it. Here—I'll take three and you take three— What's the matter?"

He had trouble meeting her eye. "Are you sure you trust me to tell you if I find something?" he asked.

"Now that's what I call diplomatic," she said, laughing. "All right, we look at them together. Where do we start?"

"My guess is that the answer's in this one," Barr said, holding up the volume whose spine had "1946–1950" lettered on it, and "*Glory*" stamped in gold on the cover. "But let's begin at the beginning."

"Might as well," she agreed. "We've got the rest of the evening. And all night, if we need it."

"I take it Troiano's watching the boat."

"Of course. I told him to come get us if he needed help—if more than one visitor at a time turns up," she said.

"You're expecting visitors, then?" Barr asked. He drew the rickety night table around to the side of the bed and propped the first logbook on it.

"Seems likely," she replied, rolling up the sleeves of her blouse. Her arms were slender but surprisingly muscular. "By the way, it makes him jealous, me being with you."

"Jealous?" Barr was astounded and, he was surprised to note, vaguely pleased.

"Pretty weird, no? He's watched me take on platoons of good-looking guys without batting an eyelash, but one beat-up, middle-aged sailor bugs him." She was grinning, not looking at him. "It's not supposed to make sense," she added. "I just thought it would be a good idea for you to know."

"Thanks," he said. "Does that mean he's in love with you?"

She cocked her head to one side, appraisingly. "I guess he is, in his own way."

"And you?"

She turned and made a point of looking him in the eye. "I don't think much of men," she said. "Most of them are like Johnnie—Troiano—only more subtle. He's available and I need him. And I can handle him."

"I don't suppose there are many men you can't handle," he said.

"None," she replied firmly. "Now, let's get to work."

6

~~~⋘⋙~~~

CITY ISLAND
EIGHT P.M.

Gillian sneezed, and then again, and a third time. The dust and mold in *Glory*'s accommodation were getting to her. "Bless you," said Patrick, from behind her.

"Thanks." She straightened up, easing her aching back, and stretched. *Glory*'s saloon was dimly lit by two kerosene lamps, whose glow was made almost palpable by dancing dust motes. After Barr's departure, Gillian had bullied Patrick into helping her remove the canvas that covered *Glory*'s deck over the winter. It had taken them a couple of hours to get the tarps off and folded, letting the late afternoon sunshine warm the old yacht's decks and penetrate her skylights. Gillian, who had not handled the paint- and tar-stiffened fabric before, was amazed at how intractable it was—heavy as metal sheeting, and nearly as rigid. Patrick was incredibly strong, though Gillian had been amused at the almost ladylike precision with which he had folded his starched khaki shirt to preserve the creases before setting it down gingerly on a dusty settee. His prizefighter's torso was now smeared liberally with grime as well as sweat, the muscles highlighted with streaks of dirt. Singlehanded, he had heaved at the tarpaulins, stretched over wood frames that kept them off *Glory*'s deck, until they had slithered reluctantly to the ground below. Then, after an unbelieving look at *Glory*'s highly eclectic set of tools—worn and dulled and chipped hardware from God knew where—he had set to work to dismantle the frames, while Gillian went below, ostensibly to map the first steps in cleaning up, actually to decide where to begin her search.

The intense activity had, for a couple of hours, driven the numb grief out of her. Now, as she looked around the cabin, it descended like a curtain—a sorrow that encompassed not only Uncle Dennis but, to her surprise, Jeremy Barr. Even while she was fishwifing him, she could not help observing, and resenting, the quiet self-possession he never lost. In her heart she knew, had known almost from the moment of opening her mouth, that she wanted him to stay. Then what made the hateful, patronizing words pour out like that?

When Barr had turned away to leave, stuffing the six fifty-dollar bills in his pocket (without counting or even looking at them), she saw his hand go, unbidden, to caress the old hull as he passed, a gesture of farewell for *Glory* that cut unexpectedly deep. Barr had looked desolate, with his few belongings over his back in an old drawstring laundry bag stenciled WINDHOVER. She wondered where he was now, what he would do, then came to herself with a start. Patrick was eyeing her with a watchful respect. I must have exceeded myself with Barr, she thought. Keeps Patrick in his place, anyway. At least for the moment. She had, after last night, decided that she recognized Patrick's type. By now he felt he had a proprietary right in her, and pretty soon he'd want to exercise it. She was almost looking forward to putting him down.

Now he spoke: "The tarps are folded and the frame is broken down. Will the yard's people take care of them, or are they yours?"

She had no idea—Barr had attended to this kind of thing, in his imperceptible fashion—but she was not about to admit it. "Just leave them for tomorrow. And I think we can call it a day. The showers are right behind the yard office, if you want to use them. I have a couple of phone calls to make."

She stood for a few moments in the twilight, looking down the length of *Glory*'s deck. The boat always seemed so huge at this stage—endlessly long, unbroken by the spars, which lay wrapped on deck. And unbelievably cluttered and dirty. With a sigh, she pulled a notebook from her hip pocket and consulted it before climbing slowly down the ladder and back into the world.

Old Mr. Coyle had left the yard office open, as he had promised, and she found two messages in his careful, minuscule writing. One was from the undertaker she'd called that morning. She grimaced and set it back on the desk, picked up the second slip of paper. Who was Lieutenant Barone? After a moment's reflection she placed him: the cop from the previous night. When she dialed the number, she recognized his voice immediately. "Miss Verdean? I have the autopsy report—I asked for a quick work-up." He paused, obviously waiting for some reaction, then explained: "What that means is, you can claim your uncle's remains, but you have to go down to the Medical Examiner's office, on First Avenue in Manhattan, and make a formal identification before the undertaker can pick the body up. It's the law, I'm afraid."

That must be what the call from the funeral home is about, she told herself. "Thank you, Mr. Barone. Thanks again."

"And we may have a line on the man who killed your great-uncle. Do you know a Thomas or Timothy Jefferson?"

"No. Is he . . ."

"Didn't think you would. A vagrant. He was found this morning, in a vacant lot on 255th Street. O.D., with a paper bag full of pills. Some of them match the ones on your great-uncle's prescriptions."

She knew she should say something, but she didn't feel anything. "That was fast work," she managed. "That's great."

"Well, it fell in our lap: we got a phone tip," said Barone. "I just thought you'd want to know."

Five minutes on the phone with the undertaker, an indescribably slippery person, left her drained. It all felt so unreal, she was thinking as she emerged into the sunset, but Uncle Dennis was really dead, along with the man who'd killed him. As she locked the office door, a woman's voice said, right beside her, "So you're the one."

She was tall. And overweight. The voice was harsh, flat. Long Island, was Gillian's first thought. "The one who?" she said.

"Don't give me that shit. The one who's trying to steal Patrick. His landlady told me, but I wanted to see for myself."

This is too crazy, Gillian thought. I don't need this crap. The woman standing in her path was in her late twenties; heavy makeup on top of a careful tan, Gillian judged. Too much eye shadow, too much lipstick. A too-tight sweater that barely constrained her above, and too-tight designer jeans that were fighting a losing battle below. She was like a caricature of a *Playboy* centerfold, but maybe she was a tiger between the sheets. Gillian sniffed the air experimentally: "You're the daughter," she said.

"He told you about me, then," she said, with belligerent satisfaction. "Bobbie Thayer. My father's Senator Cardegan."

Gillian felt some reaction was required. "That's nice," she said, in her best Seven Sisters voice. Bobbie goggled at her, and Gillian realized she was in a fury. She looked like a woman who exercised her emotions hourly, and who was unaccustomed to being thwarted. "Did you want to talk to Patrick?"

"I never want to talk to that bastard again," said Bobbie. "Where is he?"

Gillian restrained herself. "He's around someplace," she said vaguely.

"Well, you better keep an eye on him," said Bobbie. "He'll be sneaking off after everything in skirts."

"Really?" said Gillian, trying not to sound lofty. "I only met him last night."

Bobbie seemed to take in Gillian's appearance for the first time. "You fall into something?" she asked. "You look terrible." She paused. "Last night, you said? You met him last night? For the first time?"

Mystified, Gillian nodded. "That's right. In that little bar down the street. The Running Light."

"That dump? He never took me there," said Bobbie, her face darkening. "But didn't you call him first? About eleven-thirty?"

"No," Gillian replied. "I didn't know he existed until after midnight."

"Two drinks and off to bed, is that how it was?" There was obviously no doubt in Bobbie's mind—and of course she was right. But she was uninterested in any answer. "I

guess you couldn't have looked the way you do now."
Gillian felt her jaw drop, but Bobbie was oblivious. "Hey,"
she continued. "If you didn't call Patrick, who did?"

"How do I know?" Gillian said. "I don't even know
what you're talking about."

"Like hell," said Bobbie. "You know, all right." She
paused, deciding whether to press her charges further, then
changed her mind. "You just tell him something for me.
You tell him nobody walks out on me like that."

"What do you want me to do—send him back?"

"I don't want him," said Bobbie, too quickly. "I don't
want to ever see him again." Horrified, Gillian saw the
large woman's eyes begin to fill with tears. "You tell him
that," she cried, her voice shrill. "Tell him I hate him."
Her hand—Gillian could not help noting the immense dia-
mond—went to her eyes. Bobbie shook her head, unable
to continue, then flung away, walking fast, then faster, and
almost running into the corner of the building. Suddenly
she turned back and called to Gillian, in a choked voice,
"Tell him to screw himself!"

Patrick, crouched by the engine, looked up as Gillian descended the companionway. "Oh, hi," he said. "I was just
fooling with the batteries. I thought maybe you'd gone
home."

She came down the rest of the steps, aware of his gaze
following her. "No, I suddenly felt in great need of a
shower." She was wrapped in a towel that had seemed
large enough as she skipped across the gravel of the boatyard but that suddenly felt wholly inadequate under Patrick's appraising stare. He was still bare to the waist,
gleaming with sweat. He seemed twice as large as when
she had seen him last. She wondered what it had been like
with Bobbie. "Your main squeeze was here looking for
you," she said, tossing the bundle of her clothing onto the
chart table. "Your landlady told her about last night."

Patrick's face registered mild embarrassment, slight concern, a little male satisfaction . . . and something else, as
if he was waiting for another shoe to drop. "I guess she
was pretty pissed off," he said, after a moment.

" 'Tell him to go screw himself,' " she said, trying to
reproduce Bobbie's harsh nasality. "What did you say?"

He colored. "Nothing. Sorry you had to get screeched at." He paused. "How'd she know I was here?"

In the shower, Gillian had considered that question— among others—and had decided to keep her own counsel. "Beats me," she replied. "It's a small island, after all— probably somebody saw you and told her."

"I suppose," he replied.

"You were a busy boy last night," Gillian went on, keeping her voice light. "You must've come straight from her to me."

She could feel his wariness, could almost hear his brain whirring, as he waited for her to go on. He set a wrench down with exaggerated care before he spoke. "I got clear of her as soon as I could—that's for sure. But I never expected to find somebody like you in that place. Not during the week, anyway." He straightened up. Standing in the engine compartment, he was almost eye to eye with her. "I already forgot about the first half of last night," he said quietly.

"Well, Bobbie hasn't. I'm not sure, but I think you may be fired. If it's up to her. On the other hand," Gillian continued, "I had the feeling you might be able to get back into her . . . good graces."

Patrick regarded her in astonishment for several seconds, before his roar of laughter filled the cabin. "Good graces!" He shook his head. "Good fucking graces!"

"That's just about it."

"You really get a charge out of needling people, don't you?" he demanded. "Listen: I already had enough of her. Only I didn't realize how much till I met you: Okay?"

The conversational ground was shifting dangerously, and there was still something she wanted to ask him about last night. But it was just beyond her memory's grasp. Awkwardly, she changed the subject. "What are you up to down there?"

"I figured if I was going to be aboard at night, I wanted some power—I can't feel my way around like Barr must've done. You don't have one-ten, so I brought the yard's line in and hooked up the battery charger. The batteries look to be all right, so at least I'll have lights."

"I see." She looked down into the engine compartment. It was as he had said—a heavy electrical cord had been led through a deck ventilator and down to where a portable battery charger was wedged against the yacht's side. The charger was whirring away, hooked up to one of *Glory*'s massive twelve-volt batteries. "It doesn't seem to be taking much of a charge," she said.

His look said clearly that he was surprised by a woman who could read the dial of a battery charger and interpret it correctly. "It's pretty near topped up," he said. "Barr must've been running them both up."

"The bilge isn't as bad as I'd have thought," she went on. "Have you been poking around down there?"

"No," Patrick gave her an odd look—her tone had been sharper than she had intended. "I was trying to do a quick survey. She's in better shape than I expected."

"Did you find anything down there?" It had slipped out before she realized how strange it must sound.

"Like what—buried treasure?" said Patrick, with a grin. She forced herself to return his smile.

"Just anything . . . unusual," she said. "You never know what's going to turn up in a boat as old as this one."

"That's for sure," said Patrick. "Your uncle must have been a real squirrel for tools. There's some old junk tucked away down here I've never seen before." He stretched and groaned. "I don't know about you, but I'm done."

She glanced at the watch on his wrist. "We've put in a good day," she said. "I was going down the street to get some food, and then I'll cook us dinner."

Reaching up, Patrick grasped the edge of the chart table and pulled himself out of the bilge. Carefully, he lowered the engine hatch over the opening. "Let me," he said. "I'm the best cook you'll ever see."

"Man of a thousand talents," she said, grinning at him. "You're on. I'll unpack in the meantime."

His eyebrows rose but he was not, she saw, terribly surprised. This kind of thing was probably standard in his life. "You're moving aboard, then," he said, his voice neutral.

"Somehow, I don't want to go home," she replied. "I'll take the after guest cabin."

"My stuff's there," he said. "But I can move up to the bow."

"No," she said quickly. "I'll take the fo'c'sle. You stay where you are."

"Anything you say. You're the skipper."

"That's right," she replied, wrapping the towel more tightly around herself. "So I am."

She watched Patrick, shopping list in hand, disappear among the boats. From the middle distance she could hear the angry whine of an electric sander, but there was no one in sight, and it felt good to sit on the deck and do something mindless like brushing her hair. She knew she ought to be scuffling about below decks, but for the moment Uncle Dennis's hoard seemed remote. Besides, it probably made more sense at this point to figure out intellectually where it might be hidden. That "it" was the nub of the problem: until she knew what she was looking for, searching a sixty-five-foot yacht, with its innumerable lockers and crevices, was just a quick way to go bonkers.

A glint of motion caught her eye. A man—no, two men—standing between the old Huckins and the even older schooner, just on *Glory*'s land side. Gillian picked up the big six-volt lantern she had brought on deck and pointed it at them. The dying yellow beam spotlighted a figure that was fashionably slender and not so much dressed as encased in a gray double-breasted suit, vaguely continental in cut and worn the way an actor wears a familiar costume, easily, but with an air. His face was aquiline, theatrically perfect, tanned to an evenness that was an end in itself, not merely a color acquired while being outdoors. His hair, brushed almost straight back, was a glossy, crow's-wing black, except for the discreet brush of gray at the temples. Even from twenty feet away his glowing black eyes were alive with humor, and he radiated an energy that made Gillian feel like an iron filing too close to a magnet.

He was looking up at her, the strong bones of his face highlighted by the lantern. "Miss Verdean, I believe?" he said. His tone was businesslike, but the impression it gave was quite otherwise; she felt momentarily as if they shared some rather risqué secret.

"Mr. Visconti," she replied, not getting up from her seat on the cockpit coaming. "I didn't expect you. Considering."

"I apologize," he said. His gaze passed over her in a considering sweep; she felt as if she had been weighed and set aside for the future. "May I present," he was saying, in his deep, vibrant, not-quite-American voice, "my captain, Mr. Joseph Arrow."

The man who stood behind and one step to the side was huge and broad. He had been dressed, by someone with conservative tastes, in a blue blazer and gray flannels, but the size of his biceps and chest and thighs put the ensemble visibly at risk every time he moved. His head seemed small for the rest of him, and his face was lumpy, with wispy thin hair and compressed features that somehow reminded her of a potato, but there was something measuring in his stare that was not at all amusing.

"You're alone," said Visconti. "I'd expected to see your attorney, Mr. Hitchcock. It may be just as well: we can be more informal."

"Informal but unyielding," Gillian replied, as sweetly as she could manage. She was very glad to be well above the two men, and she found herself wishing Patrick would hurry back. "*Glory* is mine, Mr. Visconti. Nothing's going to change that."

He smiled up at her, and she felt the force of him, almost like a blow. "I can understand your fondness for *Glory*," he said, running his fingertips along her planking. "Your uncle loved her very much, but he found her rather expensive to maintain, as I recall." Understatement of the year, she thought, forcing her expression to remain neutral. "There are not so many Herreshoffs left, unfortunately, and yours is one of the great ones," Visconti was saying. He sounded, even to her supercritical ear, quite sincere. She felt herself relax just a little.

"You know about her, then?"

"Only a little more than I might have got out of an old Lloyd's Register," he said, with a disarming smile. "I have been aboard, though, when your uncle was alive. We had drinks together, on your mooring at East Norwalk." He looked at the ladder and then up at Gillian, but she ignored the hint. "A beautiful piece of design," he said.

"You have a yacht, Mr. Visconti?" Gillian put in.

"Matt," he said, unveiling his perfect teeth in a smile that brought to her mind the wolf in Grandma's nightie. "Please—when you say 'Mr. Visconti' I always look over my shoulder to see if my father's standing there. Besides, it makes me feel ancient."

"Matt, then," she agreed. What was he? Forty, maybe. Barr's age; no, a little older. Certainly not ancient. She felt her cheeks burn.

"I wish I had the time for a sailing yacht," Visconti said. "But my *Tiamat* is the perfect example of making the best from a bad bargain."

"Tiamat?"

"A Babylonian sea goddess. Very obscure. The vessel herself was to have been a patrol boat. We were building her for a Central American government, to chase smugglers. Then the smugglers took over the government and canceled the order. These things happen . . ." His eyes were hard as onyx, though the smile never left his lips. "Anyway, a hundred-foot steel hull isn't something you can tuck away in your backyard, so I had her finished out as a yacht, for me. Good money after bad, I'm afraid. But I have my eye on a sheikh who may take her off my hands."

"A sheikh?" Gillian, against her will, was fascinated. "You sell boats to the Arabs?"

"I sell boats to anybody," Visconti replied. "Anybody with money. But I came to talk about your yacht, or the yacht you claim is yours."

Out on City Island Avenue, not a hundred yards away, there were thousands of people, and Gillian had never felt so alone. "Is mine," she said. "It's not *Glory* you want, anyway."

He was watching her intently. "What exactly do you mean, Gillian?"

"You know. It's why you've come up with this story about Uncle Dennis owing you money. You've got the same crazy idea—that Uncle Dennis had some stash or something, and you want to tear *Glory* apart to find it."

Visconti glanced at his companion and back at Gillian. " 'The same crazy idea'? The same as whose, Gillian?"

"Never mind."

"Perhaps I know," he said. The disarming smile illuminated his too-handsome face. "But you believe it, too, I see."

She shook her head, not trusting herself to speak.

"Look," he continued, after a moment of silence, "you respond to reality, Gillian. Let me put it realistically." Suddenly, he was a different person, detached, the undertone of sensuality transmuted to silky power. "I'm just a businessman. Like my father before me, I make weapons. Patrol craft, mostly, but my boatyards have done everything from landing barges to midget submarines. We sell them around the world, and most of our customers are pretty tough people. Also, most of them know one another."

"So what?"

Gillian's bluntness clearly surprised him. "So what? You mean you don't know what your late uncle was."

"Oh, sure. He was a rum runner, ages ago. And then he smuggled guns to . . . oh."

"Exactly. We were in the same business. Your uncle was once a partner of my father, in fact, but he—your uncle—retired, to Cuba. He was a wealthy man, until Castro, and he had to leave in his socks. So, since then, your uncle was sometimes a cutout . . . a middleman, you would say, but a very special kind. One who conceals the principals in a deal from one another. In this kind of work, it can be useful not to be too close to one's customers."

"Or one's suppliers?"

"True for you." The smile had returned. "People in my profession have to act somewhat like porcupines making love: very carefully. What's needed is an agent both sides are willing to trust, who holds the money until the goods are ready. It's actually more complicated than that, but never mind. Your uncle served as a cutout for me, more than once. Not the most trustworthy, I'm afraid, but one uses what's available." He looked abruptly up at her. "No offense, I hope?"

"No offense." It was fair enough: she would not have trusted Uncle Dennis with a rusty dime, much as she loved him.

"A realist," Visconti said, to Captain Arrow, as if settling an argument. The big man's face was still sullen—maybe it always was—but he nodded. "Some time ago, your uncle took money, a lot of money, to hold for a stepped deal. That is, he was to pass it on at stated—"

"Your company was building something," she interrupted, "and you were to be paid, through Uncle Dennis, as certain stages in the job were finished."

"Admirable. Exactly so. In any case, your uncle made the first payment, and the second. When it came time for the third, he was said to be very ill. Unavailable. There were rumors that he had become involved, on his own account, in a large and very foolish venture—something to do with palm oil . . ." He looked quickly up at her, but she was ready this time, and stared him down. "In any case, he is now dead."

"And you're holding the bag," Gillian said. "Or the boats."

"May I suggest," he said, in his most friendly manner, "that it's possible sometimes to be too clever?"

"It's my curse," she replied, as lightly as she could. "Look, Matt, I can see your problem—but that's what it is: your problem. Not mine. Uncle Dennis sold me the boat, and I plan to sail her."

"I would like to accommodate you," Visconti said regretfully. "Truly I would. But you must understand my position. The money itself is only part of it—I am big enough to absorb that kind of loss—"

"Then why don't you?"

"Be quiet. As I was saying, the financial loss is only part of it. More to the point, we cannot allow ourselves to be defrauded—ripped off—like this. When that happens in my small community, everyone knows. And everyone will think he can try the same thing."

"As I said, that's your problem. And as I've also said, Uncle Dennis died broke. I should know—I had to pay the hospital bills."

Visconti was shaking his head indulgently. "No, my dear, that won't do," he said, then quickly added: "It didn't work with General Hals, did it?"

Gillian knew her expression was betraying her, but she said only, "General?"

"A good question," Visconti replied, as if she had made a clever point. "The promotion was his own idea, of course. Rather a jump from a Wehrmacht major."

"West or East?"

Visconti's avuncular tone, she decided, was as annoying as Barr's. "General Hals rather predates all that. The Second World War—'the war,' as our parents called it—was his setting."

"He's a little long in the tooth to be a general, then," she said. "I mean, that would make him seventy, right?"

"Don't underestimate him, Gillian," Visconti said. "He's been a soldier, a fighting soldier, for all these years.

He fled Italy in 1945, with your uncle's help, and went to the Near East. He fought first for Arabs against the British and the Jews, and then he started his own force. For hire. Now he is said to be employed—"

Captain Arrow, looking quite shocked, cleared his throat loudly, and Visconti glanced sidelong at him. "Perhaps not," he agreed. "But I *can* say one thing more. Was Hals accompanied by a tall, thin Englishman?"

There was no point in pretending. "Tall and thin, yes," she said. "English—could be. He never spoke. Major something, Hals called him."

"Bellairs," said Visconti, his lips curling as if the name had a bitter taste. "Major Bellairs, late of the Scots Guards and several less squeamish organizations. With General Hals, he has found his level."

"What do you mean?" she asked.

"He kills people. For amusement." She remembered the shallow, protruding eyes. "I'm glad you believe me," he said, and she felt her face go hot. "Your captain won't be able to protect you from that . . . even if he wanted to."

"My captain?"

"You know how he lost his own boat, of course."

So it was Barr he meant. "On a reef. Off Anguilla, I think."

"Anegada," Visconti corrected. "He lost everything—boat, wife, the lot."

Wife? He had never mentioned a wife. She wanted desperately to ask Visconti more, decided it was best not to.

"A man like that has nothing to lose," said Visconti. "Think it over." He turned on his heel, the giant Arrow at his back, and stalked off.

"This is like a picnic," Gillian said. "All we need are ants." She pushed the plate away and leaned back. Across the table from her, Patrick had finished eating. He was like a big cat, she thought—neat, smooth and watchful. He was watching her now, his face politely attentive. "I filled one of the tanks, while you were out," she continued. "We can heat up some water for the dishes. Unless you don't do dishes."

"I don't care. I'm easy."

"You'll make some woman a great wife," she said. He

smiled, the white teeth gleaming, and she added: "I like that."

"What?" he asked. He was surveying her with lazy appreciation, and she was glad she had dug out the good slacks and the red blouse; last night he had felt sorry for her, at least at the beginning. That was not the relationship she wanted.

"You don't worry about being macho all the time. That's what I like."

"What's to worry?" He put his hands behind his head and stretched. He was wearing a fresh khaki shirt, short-sleeved, and her eyes were drawn to his powerful arms. In a way she felt safe with him. He would pop her in bed again if he could, but if things didn't work out that way he wouldn't be too disappointed. Or so she hoped.

He was watching her, and she knew it was time to get things straight between them. Well, maybe in a few minutes. "Did she—Bobbie—have a thing for muscles?"

"Muscles," he said, making his biceps jump. "There was a line, from a musical we did in high school . . . 'All he must be is a man and alive.' "

"*Brigadoon*," she said. "Are you into music, Patrick?"

"I fool around a little," he replied. "Mostly Irish songs. My dad's Irish—first-generation, that is. Very big on the IRA."

"And you're not," she said.

"I've met some of them." He hesitated, choosing his words. "Mean little bastards with bad teeth. And how can anybody, for Christ's sake, be a Catholic and a Commie at the same time?"

"You're not either one, I suppose."

"Not either," he agreed. "I brought my guitar. How about some music?"

"I'd rather hear about your past," she replied. "You want to split a beer?" She felt at ease for the first time in weeks. At ease and in control, allowing herself to respond to him. She knew she couldn't let it go too far, but she was enjoying being a woman.

"No, thanks," he said. "But I'll get you one." He returned a moment later, and set down the open can in front of her. "Wait a minute," he added. "I'll be right back."

"I'm not going anyplace." From where she sat, she could just see down the companionway passage aft. The chart table was bathed in a warm, red glow from the navigator's light with its tinted bulb. The familiar books clustered on the shelves above it. Further aft, through the open door of the ladies' cabin, the freshly scrubbed woodwork gleamed dimly. In spite of everything that had happened, it felt like home.

"Here," said Patrick, reappearing with a scarred guitar. "This is the traveling version. The good one's back in my apartment."

She folded down the leaves of the big table to give him room, and he sat down next to her. His hands were strong and well kept, like everything else about him. She glanced down at her own fingers; it would take weeks of care to make them look human again. Patrick hit a couple of experimental chords and then drew his fingers slowly across a G, letting the sound fade nearly away before his voice picked it up softly: " 'When all beside a vigil keep, the West's asleep, the West's asleep,' " he began. The trace of a brogue slid into his voice. " 'Alas and well may Erin weep, when Connaught lies in slumber deep.' "

"That's nice," Gillian murmured, dropping the words neatly into the space between verses.

Patrick nodded an acknowledgment. " 'For long a proud and haughty race honored and sentinel'd the place . . .' " The sound flowed over her. Not a trained baritone, but sweet and easy, with power to spare behind it. The tempo picked up to a martial canter: " 'And often, in O'Connor's van, to triumph dashed each Connaught clan—' " he glanced at her sidelong, amusement in his eyes: " 'And fleet as deer the Normans ran, through Corshleave's pass and Ardrahan.' " He vamped for a bar or two. "It's a French name, isn't it—Verdean?"

She laughed. "Go on, Mick. Finish it."

"I can't," he said, grinning. "Not sober, anyway. It's too dumb. They all are. Do you know 'Kevin Barry'?"

"I've heard it." Had he moved closer to her or was it vice versa? She didn't care.

" 'All around the little bake-shop,' " he sang, pushing up to a tenor, his accent outrageous now. " 'Where we fought them hand to hand. Shoot me like an Irish soldier, for I die to free Ireland.' What bullshit!"

"You want silly lyrics, try grand opera," she said.

" '*Anges purs, anges radieux!*' " she sang lightly, " '*Portez mon âme au sein des cieux!*' "

"What's that?" he asked.

"*Faust*," she replied. "The ding-a-ling Marguerite. Having killed her illegitimate child, she demands a free ticket to heaven. And gets it."

"Oh."

Something she said had jarred him. "What else can you play?" she asked.

"How about this:" His finger picked out the melody; his voice was light and straightforward. " 'The joys of love are but a moment long. The pains of love endure your whole life long.' Short and bittersweet."

" '*Plaisir d'amour*,' " she said. "I know that."

"In French? In D?"

"Try me." His fingertips were very gentle on the strings, just the ghosts of sound, and her own voice was almost a whisper. " '*Plaisir d'amour ne dure qu'un moment*,' " she sang. " '*Chagrin d'amour dure toute la vie*.' "

"I can't do French," he said. "Follow me in English?" She nodded, as he picked it up: " 'Your eyes met mine: I saw the love in them shine. You brought me heaven right then, when your eyes met mine.' "

Somehow her head was on his shoulder. He seemed not to notice, his voice gaining power: " 'My love loves me, and oh, the wonders I see: A rainbow shines in my window—my love loves me.' " She was following him easily, her light soprano twined around his baritone. " 'And now she's gone, like a dream that fades into dawn . . .' "

She made herself reach out and clamp a hand across the guitar's neck. "No," she said.

That surprised him all right. "No what?" he demanded.

"No replay of last night."

He set the guitar down on the table and turned back to her. His big hands took her gently by the arms, and she felt a thrill of fear. *My God, his fingers go clear around my biceps.* "No," she said again. She had meant to sound calm, dignified, immovable, the way Hepburn would have sounded, but what came out was a squeak more like Olive Oyl.

After a long moment, his hands dropped. "I guess it's my turn to apologize," he said. He looked puzzled.

"That's okay," she replied, her voice nearly as steady as she wanted it to be. "You were just running on automatic pilot."

"Not that at all." He clearly wanted to say something, and just as clearly could not find the words.

"The thing is," Gillian said, "sex is just no good if you're working together. I had to learn that the hard way."

He looked at her without speaking, but she could feel him willing her into his arms.

"I think we'd better call it a night," she said firmly, getting to her feet. Virtue intact, damn it.

"Okay," he agreed, rising. He picked up the guitar.

"Good-night, Patrick—thanks for the song."

"My pleasure," he replied. "See you in the morning." He opened the door to his small cabin. "You want this chart table light on?"

"I'll turn it off," she replied.

"Right," he said. "Good-night again."

For several minutes she stood in the main cabin, letting the feel of the old yacht sweep over her. *Glory* was really hers, now. And somewhere aboard, she was sure of it, was enough money to make her and the boat independent. She ought to feel triumphant—part of her did. But another part of her was still grieving over Uncle Dennis, and feeling guilty because the grief was not keener. She heard a small noise from the guest cabin. That would've been nice, she thought. Nice, but a mistake. I like you, Patrick O'Mara, and I'm pretty sure you like me; if only I could trust you, too. She walked slowly through the saloon, back to the chart table. Damn it, I miss Barr. As she reached up to turn off the red-tinted light, her gaze fixed on the open locker door in the ladies' cabin, and on the gaping emptiness within. In her mind's eye was a picture of Barr walking away from her, across the boatyard, with that lumpy, heavy sack over his shoulder. In a flash of perception she realized what he had taken. And why.

7

CITY ISLAND
FRIDAY, MAY 10
ONE A.M.

Patrick went from asleep to completely awake in an
instant. He was lying on his back in the cramped
berth. The cabin was as black as a closed coffin, although
a slight breath of fresh air whispered down through the
deck ventilator above his face. He brought his wristwatch
up to eye level and triggered the faint illumination on the
dial: one in the morning. From long habit, he forced himself to lie completely still while he took inventory of the
space around him. He had known in the moment of waking
where he was—the smell of old wood and bilge and mildew
must have been pressing on his sleeping mind. Around
him was the slow chorus of tiny squeaks and groans that
marked *Glory*'s discomfort in her cradle. He had slept
aboard old wooden vessels like this one before, as a boy,
and had not forgotten the sounds they never stopped
making.

A sudden thump and scrape made him start. It seemed
to be coming from right next to his head, and for a moment
he thought Gillian had changed her mind and come into
his cabin. Then he realized that the sound was on the
outside of the hull, and his gut knotted, remembering:
They had picked him up as he came out of Tremaine's
gate on his way to the grocery. From fifty yards off, he
had recognized Bellairs behind the wheel of the tan Fairlane at the curb. Patrick had had to force himself to move
forward, toward that hated, feared face. Only steps away,

he saw who was sitting beside the adjutant—he had not known till that moment that the General was here, too. Not that it made much difference: in his whole two-year hitch, Patrick had not said five sentences to the General. The old man—he looked much older, and smaller, in civilian clothes—had remained a distant figure, always near but never actually present. As Patrick came up to the car, Bellairs rolled down his window. He had been brief, and the General had said nothing at all. "Stay put, lie doggo till we tell you what to do. You don't need to know what it's all about, so don't ask."

Now the sound outside changed, to a slow, irregular squeak. Of course: someone had placed the ladder against *Glory*'s side and was climbing it, trying to make as little noise as possible. Patrick's first thought was Bellairs. But why would Bellairs turn up at this hour? And if not him, who could it be? Patrick slipped out of his berth, pulled on his pants. He groped his way quietly to the door and eased it open. A faint scuffling on deck, and a muffled metallic thump as whoever it was tripped over a fitting.

The main hatch was open, a square of starry sky. As Patrick watched, a black outline moved across the opening. It was not Bellairs, nor was it Barr returning; the man coming slowly and carefully down the ladder was far wider than either the Englishman or *Glory*'s ex-skipper. The companionway ladder creaked under his weight, and Patrick shrank back, tense but ready—this was something combat had trained him to handle, trained him over and over until darkness and unfamiliar surroundings were immaterial.

The boat was even more unfamiliar to the visitor, apparently: Patrick heard him swear under his breath as he collided with the rounded edge of the chart table. He was within easy reach, but Patrick remained silent and still, waiting. A sudden tiny beam of light darted out, illuminating the passageway and the door, but not strong enough to light the saloon beyond. It silhouetted the man holding it; he was carrying the flash in his left hand, extended to one side, and something shiny in his right, close to his body. A handgun, from the way he held it.

The intruder halted in the doorway to the saloon, playing the beam of his flash around the compartment. He was breathing hard, whether from nerves or from the climb. He was a little shorter than Patrick, but his bulk filled the door frame—two hundred or two-twenty, at least. Strong enough, with all that beef, but out of shape and clumsy. He was looking, Patrick guessed, for something, rather than someone, and he was unsure where to start. Without warning, the stranger turned, the beam of his light sweeping around toward where Patrick crouched. Up forward in the fo'c'sle a board creaked, and the heavy-set man paused, listening. But he would be coming aft in a second, Patrick knew, and took his chance, fading back through the open doorway behind him that led to the ladies' cabin, at the stern of the accommodation. It was much too much like a trap, and Patrick felt the sweat running down the inside of his arms.

Easy does it. He's blinded by his own light. I know he's here and he hasn't seen me yet. And I can handle any man alive, if I can get to him. Patrick heard inside his head the long-ago voice of his unarmed combat instructor: "Until he's made up his mind, the man with a pistol hasn't decided if he's holding a gun or a club. That gives you—just maybe—a clear half second."

The intruder took a step down the passageway. Another, and a third—each marked by a soft creaking of floorboards. Now he must be abreast of the companionway ladder. The flashlight beam played through the open door of the ladies' cabin, and Patrick tensed himself to spring. Then it passed on, and wobbled strangely. Patrick risked a look, saw that the unknown had apparently pocketed his weapon, and his right hand, gleaming black—a leather glove?—was slowly opening the door of the guest cabin where Patrick had been sleeping. Would he guess someone had been there only moments before? If he felt the rumpled blanket, it would still be warm. Apparently, the fact of the cabin's emptiness was enough. The intruder stepped back and Patrick retreated into the shadows as the beam of light swung around again and paused, playing over the chart table.

The man was in profile from where Patrick stood, and bits of him were sharply illuminated by the reflection of his flash off the varnished woodwork: shiny hair that looked as if it was glued in place, maroon shirt with some kind of metallic threads in it and black pants. He was scanning the shelves, moving the beam of light over the books. Whatever he was looking for was not there, and he opened the topmost of the wide drawers under the chart table's surface, lifting the charts one by one. Not there, either; he closed the first drawer and was opening the second when a clear, unafraid voice called out from the saloon, "Patrick, is that you? What're you doing?"

The heavy man moved fast. The beam of light was on Gillian's white face before Patrick could take a step. "Hold it!" said a deep, harsh voice. "Right there, sweetie. This is a gun in my hand."

She was wearing an old-fashioned man's nightshirt; it made her seem about twelve years old, except for where the tips of her small, high breasts thrust the fabric out. Her expression never changed; she looked, if anything, mildly irritated. "Well, which of them sent you—Visconti or Hals?"

So she knew about the General. But who was this Visconti? Patrick's eyes never left the gun, a big army .45. The stranger said nothing. "If you're looking for charts," she continued (and now Patrick thought he detected the slightest tremor in her voice), "I have to tell you ours are very out of date."

"Don't be a wise-ass, kid," said the man with the gun. "I want the plans for this old tub. You just show me where they are—stay right there!—and I'll be on my way."

Patrick could hear the edge in her voice: "You're out of luck—who'd keep a set of plans on a boat? Why don't you try the Herreshoff Museum? They have a set."

"You're asking for a working over," said the man, plainly angered. "You might get more than you're looking for, too."

Jesus, Gillian, give the sucker what he wants, thought Patrick. He won't be jerked around: can't you hear it? Maybe she could: "Honest, they're not here," she insisted. "We had a set, but they were with Uncle Dennis's stuff. Mr. Hitchcock has them."

"No, he doesn't. You're lying."

"Well, maybe they're at home. In Westport. What do you want with them, anyway?"

"Never you mind. Okay, then—we'll go to Westport, and you'll show me where that stuff is."

In the flashlight's beam her face had been white, but

suddenly it went whiter still. "At least let me get some clothes on," she said.

"No more stalling," the man replied. "You'll do fine the way you are. Come on—or I'll come get you."

Wordlessly, she shook her head, and the big man took a step toward her. Patrick tensed, ready to jump but knowing he was too far away. At the last instant, she put up her hand. "Okay," she said.

"That's better," he growled. As she stepped forward he backed away ahead of her. In the shadows, Patrick crouched, but the intruder stopped, well out of reach. "Put your hands up on the bulkhead," he ordered.

Gillian gave him a look of hatred, but to Patrick's relief she did what he told her. The man set the flashlight down on the edge of the chart table, where it illuminated the girl, picking out the curve of her buttocks against the night-shirt. His Cupid's-bow mouth shaped a private smile as he ran his free hand over her, letting it linger on her breast. "Pretty skinny," he said. She was as rigid and motionless as stone, even when he pushed his hand between her legs.

That's right, Gillian, thought Patrick, willing her to be still. The man stepped back. "All right," he said reluctantly, picking up the flashlight. "Up the ladder. Slowly."

She was between Patrick and the stranger, withdrawn into herself. Her pale face was blank, and then she saw the open door of the guest cabin. She turned on the heavy-set man so quickly that he took an automatic step backward. "Where's Patrick?" she demanded.

For an instant, the man looked almost comically baffled, and then the penny dropped. "In here?" he said suspiciously. "Face the bulkhead, sweetie. Hands up on it. Feet back—like that." She was immobilized, and the intruder cautiously aimed gun and flashlight through the door of the cabin.

Now or never, Patrick told himself. Two steps down the passage, brushing Gillian clear with a stroke of his arm. The man was halfway into his turn, the light and the pistol coming around together. Patrick dropped his shoulder, caught the man just under the ribcage in a savage block that hurled him against the door frame with a force that shook the boat. A lighter, weaker man would have been down for the count, but this one just grunted. He started to fold his powerful arms around Patrick, who slipped free

at the last moment. As the stranger battered at his back
with the flashlight, Patrick grabbed the man's right wrist
with both hands and slammed his hand into the bulkhead's
ridged moulding. The automatic fell and hit the floorboards, going off with a thunderous crash.

Abruptly, the flashlight went out, although the intruder
was still smashing at Patrick's back and shoulder with it.
The sudden blackness was welcome—it more than evened
things up. Unable to see, the heavy man could scarcely
use his weight effectively, and he was already gasping like
a beached whale. Patrick pressed in, knowing he had to
end it fast before a lucky blow stopped him. He slammed
the edge of his hand at the other man's throat, and felt it
hit what must have been collarbone. His other hand came
up hard, but struck a heavy thigh instead of the groin.
Timing's off. I'm out of practice.

Something—the flashlight—crashed into the side of Patrick's head. He shook it off and bored in again, behind a
barrage of short lefts and rights. The big man had his back
to a bulkhead, trying to fend off the punishing blows with
the jagged wreck of the flash.

The cabin lights came on. Patrick caught a glimpse of a
pale-faced Gillian standing by the switch. With an inartic-
ulate bellow, the man hurled himself at Patrick, swinging
the stump of the light in a vicious downward arc. Patrick
stepped inside it, feeling a burning sensation, like a red-
hot wire, across his shoulder. He drove a quick left-right-
left just under the man's heart, and followed it up with a
savage upward jerk of his knee.

This time he did not miss. His opponent jackknifed forward, his hands going to his crotch. Patrick stepped back,
felt a blow in the small of his back as he hit the edge
of the chart table. Measuring his man, he waited till the
intruder began to straighten up, hearing the agonized,
wheezing intake of his breath. Down came Patrick's linked
hands in a blow like the blade of a guillotine, striking just
behind the base of the neck. The heavy-set man began to
topple, and Patrick brought his knee up one more time,
felt the crunching give of cartilage. His opponent straightened, his eyes as blank as saucers, and Patrick grabbed
the front of his shirt to steady him, then crossed his right
with a crisp, economical crack to the jaw. The man
bounced off the bulkhead and slid to the deck, the blood

from his broken nose already streaming down his shirt front. Amazingly, he was not unconscious, although he was, for the moment, as helpless as a side of beef.

"Stop!" Behind him, Gillian's voice was peremptory. Patrick, his chest heaving, half turned. She had the gun, was holding it steadily in both hands, the muzzle pointed at the seated man. "That's enough, Patrick. You almost killed him."

Patrick shook his head, feeling the stab of pain in his shoulder. "Take a lot more than that," he gasped. He sagged against the chart table. On the floorboards, the man was watching them. He was a mess: one eye was nearly closed, the blood from his nose seemed to be all over the front of his shirt.

"Here, Mister," said Gillian. She tossed him a rag. "Don't you bleed on my woodwork." He pressed the cloth to his face, still watching her with his good eye. "Get up," she ordered.

He struggled to his feet. Patrick watched him narrowly, but the man was just barely able to stand. Gillian was still pointing the automatic at him, and looked fully capable of using it. Patrick saw a gleam of leather at the man's hip pocket, reached out for it. "His wallet," he said, flipping it open. "John Troiano," Patrick said aloud. "Heard of him?"

Gillian shook her head. "Give it back to him." Patrick tossed it to the deck, and Troiano bent forward, painfully, to retrieve it. "Get off my boat," Gillian said coldly. "Get off my boat and don't come back."

The cloth still pressed to his face, Troiano mumbled something.

"What?" she said.

"By dose," Troiano replied. "Bastard broke by dose."

"If you're not out of here in two minutes, I'll let him break your neck." She waved the gun dramatically at the companionway ladder, and Patrick flinched. "Up," she said.

Weaving slightly, Troiano moved toward the ladder. Patrick half expected him to grab for the .45—the man was a long way from done—but he saw Patrick was ready for his move.

"Wait," Gillian said when they were on deck. "Can you see anybody down there, Patrick?"

There was only the glow from the open hatch, and the distant glitter of streetlights. "No," he replied, controlling his breathing with an effort.

"Down you go," she said to Troiano. He threw a leg over the side, feeling clumsily for the rung. For a moment Patrick thought the ladder would go over. The heavy man's bloody face was level with Gillian's. "You tell your boss, whoever he is, to stay away from me," she said. "You hear?"

Troiano said nothing, staring her down with his one good eye. Slowly, she raised the pistol until it was pointing right at his face, a foot away. "You hear me, Mr. Troiano?" she repeated. Patrick, who had seen the wrong end of more than one gun from about the same distance, was not surprised when Troiano's eyes lowered, and he muttered, "I hear."

Patrick watched him go slowly, painfully down the ladder; heard him blunder off in the dark. He turned back to Gillian, who was sitting on the edge of the companionway, and put his hand on her shoulder. "You're shaking," he said.

"Damn straight," she replied, the tremor in her voice, too.

"Maybe you better give me that thing," he said. "Before you hurt somebody."

She started, and he flinched again. "Here," she said, extending it. "Christ, it's heavy."

He took it by the barrel, slid the clip out of the butt. "Good for driving nails, breaking down doors and holding stacks of papers in place, but not a whole hell of a lot else."

"It looks pretty businesslike to me," she said, her voice steady again. "We'd better go get the first-aid kit: your back's a mess."

In the main cabin, she turned him around. "Sit on the end of the table," she said. "No, not the—"

The gimbaled table swung under his weight, almost spilling him to the deck. He repositioned himself cautiously. "We don't have these on powerboats," he said.

"Uh-huh," she murmured abstractedly. "Hold still: this is iodine—it's going to sting."

It did. "The flashlight?"

"The lens broke," she said. "There's a piece of glass here. I'd better fish it out."

He bent forward, holding the edge of the saloon table with both hands. "Go ahead."

"There." She held it up for his inspection, a shard an inch across. "That's twice I've watched you wipe somebody out—"

"Listen," he interrupted, "what's going on here, anyway? You didn't seem all that surprised when what's-his-name Troiano turned up. Are we supposed to be expecting more of them? And what in hell do they want?"

"Mr. Troiano? He works for someone who wants . . . who wants to get their hands on this boat."

"Someone named Visconti or Hals?" Patrick asked. "Who are they?"

She hesitated for several seconds before she said, "They want *Glory*—both of them think they have some claim on her, but they don't."

He straightened up and turned around. She was avoiding his eye. "He didn't want the boat, he wanted the plans. Or that's what he said."

"The plans," she said. "Well—"

"Look," Patrick said. "I know I'm the new guy, but after tonight I think you could trust me a little."

Her smile, unexpected, made his heart turn over. "Yes," she said. "I guess you've earned that. Sit down and I'll tell you about it."

Fifteen minutes later, Gillian stopped talking and looked at Patrick apprehensively. He shook his head. "That's wild," he said.

"It's true," she insisted. "All of it."

"Sure. Whatever you say," he agreed, trying to order his racing thoughts. One thing was certain: Gillian was in twice as much of a mess as she knew. "So what're you going to do?" he asked.

"That depends on you," she replied, startling him. "While I was talking just now, I came to a conclusion. I can't handle this myself. Alone."

This wasn't the way he wanted her to go. "Look," he said, "why not just give the damn boat up? Let this Hals and his buddy go over it and find what they want." He saw her face close off, wanted to grab her thin shoulders and shake her. But he forced himself to continue, calmly: "They won't want her after they find it—and they can duke it out with Visconti and whoever's behind Troiano. You'll be in the clear."

"You don't understand," she said, shaking her head. "I want it too, whatever it is." Her small, callused hand took his arm, and he felt her touch all the way to his fingertips. "I love this boat. She's all I have. But if I'm going to sail *Glory*, I've got to have money, a lot of it."

Her hand fell away, and he took a deep, shuddering breath to steady himself. He forced himself to look past her, around the grimy cabin. "Well, you're right about that. Fixing this boat'll take a bundle."

"So will you be my skipper, Patrick?" she blurted out. "Help me get *Glory* launched. Help me find Uncle Dennis's stash. And split fifty-fifty."

It was perfect, just what Bellairs and Hals wanted. "Okay, I'll do it," he said, and his heart felt like lead.

8

CITY ISLAND
TWO A.M.

Barr had been aware for some time of his growing irritation, as he worked his way through *Glory*'s old logbooks, but he did not realize how much his distaste was showing until Emerald straightened, pushed her glasses up on her head and said, "Well, what's the matter?"

It was hard to explain, especially to a nonsailor. "All this," he said, tapping the book on his lap. "I mean, there's one right way to keep a log, and this is garbage. It's like *True Romances*."

"Come off it," Emerald replied. "You've never read *True Romances* in your life. I don't know why you're so pissed off," she continued. "If Dennis hadn't put all his hopes, fears and ambitions in here, we wouldn't know where to start. But we've done two of these books, up through 1939, and what do we know so far? Damn little."

"Well, we haven't got to the real meat yet," he said, "but we've got a good deal of background."

"Maybe I'm slow," she said. "Explain it to me."

He sat back for a moment and collected his thoughts. "All right, here goes: Falk buys *Titania*—as she was called then—in 1934. If I remember right, that was the year after Prohibition ended, so I suppose he was using money he made running booze. It was also the bottom of the Depression, but Falk must've been in good shape. I figure he got the boat cheap—"

85

"Why?" Her sharp question stopped him for a second, and he had to pull his thoughts back.

"Why? Well, she'd been out of the water for a whole year, and Falk had to do a lot of little repairs—the kind of things that tell you the original owner didn't have enough money to keep her up. I'm an expert," he added, with a wry smile, "on that state of affairs."

"Fair enough," she said. "What next?"

"He fixes her up, and spends the next couple of years doodling around. Summer in New England, winter in Florida. On the boat all the time, so he must not have had a job. But he's getting a little pinched toward the end. There's entries," he explained, seeing her eyebrows go up, "about work that needed to be done but wasn't. No reason given. Even so, he's got the money to keep her sailing—and with a live-aboard captain, a deckhand and a cook—"

"Not to mention money for Inez in Baltimore, Clarissa in Palm Beach and a light dusting of other cuties in Newport, Bar Harbor and Shelter Island," Emerald put in.

"Right," Barr agreed. "So where are we? Middle of '36. Money's getting low, but he sees a great new way to recoup."

"You lost me again," Emerald complained. She was following the dates in the log, and shaking her head.

"Look," Barr said, pointing. "He has the boat hauled for a full refit—and in July. You don't do that kind of thing in July, you go sailing. And look here at the work he's having done: New chain plates, twice as heavy as the original ones—"

"I don't even know what chain plates are," said Emerald plaintively.

"Long, flat bars. Bronze or stainless steel," Barr replied, slightly distracted. "The standing rigging connects to them with turnbuckles." He looked up, saw the expression on her face and revised his remarks. "They anchor the masts. If you replace them—and the wire rigging, too—it means you're planning for some really heavy going. And look here," he pointed, "new storm jib, new trysail, extra sets of reef points in the staysail and mizzen—"

"Okay, okay," she said, throwing up her hands. "I told you I was a dry-land lady. I did see that he replaced the crew, at the same time."

"Yes. Six men instead of three, so he'd have two

watches, for round-the-clock passage making. But the important point is the cargo."

"What cargo? He doesn't say anything about that."

"Not directly," Barr replied. "But look here—and here. And there's another reference later, I'm sure."

" 'Miss Thompson,' " she read aloud. " 'Sharing the ladies' cabin with Miss Thompson.' I thought he was taking one of his sweeties along."

"So did I, at first," Barr said, turning the pages rapidly. "But—here it is—look at this."

" 'Miss Thompson's sisters forward, under the galley, bring the waterline level again.' " Emerald shook her head. "I missed it, but I wouldn't have got it anyway. What does that stuff mean in English?"

"Look, there used to be a big storage area underneath the galley floorboards. It was intended for food—a metal-lined box, about eight feet by four by four. I'd bet 'Miss Thompson' is Falk being cute, shorthand for Thompson submachine guns. During Prohibition, they were a big thing—the weapon of choice. But afterward the demand went way down, at least in the U.S. Overseas, it was a different story, especially in a war."

"World War Two, you mean? That didn't begin till 1941," she said. "Even I know that: December seventh, 1941."

He regarded her with awe. "You don't know how old you make me feel, Emerald. Look, the war—as we old folks call it—began in Europe in 1939, but the war I was thinking of is the curtain raiser, the Spanish Civil War, and that started in '36."

"Learn something new every day," she replied. "So he sailed to Spain, but I'd be willing to swear the word 'Spain' isn't in here anyplace. I suppose these numbers—latitude and longitude, right?—tell you where he was going."

"Pretty much," Barr said. "I'd need charts or an atlas to be precise, but I can pick off the route generally. And that says something in itself."

"Like what?"

"The normal transatlantic route from New York to Spain is via the Azores. I've made that passage myself: the islands are right on your course, about two-thirds the way across. But Falk didn't even stop—probably didn't want to be seen."

She pursed her lips. "Does that tell you which side he was on?"

"No, but the boat's name does."

"I saw he changed it, but I don't read Spanish. What's a *pasionaria*?"

"*La Pasionaria*. The great heroine of the Spanish Republicans," Barr said. "He really gave himself away that time. And you notice something else?"

"Less words," she said after a moment. "Mostly numbers and a little stuff about the weather."

"More like the way a logbook ought to be," said Barr, unable to keep the approval out of his voice.

She regarded him in mock exasperation. "Not bad enough you're a Puritan," she said, "but a goddamn nautical Puritan. I guess it serves me right, though—same as it serves you right, being partners with a whore."

"Please," he said. " 'Porno queen.' Isn't that the right title?"

She laughed. "Absolutely. Where'd you pick up that one."

"Gillian, believe it or not. When she was telling Dennis about your magnum opus."

"My what? Oh, *King's Mistress*, you mean. That's right, she saw it. I wish I'd been a fly on the wall for that conversation—it must've blown Dennis away."

"He didn't seem too pleased," Barr agreed.

"That was what split us up. Me making that movie— hell, I was trying to help him."

He looked the question he was at a loss to phrase, and she explained. "He was between scams—flat broke, and he owed somebody a lot of dough. Somebody really nasty. We came in one evening after dinner, and they'd beaten up his car with a sledgehammer."

"What? That's incredible," said Barr. "Didn't anyone see it?"

"The garage guy, I'm sure. But he was so scared he couldn't talk. Anyway, I'd been with Dennis two, nearly three years by then, and I owed him a lot. He sent me to drama school, bought me clothes, taught me how to sit through an opera without going to sleep. I wanted to do something in return. When I saw he was broke, that seemed like a good opportunity."

"But he didn't see it that way?"

She shook her head. "Macho stuff: 'I'll solve it myself, dear.'" Her eyes widened. "Come to think of it, that's when he told me about his nest egg. That's what he called it—nest egg."

Barr leaned forward. "What did he say? As near as you can remember?"

"I thought he was lying, at first." She looked at Barr. "He lied a lot, you know."

"I remember."

"It was all about how he'd had this stash for years," she continued. "He'd never touched it, even when he was broke. He was never going to spend a dime of it till he was too old to work." She seemed to be listening to her memory. "He seemed to be scared of the money . . . I don't know. I was hurt and angry. I'd been real fond of him, you know?"

"How did you meet him?" Barr asked, fascinated in spite of himself.

"He picked me up," she replied matter-of-factly. "It was my second week in New York. I was working the phone nights and waitressing days, in one of those nothing places down near Grand Central. He used to eat breakfast there, and he just kind of scooped me up, between the Danish and the coffee."

"Fast worker."

"I like a man who can make up his mind. Anyway, I moved in with him that same evening—I'd been sharing a room with another girl, but she O.D.'d." A quick shadow brushed across Emerald's face. "Maybe that's why I went with Dennis. I could see it happening to me, and I was scared. He was nice. Not many demands—mostly just a little flattery afterward, if you know what I mean . . . Barr, are you blushing?"

He managed a smile. "I don't know many people like you, Emerald."

"You don't know anybody like me," she said, with satisfaction. "Dennis got the idea he was, you know, Pygmalion: he was going to invent me. What he didn't see was that I was inventing myself at the same time. He never told me when he started to run out of money, of course, but a girl can figure those things. I just wanted to help, and I had this great idea for a movie. I talked to some of the kids in the acting group I was with, and some of the girls I knew . . . before. It would've been a cinch to finance."

"But you did make the movie," Barr said.

"Sure. But not then. Dennis hit the roof when I told him what I wanted to do. And I walked out. I got an apartment and went back on the phone for a while, before I got into X. Dennis cooled down some, and we'd have lunch or dinner once in a while—like when you and I met, that time I came up to Norwalk to go sailing, and up-chucked all over you. But Dennis and I were through. I was out of the nest."

"You knew about Gillian, though?"

"Of course. I thought he was getting ready to move in on her, when he got sick. But he didn't quite get around to introducing us."

"A pity," Barr said.

"I sometimes think so," she replied. "She sounds like a girl with balls, if you'll pardon the expression. But what about you, Barr? Where do you come from?"

"I'll tell you sometime," he said. "But I think we've gotten off the track."

"Don't think you're getting out of it that easily," she replied. "I've got a raincheck. Where were we?"

"Late summer, 1936. Just entering the Med. He sails east, past Spain, to Marseille."

"Right. That's in the book. What do you figure he did there?"

"Made some contacts, I suppose. Two weeks later, he heads west."

"To Spain?"

"Probably. Maybe Barcelona. Anyway, now he's got money again. . . . At least he's spending it. He heads east to Monaco and pays off his crew."

"So he sailed this big, slow old boat right into the middle of a war. Is that as dangerous as it sounds?"

"It isn't dangerous," said Barr, with deep conviction. "It's lunatic. And I doubt he did it for the money. I think he was having fun."

Emerald cocked her head to one side and considered. "You may be right," she said. "He certainly had that streak. It was one of the things I liked about him."

Barr shrugged. "Whatever. So he's based on Monaco and makes a couple more trips each year, until '39, when the Fascists won and the war was over." He put the book down and picked up the next. "In July of '39, he changes the boat's name to *Glory*—no more mileage in *La Pa-sionaria*—sails to Portugal and has her laid up there."

"Why?"

"He must have been able to see the big war coming—it was pretty obvious by then, I think. It wasn't certain, in 1939, who was going to be neutral, but Portugal was a good bet, and he hadn't made it too hot to hold him. Besides—and this is just a feeling I get—I think he was waiting for something."

She was nodding even before he finished. "Yes," she said. "I thought so, too. He was still making entries, but the style is different—as if his heart wasn't in it. And this last entry—" She hesitated. "He was saying good-bye, as if he might not come back."

"My feeling exactly," Barr said. "Okay, the log picks up again in 1946. April fifth," he added. "He's in Lisbon, but he doesn't say how he got there or what he's been doing."

"His handwriting's changed, too," Emerald observed. "More restrained, somehow."

"Well, he's six years older," Barr said. "And he's been through a world war."

"So he has," she said. "Doing what?"

"He was in intelligence, right?" It was hardly a question at all.

"Something like that," she admitted. "He talked a lot about a place called Lugano. I looked it up last night—it's in Switzerland. Why would he be there?"

"Because it's right down near the Italian border," said Barr. "Switzerland was full of spies during the war—theirs, ours, everybody's. The Italians were open to a deal pretty early on, and of course their government dropped out of the war in '43. Did Falk ever tell you what he was doing there?"

"Probably, only I wasn't listening," she said. "Christ, he could talk a blue streak, and most of it seemed like ancient history."

"I guess it might. I heard a lot about war when I was a kid. From my mother. My father was in the army—in the first assault on Omaha Beach. June sixth, 1944. He was called back for Korea—killed at Inch'on, just before I was born. My mother always said he was a hero."

"Was he?"

"As much as anybody, I suppose," Barr replied. "He got shot trying to help one of his men out of the water. If you have to go, that's as good a way as any—helping somebody else."

"Barr, sometimes I think you're not cut out for this kind of thing," Emerald said. "How about we get back to helping ourselves?"

"Fair enough," Barr said. "You know, two things strike me about these first postwar entries: first, Falk's spending money as if they were going to stop printing it. New engine, new fuel tanks, yank out the old food locker under the galley, drilling for new keelbolts. . . . That's a hell of a job, by the way: right through three or four feet of solid lead. Maybe the old bolts were rusted in and they couldn't get them out—"

"He wasn't hurting for money," she agreed, interrupting Barr's train of thought. "And he was in a hurry, too. He's run half the words together in this entry, and here he left one out, he was writing so fast." She turned the page. "And this: 'Lose not an hour,' all in capital letters, and underlined."

"A note to himself, quoting Lord Nelson," said Barr. "But look at this: 'To Antwerp tonight. João Figueroa will finish the work, so everything should be ready on my return.' I think we're getting close."

Her head was next to his, her body touching him, but he was virtually unaware of it. "Three days," she said, pointing to the date. "He's back again." She turned the page. The writing at the top was a manic scrawl: "Done, done, done!!!!!" Falk had written clear across the page. And under it, "From 88s to 88—safely completed."

"He's flipped," said Emerald, after staring at the entry for a long moment. "Maybe he was drunk when he wrote it."

"Maybe," Barr said. "But look here." The writing had settled down to unusually small printing, as if the author had been adding a footnote to his first outpouring: "Slight confusion between metric and real measurements; so João transferred the contents to .50 casings, sawed off and capped on the spot. A nervous operation, but successful."

"I see it, but I don't get it all," she said. "I mean, it's obvious that he's talking about whatever he brought from Antwerp, but what's a point-five-oh casing?"

"Empty shell from a fifty-caliber machine-gun round,"

Barr replied, not lifting his eyes from the page. "Common as dirt in 1946, I imagine. Half an inch across at the top, wider below. Diamonds, I bet," he added, answering the question that was clearly trembling on her lips. "Or jewels, anyway—something small and portable."

"Sounds reasonable. But why 'a nervous operation'?"

"Maybe he was afraid of spilling them all over the deck. I don't know."

"Okay," she said slowly. "But we still don't know where it's stashed, just that it's in these shells."

"And they're sealed," he added. "Let's keep going. It's only a little after two—or are you tired?"

"I do a lot of night work," she said, deadpan, and he felt his ears burn. "But I ought to check in with the store. You got a phone I don't see?"

"In the hall downstairs," he said. "But Mrs. Pearse— the landlady—doesn't like people to use it after ten."

"Screw her," said Emerald, getting to her feet with graceful economy. "Christ, I'm stiff." She stretched, her arms extended full-length above her head, then arched her spine, kneading the small of her back. Barr watched, transfixed. Her muscular buttocks—small and firm like a boy's—flexed under the fabric of her slacks. Although her blouse was loose-fitting, Barr could imagine perfectly the slender, smooth body beneath. Her face was lit from below by the harsh light of the desk lamp, and she was the most beautiful woman he had ever seen. Yet, he realized, beautiful in a somehow asexual way, at least for him.

"After a while," she said, reading his face, "you get to be able to switch it on and off."

"Oh, really?"

She smiled. "Relax. I'll be back in a couple of minutes."

She left the door open and he did not close it, but as the top of her head disappeared down the stairs, he slipped out his pocketknife and neatly removed the page they had been reading; he folded it in quarters and put it in his shirt pocket. He heard, from the foot of the stairs, the burring dial of the old-fashioned phone, and began turning the pages of the logbook. When he stopped, it was the handwriting that had caught his eye. It was stark, angular— Falk's big letters not quite under control. Barr's lips pursed as he read the entry. It was dated September 15, 1946; had been written while *Glory* was lying at rest after recrossing the Atlantic to America. "Letter from João," it said. "He has been very sick. He is scared. So am I." Barr's face was thoughtful, his mind a turmoil. He cut out the page, folded it and stuffed it in his pocket with the first.

Emerald's tone was audible from downstairs, if the words were not. Firm. She was giving orders to somebody. He kept turning the pages, more rapidly now. In late 1947 he found what he was looking for, between two entries recording an otherwise uneventful passage down the East Coast to Florida. "João is dead. A letter from his wife— his widow, God save her, whom I have never met. It was as bad as Dr. Tureck said it might be—but why didn't he tell us earlier? I would like to send her something, but I don't dare extract it for conversion. Enough cash to live well for a while, but a life of leisure is out of reach again."

He stared at the words, feeling himself right on the brink of comprehension, when he heard the front door open and then slam, and a muffled exclamation from Emerald. Quickly, he slit the page free, jammed it in his pocket and put the knife away. Emerald and someone else were nearly up the stairs, and he heard her say, in a voice that barely contained her fury, "You tried to do what, you pinhead? Jesus, Johnnie, I leave you alone for a couple of hours, and—"

"What's happened?" Barr was on his feet, at the door, when Troiano stumbled through it, propelled by a shove from Emerald that nearly knocked him flat.

She shut the door hard. "Show him your face, Johnnie." Troiano mumbled something, his head down. Barr could see a dark stain down the front of his maroon shirt. "Go on, show him," she said, her voice icy. Slowly, Troiano straightened up; his nose—no small matter earlier—was now mashed and swollen, and spread across most of his face. Both his eyes were blackening, and a patch of skin over one cheekbone was raw. He had apparently tried to wash off what must have been a great deal of blood, but traces of it lay at the corners of his mouth and crusted in his nostrils. He had no human expression left at all, and Barr could feel the waves of rage and shame coming off the battered man like steam.

"What happened?" Barr demanded again. "Did Visconti try something down at the boat? Is she all right?"

Troiano looked at Emerald. "The boat," she said, with biting amusement. "The boat is fine, your ex-boss is fine and the frog prince here has just had a little boxing lesson from the new skipper." Troiano attempted a snarl but it died in pain.

"Johnnie mostly does what I tell him," Emerald said, speaking more to her smoldering employee than to Barr. "But sometimes he gets the urge to do things on his own, and when he does"—she leaned forward, speaking slowly and distinctly right into the unfortunate Troiano's face— "he Invariably. Fucks. Up." She turned to Barr. "Johnnie decided he'd ask Miss Verdean some questions. Bounce her around a little, though he won't say so. He was going to solve our little mystery all by himself."

"It doesn't look like a great success," Barr said, in his mildest tone, and received a sullen glare from Troiano.

"It's never a great success," Emerald said. "At least nobody got killed this time. Johnnie climbed aboard and stuck up the Verdean girl, and then the new guy—"

"O'Mara."

"—O'Mara, jumped him . . ."

"Frob behide," said Troiano.

"From behind," she agreed, coldly. "Beat the shit out of him, took his gun away and ran him off. Beautiful."

What little of Troiano's face that had not been purpled by O'Mara's fists was now scarlet from emotion. Barr wondered just how much of Emerald's commentary the man would stand. "He looked like a boxer to me," Barr observed, trying for a neutral tone. "He's got arms like one."

Troiano responded gratefully: "He's a pro, for sure. I dever bid hit like that. He broke by dose, the bastard."

"Well, we better get you patched up," Emerald said. Her sudden fury seemed to have ebbed completely. She turned back to Barr: "Did you find anything else that might be useful?"

"Not a thing," he said.

She looked at him thoughtfully. "My tame doctor will fix Johnnie up—it'll be the first time this year the old fool's worked above the waist. It'll be a change for him, looking a patient in the eyes—such as they are. You want to come, Barr?"

"No, I'd better stay here. Keep an eye on *Glory*."

"Suit yourself." She scooped up the books. "Maybe we'll just take these along anyway. A little light reading." She smiled at him innocently.

9

CITY ISLAND
EIGHT A.M.

As a rule, Gillian enjoyed waking up, whether it was five minutes of slow, luxurious stretching and wriggling in her big old bed at home, or—on occasion—rolling over to delight in the first look at last night's love. But this morning she surfaced with a painfully bright beam of sunlight in her eyes, coming down through the old-fashioned lemon-squeezer prism set in the deck over her berth. The air in the fo'c'sle was stuffy, and she could smell traces of bilge and mildew. She had slept, when she finally dropped off, as if hit over the head—without dreams and, as far as she could tell, in the same position as when her head had touched the flat, stale-smelling pillow, but she was exhausted. She rolled over cautiously, sampling the stiffness in her shoulder muscles from the previous day's work. Her wristwatch was on the shelf above the berth, and she reached out for it. My God—I haven't slept that late in months. With that, the full realization of where she was and why surged over her, like a breaking wave. Last night—that awful Troiano. She could still feel him touching her, and she shuddered. The look on Patrick's face, as he brushed her aside. He would have killed Troiano with his bare hands, if I hadn't stopped him. I almost didn't stop him.

Patrick. Was I right to tell him? A momentary surge of panic. Something in his manner had felt wrong. And there was something she wanted to ask him, and had forgotten.

How much could she trust him? He liked her—she was sure of that—and she thought he respected her, too. But there was so much to bear in mind, so many people to consider: Barr. And Uncle Hitch. And what about Visconti and his friends? . . . She was out of the bunk, peeling off the nightshirt and pulling on her panties. The mirror screwed to the back of the fo'c'sle door was losing its silvering from one side, and her nearly naked image dissolved at that edge into eerie loops and whorls. Her anxious eyes stared back at her. Too skinny, she thought. And no tits, or hardly any. Shivering, she dived into a sweatshirt and pulled on her jeans.

Who had sent Troiano last night? And where, in all of this, was Jeremy Barr? He had the logbooks, too—had he found any leads in them? What might there be? Maybe the plans Troiano had wanted were the answer, showing some built-in hiding place even Barr didn't know about. . . .

She smoothed her hair down and stepped out into the main cabin. Patrick was stretched out on the settee, with a chipped mug of what smelled only approximately like coffee. He was holding a paperback novel with a faded but still-lurid cover; he eyed her with appreciation, and maybe something more. "Morning," he said. Except for a bruise on one cheekbone, last night's fight had left no marks above the collar of his starched and ironed khaki shirt. He was obviously freshly shaved—presumably with cold water—and his blond hair was brushed. So much neatness made her feel intolerably grubby. "I found the instant coffee in the galley," he said. "It's stale. I thought we could go down the street and . . ."

"No," she interrupted, flatly certain. "From now on, one of us always stays aboard." She fished in her pocket and came up with three or four crumpled bills and some change. "Here. I'll have the gooiest Danish they've got. And coffee, please."

"Right, Skip," he said, adopting her businesslike tone. Clearly, he was willing to go along with her mood, whatever it might be, but she was less sure what was happening below his immaculate surface. He took the money without counting it and went up the companionway two steps at a time. Thinking gloomy thoughts about the stale-smelling, icy water in the yacht's tanks, Gillian went into the head compartment and slammed the sticking door behind her.

On deck, a few minutes later, the cool northwest breeze blew the smog out of her head and back down into the Bronx and Queens; a hovering pale-gray miasma hung over the Throgs Neck Bridge. On City Island, though, the day was cloudless and preternaturally bright, the kind of May morning that would normally have sent the blood coursing through her veins. The cold water against her skin had brought her fully, shiveringly awake, and her brain had become obsessed by *Glory*'s missing plans—not that they were really missing; she knew exactly which drawer they were in at home, and had the feeling that if she could only concentrate a little harder she could create a mental picture of them. But just as the big faded sheets seemed about to come into focus, they evaporated. She heard a deep sigh, her own. Oh, shit, Gillian—pull your socks up, she told herself angrily. There's no time to sit around moaning. She took a small notebook from her back pocket and found the stub of pencil she had jammed inside its spiral binding. It was time to make a list—time to impose some order on the untidiness of life, and never had life needed ordering more.

"What're you doing?" Patrick's voice came from directly below, and she jumped.

"Just making a few notes," she replied. "I didn't hear you."

"So I saw," he replied cheerfully. He came up the ladder with a large paper bag clamped in his teeth. "I could've been an armored division," he added, when he had set the bag down. For a moment he stood motionless, surveying the view. *Glory*'s deck was higher than most of the others around her, and you could see the whole extent of the yard from it—or at least the herd of close-packed canvas cocoons, each containing a sleeping yacht.

"See anything?" she asked. Something inside the bag smelled delicious, and she realized she was ravenous.

"For a minute . . . I guess not." He sat down beside her and began extracting containers and paper-wrapped packages. "This is a terrible place for people sneaking up on you," he continued. "Cover in every direction; no way to command the lines of approach." He was unwrapping

one of the packages. "Here: orange juice, two plain doughnuts, milk and coffee."

"I wanted a Danish," she objected.

"No food value," he said. "And the icing rots your
teeth."

"I'll be damned," she said. "Do you have kids— Hey,
watch out with that coffee! Here's a paper napkin . . . Do
you have kids? You're a natural-born nanny."

He was wiping up the puddle of black coffee, not looking
at her. "I've never been married."

She took a long sip of orange juice. It tasted good, but
she decided not to say so. "That wasn't what I asked,"
she replied, but the look he gave her wiped the smile from
her face. "Only a joke, Patrick."

His own smile was painfully artificial, and she rushed
into the awkward silence. "I guess you never had time,"
she said. "What with the army and all. You must've en-
listed right after high school." He had showed her—had
insisted on showing her—his service record and discharge.

"Right after," he said, eyeing her cautiously.

"Did you like the army?"

This time, the smile was something more like his usual
easy grin. "I swallowed it whole," he said. "After Basic,
I did Advanced Infantry. And then Airborne, and Rang-
ers—volunteered, if you believe that. The whole nine
yards. I figured"—answering the question in her eyes—
"as long as I was going to do three years, I might as well
be busy. And it came easy."

"And then you reenlisted," she said. "Did you ever
think about a commission?"

"For about five minutes. I have the soul of a noncom—
a sergeant."

"I know what a noncom is," she said. "I'm an army
brat, in a way: I was born in Germany, when my father
was an ROTC lieutenant."

"Seventh Army?"

"Near Frankfurt. Daddy married a German girl. Rather
suddenly. I was the result. Or the cause. Or both."

"What happened?" He seemed genuinely interested.

"To her?" Gillian was almost as detached, by now, as
she had taught herself to sound. "When we got back to
the States, she hung around just long enough to get her

papers. I haven't seen her in years. No, that's wrong: She did come to Daddy's funeral." He opened his mouth to say something, but she forestalled him. "Two years ago. Car accident. That was when I sort of descended on Uncle Dennis. You know, these doughnuts are still warm? I never knew that place had homemade doughnuts. What made you leave the army, anyway?"

"Oh, my tour was up," he said, in the just-too-easy tone she was beginning to be able to distinguish from his normal way of speaking. "Time to try something different."

Never, she thought, had a subject been turned off so clearly. "Like what?" she asked.

"Boats, for one," he said. And then he stiffened. "There is somebody . . . on the deck of that big boat over your right shoulder. No, don't look. He's under the tarp, but I saw his face for a moment."

"You recognize him?" She was sitting stiffly, forcing herself not to turn her head.

"It might have been that skipper of yours, Barr. But it might not, too."

"Could be an owner, getting an early start," she said.

"Maybe." He picked up a small cereal container and slit it lengthwise with his thumbnail. "Could I borrow some of your milk?"

"Sure," she replied. "What in God's name is that?"

"Shredded wheat," he said, through a mouthful of what looked like hay. " 'Sgood for you."

"It would have to be," she replied. She took a long swallow of coffee. "I made a list," she went on. "Of things we have to do."

He nodded, crunching away.

"I have a bunch of phone calls to make, as soon as the yard office is open," she said. "And after that, I have to drive up home."

"To Connecticut?" he said, his mouth empty now. "How come?"

"I need some things," she replied. "Clothes. For to-morrow." His eyes dropped. "Tomorrow" meant Uncle Dennis's funeral, and Patrick had picked it up from her voice. "I'll be back in the afternoon," she went on, "but I want you to put the heat on the yard. I want *Glory* in the water as soon as possible."

He looked around him at the chaos on deck, his doubts in his eyes. "What do you figure has to be done?"

"Not as much as you might think," she replied firmly. "Launched. Masts stepped. Rigging set up. Sails bent on. How about the engine—will it run?"

His eyebrows shot up. "Beats me, but we'll give it a try. Was it running last year?"

"Absolutely. Well, more or less." If only Barr were here. He could make the tired old piece of junk turn over when no one else could.

"When she goes in," said Patrick, pursuing a thought of his own, "how long for her seams to take up?"

"Say again?"

"Her seams," he repeated. "I know they're caulked, but they'll be at least a little open, on such an old boat. How long before the planking swells and she stops leaking?"

Barr had attended to the launch last year. She had no idea. "Would she leak a lot?" she asked.

"It's your boat," he said. "I thought you'd know. On my uncle's old boat, we had to have two big electric pumps going for half a day, and then all of a sudden she'd be tight as a drum."

"Maybe the yard'll know," she said, making a note. "I'll ask them when the office opens."

"It's open now," said Patrick. "I just saw the old man go in. Maybe I'd better get started on the engine."

"Good idea. And listen: If we have visitors while I'm away, Troiano's gun is on that shelf in the companionway."

"Great," he said, with no trace of enthusiasm. "You sure you don't want to take it with you?"

"That's okay," she replied, more confidently than she felt. "I've got one at home." He stared at her wordlessly, shaking his head.

"No, Uncle Hitch," she said again, "I'm sure I didn't say anything to Patrick except that somebody—somebodies—were trying to get *Glory* away from me." The old man sounded quite agitated, but instead of worrying her, his persistent questions only annoyed her. She should have known better than to tell him about Troiano.

"Remember, Gillian," he was saying, the phone connection making his voice reedier than ever, "you can't trust anyone. Anyone at all."

He sounds as if he were talking to a nine-year-old, she thought, and on an instantly regretted impulse: "Not even you, Uncle Hitch?"

The silence meant he was either flabbergasted or trying to get a grip on his temper, and when he spoke again, she knew which. "Gillian, try and get it through your head that this is serious," he said evenly, spacing out the words.

"When somebody points a gun at me, I take it seriously," she snapped. "But Patrick risked his life for me—and he took care of that clown easily." Well, that might be putting it a little strongly; she suddenly saw the two men grappling in *Glory*'s narrow passageway. Patrick could be dead this morning. And she herself . . .

"If you'll just listen for a moment, I want to tell you about something that your young man can't handle with his fists." Uncle Hitch sounded thoroughly angry, and Gillian held her tongue. "Visconti's attorneys have applied for an injunction to prevent you from moving or disturbing *Glory*. They want her sealed—they say you might damage her, and they've made a formal claim that she should have been part of your Uncle Dennis's estate."

"What?" She was instantly furious. "I thought you said they couldn't get away with that, Uncle Hitch."

"Once we get them to court, they haven't a chance," he replied. "But what they want to do, clearly, is immobilize *Glory* and keep you off her, while they set up some more effective way of getting inside her."

Gillian forced her racing thoughts to slow down. "Do they have this injunction yet?"

"Not yet. The hearing's this afternoon. I was able to stall that long. But I have to say, Gillian, that if they can show any shadow of a reason—and Visconti's attorney is no fool at all—it's normal to grant at least a temporary injunction. What did you say?"

"Nothing, Uncle Hitch." She hesitated, phrasing her question carefully. "What if *Glory* were to leave the yard before an injunction came through?"

"It wouldn't matter," he replied. "That is, it wouldn't matter, if *Glory* could be found—she'd just be sealed someplace else." He waited. "You understand, there's very little advice I can give you, being an officer of the court."

She doubted that Visconti's lawyer was so scrupulous,

but did not say so; her not saying so hung on the phone line between them. "What if I found something on *Glory* before this afternoon? Could I take it?"

He sounded relieved. "Who would know? Have you any . . . leads, any clues?"

She was certainly not going to tell him about *Glory*'s plans, about driving alone up to Westport. "In a manner of speaking," she said. "I don't want to say on the phone. Change of subject: What did you find out about General Hals from your Washington friends?"

"Quite a lot, really." He sounded more cheerful, and she realized that half his anger must be simple frustration. "What Visconti told you about him is true. As far as it goes."

"How far is that?"

"He did disappear from Italy in early 1945, with a great deal of working matériel: tanks, self-propelled artillery, small arms—his unit hardly saw combat for the last year of the war. Hals was a battalion commander, and the Italian partisans wanted him for a number of atrocities. He apparently made some arrangement with certain Arab princes, and later, with the Egyptian independence movement. After that, he went on his own, with his own army, as it were, for hire. He recruits his officers and senior noncommissioned officers from bored or cashiered soldiers in a number of western countries. That's how he got the unattractive Major Bellairs. And Bellairs seems to be a singularly dangerous person."

"How so?" she asked, wondering if she really wanted to know.

There was a sound of rustling papers at the other end. "He comes from a rather ordinary military family in the south of England. Father retired as a colonel—in the Service Corps, but was able to get young Bellairs a commission in the Scots Guards. Sent to Northern Ireland and got in trouble . . ."

"What kind?"

"My friends say it's not too clear. Few things in Ireland are, I daresay. Something to do with mistreating prisoners. He was allowed to transfer into the Ulster Defence Regiment, but they couldn't stomach him. He went to South Africa, first as an officer in the army, and then, after a similar kind of trouble, in a really rough semiprivate group on the northern frontier. He resigned two years ago, and after about six months turned up as General Hals's adjutant, when the General accepted a commission from Mr. Qaddafi, the dictator of Libya."

"All this 'trouble' Bellairs keeps getting into, Uncle Hitch," said Gillian firmly. "You're not telling me what it is, and I think I should know."

"Well, it's not proven, you understand," said Hitchcock slowly. "But it sounds reliable, and it holds together." He must have heard the impatient noises she was making. "All right, Gillian. He kills people, Major Bellairs. Helpless people—prisoners, by choice. He seems to get some satisfaction from it."

In the warm, cluttered shipyard office, Gillian felt cold for a moment. It might not be proven, as Uncle Hitch had said, but she believed it utterly. He was speaking again, and she came back to herself quickly.

". . . Better news, at least in one respect."

"I can use it," she said. "Tell me."

"Jeremy Barr. I asked my friends about him, too. His late wife, a young lady of great charm and absolute irresponsibility, seems to have been involved in drugs. She was using him, and he was probably unaware of it."

"Using him? You mean she was a drug smuggler?"

"Nothing so well organized. She was apparently an occasional employee of drug runners, and she may have used Captain Barr's boat after they married. It was, of course, her boat, too. But Captain Barr was also employed—also occasionally—by certain people in Washington, to report on conditions in the West Indian islands. He was known throughout the Windwards and Leewards—known and trusted by nearly everyone. But that kind of person can be just as useful as a mysterious agent is."

"Barr was a spy?" It was too ridiculous to consider.

"That's not how these things work," said Hitchcock. "Most intelligence is just research, of one sort or another. People who travel a great deal—businessmen, journalists, some academics—often have an informal contact in their government to whom they make reports of things they see. Captain Barr was just such a person."

"Is he still supposed to be doing this?" Maybe the idea was just barely conceivable, at least in the terms Uncle Hitch put it.

"He is, I understand, still on their books," said Hitchcock cautiously. "But his unfortunate marriage made them put him on the shelf, so to speak. When he first became infatuated with the lady, he was warned off; he chose her instead of them."

"But they might still look out for him?"

"They might. They apparently would like him back."

"But would they help him in something like this? To get hold of *Glory*?"

The thought had obviously occurred to him. "Absolutely not. They knew nothing about it. I'm sure of that."

She felt herself start to relax, but there was something in his voice . . . "What aren't you telling me, Uncle Hitch?"

"There is one other person involved in this whom Washington would assist, if they were asked. Someone who is so important he can't even be discussed."

She knew, but had to ask. "Who?"

"Matt Visconti. It has something to do with Qaddafi, but no one will say what."

You have to trust somebody, she told herself. No matter what Uncle Hitch said. And she couldn't be in two places at once. With unconscious skill, she took the Mazda down through the gears, as traffic, already heavy, clotted for the Mamaroneck toll booths. Surveying the jam ahead, she spun the wheel and the little car darted over to the right-hand lane, behind a huge semitrailer that was just easing through. Another driver with the same idea pulled up right behind her. Fishing for change, she glanced up into the rearview mirror. The man in the car behind had his head down, so his face was invisible—but what of it? She allowed the quarter to escape from her hand, and the toll-taker looked at her reproachfully. "It's under the car, lady," he said.

"I know," she replied, handing him a dime and a nickel, and tramping on the accelerator. Over her shoulder, she saw the toll-taker come out of his booth, pick up the coin and return, and then the scene was obscured by a van that swung in behind her. For the next fifteen minutes, she played faster and looser than usual with the traffic laws, weaving from lane to lane, accelerating and then braking quickly, in an effort to shake loose any possible tracker.

At last she was satisfied that no one was following the

Mazda—but just in case, she got off an exit early and doubled through a maze of back streets for five minutes before coming out onto the Post Road, just beyond downtown Westport. The road was crowded with shoppers and trucks, and she dropped the Mazda between a couple of big vans, then whipped left at her intersection, without signaling. The side road, up the familiar hill, was straight as well as steep, and she was sure no one followed her. Two more turns, and she pulled into her own driveway, feeling a small sense of triumph.

The door was wide open, behind the screen. In an instant, her fears from the night before returned. There must be someone inside. But more coherent reflection said no: there was no car but hers in the driveway, and none was parked in the road behind her. Slowly, watching the door, she got out of the car, wishing she had not left Bellairs's revolver in her bureau. The slightly seedy garage seemed cold and forbidding. She had made it home, but she would be happy to see the last of it now. Even so, it was outrageous that someone should have broken in. She felt a rush of the same helpless anger as when Troiano had pawed her, and buoyed by fury she stalked up the wobbly flagstones and flung open the screen door. "Bugger off!" she heard herself yell, and then, "Oh, no!" The living room was wrecked: the intruders had torn three days' mail to shreds, had pulled the drawer out of the little table—the only genuine antique in the house—and emptied its innocent but very personal contents all over the floor. Clearly, they had had all the time in the world: with a kind of casual arrogance, every drawer in the tiny room had been pulled out and upturned on the carpet. The bedroom, just big enough for a bed and a bureau, showed the highwater mark of the search. Exactly half of it had simply been annihilated—there was no other word. I suppose, she thought, forcing calm on herself, they knew this was the most likely place. And when they found the plans (the big, yellowed envelope, torn across, lay empty on the floor), they just stopped. Absently, she bent and picked up a framed photograph of herself. Her graduation picture, from Conn. College: longer hair than now and—even then—a determined jaw. Someone had stepped on the picture, and the glass was cracked in a spiderweb pattern. She set it upright where it had always stood, on what had been her father's bureau. She began to pick up the scattered papers, and then paused and straightened up. "No," she said, aloud. Looking straight ahead, she went to the closet, yanked a dark dress off a hanger and scooped up a pair of shoes. She took one long look around her raped apartment, then turned and walked out.

So they—whoever—had *Glory*'s plans. And Barr had Uncle Dennis's logbooks. His nest egg, if there was one, might be indicated in either place. And she, meanwhile, had nothing. Maybe less than nothing: what if Patrick were working for someone, too—had found Uncle Dennis's hoard while she'd been away. What if Visconti had managed to get *Glory* sealed by the cops? In a mood that approached despair, she swung the Mazda off the parkway, onto the City Island approach road, not even looking behind her. What did it matter now if someone was following?

Her heart lifted slightly when she saw Patrick on *Glory*'s deck, and he waved to her. His khaki pants were rumpled and splotched with grime, and he had shed both his uniform shirt and the T-shirt under it. Sweat gleamed on his smudged face and torso. She ran up the ladder to the deck. "How's it going?" she asked.

"Good and bad." Up close, he looked exhausted under the dirt. "The engine works—I had it running. And the hull looks tight. I checked the whole underbody, and unless there's a big leak I missed, the bilge pump should take care of it."

"That sounds great, Patrick," she replied. "Now give me the bad part."

"There's no way of launching her till they get the crane fixed," he said, sitting down on the cockpit coaming with a groan. "And they won't have that fixed, if you want my opinion, for goddamn weeks. It hasn't been run since the fall, and it's a mess."

"But they don't launch us with the crane anyway," she objected. "*Glory*'s too heavy. They use the railway." She pointed to the rusty tracks, half hidden by weeds and trash.

"I know," Patrick said. "But the two boats that're sitting on the tracks ahead of us—they have to be launched by crane before *Glory* can go down the ways." It was true: the forty-foot sloop right under *Glory*'s massive bow and the dejected-looking cruiser beyond were simply shored up and not, like *Glory*, sitting on a wheeled frame of massive eight-by-eights. Move the two boats and the shoring would fall away: they would simply topple over.

Gillian's heart sank. "I'll go up to the office and talk to them," she said dully. As she walked across the gritty yard, she felt frustrated rage welling up inside her; she knew that it had to be tamped down if anything was to be accomplished. Her normal reaction to slowness or laziness was incandescent anger, but she recognized that in this case the yard held all the cards, and she managed to arrange her features into some semblance of a smile as she went in the door.

Billy Fenton, a large and amiable man who supposedly ran the outside work, was on the phone, but he raised his eyebrows at her in greeting. "I know," he was saying. "I know, Mr. Hoskins: we promised to get her launched this week. But what am I supposed to do—hire a helicopter and lift her out? No, sir. I didn't mean that seriously. Look, as soon . . ." Gillian could hear the crash at the other end of the line from ten feet away. Billy winced and set the receiver down gently. "Every year, I tell myself I'm getting out of this business," he said.

"What's happening, Billy?" she said, in what she hoped was a calm voice. "Patrick tells me the crane is down."

" 'Fraid so, Gillian," he replied. "And even if it was working, the engine for the railway has to be overhauled before we can launch you."

"How long do you think it'll be?" she asked. "Yesterday, you said the part you needed would be in by noon, for sure."

He gestured at a grubby cardboard box on his desk. "The usual shit," he said. "They sent the wrong part. We'll send it back tomorrow, and they'll send the right one. Maybe."

It sounded plausible enough, but there was something very odd about Billy, who usually addressed most of his remarks to the ground, as if years of his own incompetence had beaten him down. Today he was looking her right in the eye, sincere as the day was long. On an impulse, she said, "Has anybody been looking for me, Billy? Or asking about *Glory*?"

His eyes dropped, and he seemed to redden under the

permanent coating of grease and sunburn. "Nope. Nobody at all. You got some phone messages, though. Now where are they . . . ?" He turned away and began pawing through the untidy stack of papers. "Here. The funeral home—say, I'm real sorry about Dennis. That was a real tragedy."

Amazingly, she had not thought about Uncle Dennis since she had pulled out of the driveway back in Westport, and yet the shadow of his death was over her all the same. "Thanks," she said, taking the other scraps of paper. Uncle Hitch, a name she didn't know from the insurance company and Mr. Matt Visconti, twice.

The odious undertaker was just confirming. "One-thirty tomorrow, in our chapel. Great-uncle looks very peaceful, if I may say so." She shuddered, managed to thank him, and hung up.

Uncle Hitch was concerned. "No injunction," he said, "but it was a damned near-run thing. Fortunately, the judge was a classmate of mine at Harvard Law, back in the Jurassic period. I assured him you had no intention of moving the boat, and he took my word for it. But one might wish that *Glory* were someplace else."

She debated telling him about her discovery at Westport, and finally decided against it. "Matt Visconti called me here, twice," she said. "They couldn't find me in the yard."

"Don't call him back," said Hitchcock quickly. "And if he should turn up there, don't talk to him—send him to me." She barely heard him, her attention being focused on Billy Fenton, not quite out of earshot, who had jumped six inches at the name "Visconti."

"It's okay, Uncle Hitch," she said soothingly. "It's okay." But she knew it was not: Visconti had been here today, had taken his own steps to make sure that *Glory* stayed put. Pinned like a bug to a card. The only question was what would he do next. And when.

10

CITY ISLAND
SIX P.M.

Gillian looked beaten, Patrick thought, watching her walking toward him across the boatyard. Her back, usually as straight as a marine's on parade, was slumped, and her face was haggard. Painfully, she climbed the ladder she had run up only minutes before. "Not good?" he asked.

"Not good." She produced a stiff smile for him.

"They can't launch the boat, is that it?"

"That's what they say," she said. "But I don't believe it." He looked his question. "Billy Fenton's got that crane part in a box on his desk," she said. "I'm as sure as if I could see through the cardboard. And somebody—Visconti, I bet—has got to him. Patrick, what do you know about cranes?"

"Practically nothing," he admitted. "I doubt I could fix one." She was practically quivering with frustration. Before she could speak, he added, "And even if I did fix the crane, I don't know how to work it. Do you?"

She shook her head. All at once she sagged to the deck, her head in her hands. "Don't worry, Patrick," she said from behind the screen of her fingers. "I'm not going to come apart on you." She looked up, and he avoided her reddened eyes. "I just don't handle being thwarted very well," she said, her voice level.

He wanted to take her in his arms, but he knew it would

be a mistake. "What you need is a drink," he said. "And something to eat—I bet you didn't have lunch."

She managed an unsteady laugh. "Nurse Patrick strikes again," she said. "Food it is." She inspected her wallet. "How well can we do on a ten?"

"Don't worry," he replied, pushing the bill away. "Tonight it's on me."

He knew the Fairlane would be waiting outside Tremaine's gate, but this time only Bellairs was in it. Patrick got in the passenger seat. "Where's the General?"

"It may be difficult for you to believe, Mister O'Mara, but you scarcely rate the attention of a field officer, much less a general," said Bellairs. "Where were you going?"

"Bella Napoli—the pizza place down the street," Patrick replied. "She's expecting me back pretty quick."

"You'll get back to your chippie when I'm done with you," said Bellairs. He drove badly: arrogance and bad coordination, made worse by his obvious dislike for the automatic shift and his discomfort at having to drive on the right.

They pulled up in front of the Bella Napoli, which was jammed to the doors, as usual, and Patrick said, "Look, if you told me exactly what you wanted, I'd be a hell of a lot more useful, and we could probably get this whole exercise over with a lot quicker."

Bellairs's close-set, bulbous eyes watched him for a moment. "Why don't you just tell me what's been going on," he said, opening the car door. Patrick got out, as the Englishman continued: "I'll explain as much as you need to know."

Patrick's brain was already working in overdrive, sifting what he intended to tell Bellairs from what Gillian had told him. "She says there's all these people after the boat," he began, as they walked into the steamy hot restaurant. Edging his way between the closely set tables, he pitched his voice over the crowd noise. "But that's bullshit. The boat's worth maybe twenty-five thousand, tops. Anyway, what's the General want with a beat-up old yacht? It doesn't make sense. Hi, Rosie."

The girl behind the counter beamed at him. "Long time no see, Patrick. What'll it be?"

"Large pie, half sausage, half mushroom," he said.

"And a salad?" she asked, scribbling on the pad in front of her.

"Large salad," he replied. "And two sodas—ginger ale, I guess."

"You got it. Maybe five minutes, for a special customer." She was looking oddly at Bellairs. His height set him apart from the other patrons, and his unnatural thinness, and the disdain that froze his face.

"Thanks, Rosie." He drew Bellairs off to one side. Lowering his voice just under the chatter that surrounded them, he continued: "Anyway, I figure if it's not the boat it must be something *on* the boat. Something stashed away, that nobody can find and that nobody knows what it is."

Bellairs winced. "Acute, Mister O'Mara. Ungrammatical but acute." He pursed his lips, obviously deciding how much to confide. "Dennis Falk, the last owner of the yacht, died owing a good many people a great deal of money. As far as we can tell, he didn't have any cash, but the General is sure he had other . . . resources. We have to find those resources before Falk's other creditors. One in particular, a most unscrupulous person."

"Which one is that—Visconti or Troiano?" Patrick asked quickly.

"She told you about Visconti?" Bellairs's tone gave nothing away.

"Just the name, and that he's a millionaire," Patrick answered.

"That's enough for you to know. We're acquainted with Mr. Visconti." Bellairs's lips twisted momentarily in what passed with him for a smile. "What was the other name? Something Eytie."

"Troiano."

"Doesn't mean a thing to me."

"Well, maybe it better," said Patrick. "Son of a bitch damn near killed me last night."

"Don't be insolent," snapped Bellairs. His words had fallen into a semisilence, and he looked around him to see if anyone was listening. Satisfied that no one was paying them undue attention, he turned back to Patrick. "You've been working on the boat all day. Have you any idea where something fairly small, no bigger than a . . . a carton of cigarettes might be hidden?"

Patrick shrugged. "A boat as old as *Glory* is just a

Chinese puzzle sixty-five feet long. If you told me what I was looking for, it'd give me some idea where it might be."

Bellairs was clearly reluctant to admit it, but he said, "We don't know. Small—the General is reasonably sure that whatever it is will turn out to be very compact."

"Drugs?"

"We think not," Bellairs replied slowly. "But it's possible—apparently, there is some medical connection."

"What's that supposed to mean?" Patrick demanded.

Bellairs had obviously come to a decision. He lowered his voice even more, looking Patrick directly in the eyes. "Let me tell you a story, Mister O'Mara: Long ago, there was a young Wehrmacht officer, commanding a battalion in the north of Italy. The war—my father's war—was going badly for the Germans, and their Italian allies, the bloody wogs, had changed sides."

"You want to be careful with that kind of talk in here."

"Cowards then and cowards now," said Bellairs coldly. "In any case, our young German officer—a major, like me—was concerned. He had made some enemies among the Eyties, shot some of their partisans and a few sods who happened to be in the way. There was a lot of talk about 'war criminals,' and it seemed likely that when the Germans lost, the Italians would want to make examples of a few of their former allies."

"Our young German major wouldn't have been named Hals, would he?" said Patrick.

Bellairs ignored the interruption. "He decided, at all events, to finesse the Italians' obvious play, and there was only one way to do that." He paused, but Patrick refused to oblige him. "He did a deal with American intelligence, who were hovering just over the border in Switzerland. Arranged the surrender of his whole division to the Americans, in return for a passport and a blind eye."

"Fascinating," said Patrick, in his best approximation of Bellairs's drawl. "But so what?"

"So this," hissed Bellairs. "Our major's contact among the Yanks was a young man with a very checkered prewar past, a young man with large ideas. He forced the major to turn over a vast quantity—a freighter-load, actually—of Panzer hardware, all of it in working condition, in return for his own ticket to freedom. Ship with Persian registry materializes at a North Italian port, takes on cargo, including young German major, and sails away. Yank gets the cash and our German major gets a new name and a job with the wogs."

"The Arab wogs," said Patrick.

"Correct."

"And the American was Dennis Falk."

"Correct again. He was discovered, of course—it was far too big an operation to go unnoticed, even in the last days of the war. But he'd put most of a German division in the bag, so he was only cashiered, rather quietly. There were other Yanks involved, and nobody really cared anyway."

"And that's the money you're hunting for?"

"Essentially, yes. But converted, we think, to something more compact than cash."

"How much?" said Patrick.

"I've no idea, really," Bellairs said. "Several million of today's dollars, I should think."

No wonder Gillian was so hot to get hold of it, Patrick thought, and then: fifty-fifty, she said. Aloud, he asked, "So how does General Hals figure he's got a claim? Sounds to me like the deal went down fair enough."

"That's too complicated to explain," Bellairs snapped. "And none of your affair, in any case."

"And the other guys who're chasing this loot?" Patrick asked, watching Bellairs from the corner of his eye. "I suppose they're none of my affair, either?"

The Englishman had been staring arrogantly about him, like a man at a freak show. He turned on Patrick coldly. "Exactly." He pointed to the counter: "Isn't that rather sweaty girl trying to get your attention?"

Patrick turned. "Coming, Rosie." He ignored the glares of customers who had been waiting far longer than he, paid for his order, blew Rosie a kiss and followed Bellairs out to the car. "So at least tell me about the medical thing," he said, the pizza box warm on his lap.

Bellairs pulled into the traffic without signaling, was almost nailed by a passing car. Ignoring it, he went on: "That's just the General's recollection. He was at the pier when the man Falk was paid off by the Arabs—mostly in gold, I gather. Falk said something about transforming it into more portable form, and the General—or major—

asked what. At which young Master Falk became very coy. Said it was a secret, but it was something very small that his doctor recommended. Or words to that effect."

"Sounds like drugs to me," said Patrick. "You better let me off here."

"Drugs weren't so valuable then," said Bellairs, pulling over to the curb. "But you may be right. Not so fast," he added, as Patrick started to get out the door.

"This thing's getting cold," Patrick objected, but he sat back.

"Just a moment more. I have a little present for you." He took an envelope from inside his jacket, showing Patrick a flash of checkered pistol grip. "Here: I think it's newer than anything you've got—took it yesterday, in point of fact."

Patrick went cold. His hands, tearing it open, were unsteady. The photograph was of a little girl's laughing face, a sharply focused closeup that nearly filled the frame, obscuring the background. "There is no better portrait lens than the old one-thirty-five Nikon," Bellairs observed. "And it makes a passable telephoto as well."

"I hear what you're saying," said Patrick. He wanted desperately to pick the photo up, but it was somehow contaminated for him.

"Take it," said Bellairs. "And think about it."

Patrick got slowly out of the car, his head spinning. Bellairs leaned over, and Patrick bent down to hear him over the traffic. "Stay with Miss Verdean and the boat. If you need to get in touch with us, there's a number on the back of the photo." The car shot away from the curb. He watched its taillights vanish among a hundred others, and turned back toward the boatyard.

One thought kept coming to the surface: Gillian had been straight with him. He didn't see why that should seem so important, but it was. God, she had nerve. If only . . . He suddenly remembered the photo he was carrying, glanced down at his little girl's face. What could he do? Call Joanie and warn her—but he could almost hear her scornful voice. She would never believe that she or Tracy was in danger. She and that wimp husband, and their ugly little house with the dead grass from the bad septic system, and their beat-up Plymouth—their life would drive him up the wall in a week. But Tracy wasn't their kid, she was his and Joanie's. His daughter. Part of him. Patrick's shoulder grazed a boat hull, and the pizza box tottered for a moment. He paused, breathing hard, trying to pull himself together. He slipped the photo into the pocket of his shirt, and crumpled the envelope and threw it in the dirt, wiping his hand on the seams of his trousers. He took three deep breaths, decided he was in control again, picked up the pizza box and stepped through the gate.

"Penny for your thoughts, Patrick," said Gillian. They were sitting in *Glory*'s cockpit, the empty box between them.

"You've got tomato sauce on your nose," he said. "Right on the tip . . . there, it's off." He stretched. "I was just wondering what you—what we do now," he lied.

"Well, you don't have to look so worried," she replied. "It's sweet of you, but it's my problem, and I'm damned if I know the answer. The only thing we can do . . ." Her words were cut off by a *whump!* behind Patrick's back. Gillian's eyes widened in sudden fear as he spun around to face four men who had been concealed under a canvas tarp on the deck of a big, deep-keeled boat that was propped up alongside *Glory* and less than five feet away. Led by a short man flourishing a butcher's cleaver, the four leaped onto *Glory*'s deck. Gillian's mouth was open, and before she could close it Patrick flung his half empty can of ginger ale at the first man, who ducked it and came on, waving the knife.

He was very short indeed—the raised cleaver was only at the level of Patrick's eyes—but broad and strong. Patrick caught at the arm holding the knife and drove two quick rights to the short man's neck. The man grunted, wrenching away, took a step backward to free his swing—and disappeared over the side. The remaining three stood frozen for an instant, released by a gritty crash and a yell of pain from below. Patrick found himself fighting two men, one with a policeman's nightstick, the other empty-handed, while the third, far larger than the other two, advanced deliberately on Gillian, who had snatched up a two-foot-long bronze turnbuckle.

Patrick took a punch in the side and a glancing blow from the nightstick that numbed his left arm. "The gun!" he called out. "In the cabin!" But he could see it was too

late—the big man was between Gillian and the companionway, moving toward her with his apelike arms wide.

The club-wielding man risked a vicious swipe at Patrick,
who dodged it easily and managed to get in a kick that
brought his second opponent down in a heap. Turning
back, Patrick caught another blow from the nightstick on
his left bicep, and rammed his head up against the man's
jaw, heard the grunt of pain. Even with one arm, Patrick
could hold his own as long as the other man could not get
far enough away to swing. Patrick brought up his knee,
but his opponent was too quick for it, poking at Patrick's
head with the butt of the club. Patrick gave way, acutely
aware that the gunwale was only a couple of steps behind
him, and the club-swinger held his ground, holding the
nightstick in front of him like a spear. From the corner of
his eye, Patrick saw Gillian's quick swing with the turnbuckle, heard it thwack against flesh. He darted forward,
head down, right arm wide, just as the third man leaped
on his back and bore him to the deck. They struggled
desperately; Patrick had his hand around the other's
throat, saw his eyes begin to bug out, when the club came
down on his shoulder and the pain made him yell.

Both his arms were numb—he was not sure if anything
was broken, but he was helpless. The big man, blood dripping from one hand, had grappled with Gillian. It was no
match—he was more than twice her weight—but she was
scratching furiously at his eyes. "Throw him over!" roared
the big man. "Over the edge, like he did with Arnie!"

Patrick kicked out, saw one of his opponents go white
with pain, but he knew it was no use—he was halfway over
the gunwale, and one of the men got to his feet. "Get
clear," he snarled to his friend. "I'm gonna kick his head
in."

His legs thrashing in midair, his arms nearly useless,
Patrick knew what was coming. The man drew back his
foot—black leather shoe, pointed at the toe—and paused,
to make sure Patrick could see it coming.

What the man did not see, as he watched Patrick's face,
was the hand that snaked up over the gunwale, the big,
scarred hand that grabbed his ankle, twisted and brought
him crashing to the deck. The hand was followed by the
stringy form of Jeremy Barr, death on his face. Ignoring
Patrick, Barr hurled himself like a wildcat on the would-

be kicker. There was no science in his uncoordinated fury, and no stopping him. As the man tried to sit up, Barr grabbed him by the hair and slammed his head against the deck—a solid thump, like someone dropping a pumpkin on a wood floor.

Patrick had no time to notice more. He felt himself start to go over the edge, and something caught him from below, pushed him back on the deck. Patrick's opponent, who had released his victim to let him fall, was clearly amazed to see him rise up instead. Amazed for a half second too long, as Patrick braced himself against a deck winch and launched himself like a torpedo into the man's gut. The man was writhing on the deck, whooping for air, as Patrick turned to see, climbing from the ladder over the gunwale, a squat figure whose thick-lipped face was dominated by a horrendously swollen nose and two nearly shut black eyes. "Thanks, Troiano," said Patrick.

"Go fuck yourself," said his rescuer thickly.

Now Barr was up, too. The man he had attacked lay quite still on the teak planking. "Don't come any closer!" called the big man. "I'll cut her!" He had Gillian by the hair, a knife right at the corner of her jaw, and the three men in front of him stopped. Gillian's face was more angry than frightened, but she stood like stone.

The big man looked around him. From the ground below came a scrabbling sound, punctuated by low moans. The man Barr had leveled was not even twitching, and Patrick's opponent was clearly several minutes from being able to sit up, much less fight. "All right, you bastards—over the side," said the big man. "Over the side, or the little lady gets an extra mouth."

The three men facing him did not move for a moment, and then Barr took a step backward. "We're going," he said evenly.

Patrick wanted to hurl himself at the big man, tear his arm off at the shoulder, but he knew Barr was right—and then he felt Troiano, at his side, stiffen. Behind the big man, black against the dirty gray of the next boat's heaped-up canvas cover, a slim figure had appeared. Without a sound it edged forward—but how soundless could it be? Patrick found he was able to lift his left arm, rubbed his right wrist. The action drew the big man's eye. He made a small, dismissive gesture with the knife. "Get go—" And then a cold gunbarrel was at the base of his neck.

Patrick could see the man's mind working in his eyes: he might slash Gillian, but he had no chance himself. The knife clattered to the deck. "Now let go of her," said the figure behind him. It was a woman's voice, low and cold and calm.

Gillian shook herself free. To Barr's obvious astonishment, she flung herself across the deck and into his arms, clutching him convulsively. The slender figure stepped more plainly into view, the barrel of her very businesslike revolver still caressing the huge man's neck. With her free hand she tugged off the wool watch cap, and her red hair tumbled free, gleaming in the setting sun. "I don't think we've been introduced," she said to Patrick. "My name is Emerald."

"I don't like to sound ungrateful," Patrick said, fifteen minutes later, "but why did you guys jump in like that?"

Emerald, who had just finished binding his right wrist in strips torn from his shirt, looked up from the glass of neat rum Barr had pressed on her. The moonlight somehow suited the cold beauty of her face. "Would you believe Christian charity?" she asked. "No? How about half a loaf?"

"As in half a loaf being better than none," Barr put in. His glass was already empty, Patrick noted. "We decided we had a better chance as allies than rivals."

Emerald smiled, first at Barr and then at the rest of the company. "The truth is that Captain Barr was already on his white horse, ready for the fray. Johnnie and I were just along for the ride. And for a piece of the action."

"How much?" Gillian's voice was perhaps harsher than she had intended. She had wrenched herself away from Barr as quickly as she had embraced him, and stationed herself like a sentry in the companionway.

"Maybe we ought to discuss that later," said Barr. "They'll be back."

"For sure," said Emerald. "But not tonight. Visconti's going to have a tough time getting volunteers, after they see what happened to the first batch."

Gillian, who had accepted Barr's presence without a

question, seemed unable to look directly at him, and addressed herself to Emerald: "When they do come back, they'll be ready for anything. Why did we let them go? Why didn't we just turn them over to the police?"

Emerald's smile deepened, seemed to warm her face to life. "Honey, when you call in the cops, the first thing they do is impound everything in sight. And if it's worth more than two bits, you never see it again. We can beat Visconti and we can beat Hals, but we sure as hell can't beat the NYPD."

"I don't want to rush anyone," said Barr, in his quiet, tentative voice, "but I think we ought to get *Glory* out of here."

"Oh, sure," Gillian replied. "The goddamn yard's stupid crane won't work, even though I'm sure they have the part to fix it. So we can't move the two boats in front of us and clear the tracks. And even if we could, no one's run the engine for the marine railway yet this year, and it's probably broken, too."

Barr was looking at her oddly. Maybe he had never seen her this way, giving up. Patrick hated it, wished desperately for the sassy, dauntless girl of a few hours before. He started to get to his feet, winced as a strained muscle made itself known.

"How's your arm?" Emerald asked.

"A lot better, thanks," Patrick replied. "It still hurts like hell."

"Bone bruise," she said. "Hey, where you going, Barr?"

The skinny man had got to his feet without a word and was vanishing over the side. His face reappeared. "To fix the crane."

"How're you going to do that?" Gillian demanded. "The yard office is locked up tight."

"Billy leaves the key under the top step," Barr replied. "You forget—I lived here all winter."

Her face was suddenly intent, and Patrick felt his heart bound. "You think you can fix it?"

"Why not?" He seemed mildly surprised at her question. "I had a crane like it, when I ran a boatyard in Lauderdale—they're all pretty much the same. And the engine on the railway is like the one we had at Carey & Willard in East Norwalk."

More than once, during the three hectic hours that followed, Patrick found himself wondering just whose side he was on. But part of him couldn't face the question, and it was easier to hurl himself into simple physical activity. Gillian was everywhere at once, exhorting, directing, countermanding—he was exasperated and delighted at her return of spirits. Barr worked silently and fast; it took him half an hour, by flashlight, to extract the broken gear that had crippled the crane, and then fifteen minutes to lock the new wheel in place and start up the engine. The asthmatic roar brought Troiano trotting anxiously back from the front gate, where he had been posted as watchdog, but to everyone's intense relief no one else appeared, and the sound, once the crane's engine settled down, was mostly muffled by the surrounding hulls.

Patrick was dispatched to check the two boats that had to be launched before *Glory* was free. The sloop had neat coils of dockline on deck, her seacocks closed—all ready and waiting. The cruiser, her cabin locked, was in disarray. Finally, Patrick put his shoulder to the companionway door and burst it open. The cabin had been stripped, and the only line was a spare anchor rode. When he reported this to Gillian, who was holding the flashlight for Barr, she pulled out a sailor's knife and tossed it to him. "Cut it," she said. "We'll want bow, stern and two spring lines." She sent him off with a whack across the ass, and he felt himself grinning like a madman.

He was still taping the last of the cut ends when he felt something brush across his back. He jumped, and saw the canvas-covered slings swinging just above him. Barr, watching him through the window in the crane's cab, seemed to have the trace of a smile, but in the moonlight it was hard to be sure. No instructions were required; Patrick was on familiar ground. He unhooked an end of each sling, passed them beneath the belly of the boat and scrambled back up on deck to rehook them. The crane engine's hoarse throb quickened, and Patrick felt the deck under him sway, as the boat—seven or eight tons at least— lifted neatly off her shores.

The cruiser was raised just high enough to clear the sea wall, swooped across it and dropped into the water beyond with scarcely a ripple. Moving quickly, Patrick had the slings free almost before Emerald, on the pier, had tied off the first line. "Not like that," he said. "A clove hitch is better."

"Anything you say," Emerald replied, with a dazzling smile, as she secured the second line with another granny knot. Already the dripping slings were dangling over the second boat that blocked *Glory*'s path to the water.

Barr was motioning to him. "The power switch for the railway is in that shed—you need electricity for the starter. After that, it's just a truck engine."

"You want me to hook this boat up first?"

"Gillian can do it," Barr replied. And turning to her, "Right?"

"You bet," she said, her grin bright against the dirt on her face.

"Emerald," Barr called out, as Gillian chinned herself up the yacht's side. "Take a look down below in that first boat. See if she's making any water—if there's a leak."

The shed, as Patrick had expected, was secured by a padlock. He had armed himself accordingly, with a rusty length of scrap metal, and wrenched lock and hasp from the old wood with a one-armed heave. Inside, he found the fusebox, threw the power switch, then hurried back out just as Emerald reappeared in the cruiser's cockpit. "I can't see much down there," she called to Barr. "But the water in the cabin is up over the floor."

Barr had the sloop swinging in midair, Gillian perched on its deck. "Patrick," he called, "would you take a look? There should be an electric pump in her—we can't let the poor guy sink."

Patrick scrambled aboard, hearing Emerald muttering something about "a funny time for scruples." The water in the cabin was indeed over the floorboards, and he could hear it gurgling in from someplace up forward. Groping through the inky blackness, he found the main battery switch and with an automatic, half-remembered prayer, threw it over. The pumps had been set to "On," and he heard them both kick in as he splashed through the cabin. He had overlooked the main seacock in the head, and its hose had split—probably frozen during the winter. Ignoring the stabbing pain in his forearm, he pulled desperately at the stiff lever until, with a wail of ungreased metal, it closed.

On deck again, soaked to the knees, he found that Barr and the two women had successfully launched the second boat, and Barr was already fussing with the rusty engine that powered the marine railway. Squelching over the oil-slippery old ties, Patrick kicked clear the wooden blocks that had supported the two vessels. *Glory* was resting on a pair of wheeled carriages that resembled handcars without the propelling levers and were blocked in place with triangular bits of timber. The old yacht's arching clipper bow faced the shed, from which Patrick could hear the slow grinding of a long-disused starter. A thick wire cable, encased in grease that was itself covered with filth, lay limp in the dirt. Once the wedges had been kicked away, the cable would brake the two cars, allowing *Glory* to run down the tracks under control.

The railway's engine started up on a single cylinder, sounding to Patrick's hypersensitive ears exactly like a heavy machine-gun. The echoes bounced off the boats and the shed, and Patrick glanced nervously about him: this couldn't last—somebody would call the cops, or come in to take a look. . . . A second and then a third cylinder kicked in, and finally the fourth. Patrick saw the cable squirm and writhe and slowly take up tension until it was suspended, quivering slightly. The engine raced—Barr must have taken it out of gear—and then Patrick heard running footsteps on the gravel.

"Shut it off! Shut it off!" It was Troiano, scuttling toward the shed and waving his arms.

"What's up?" Barr's voice came clearly over the engine.

"Cops!" Troiano called, and the engine coughed into silence. Patrick, who had been about to knock the wedges free, hurried up to the shed in time to hear Troiano say, "There's a patrol car right outside the gate."

"Doing what?" It was Emerald. Troiano shrugged his ignorance. "I'll take a look," she said, and glided noiselessly into the darkness. In a few minutes she reappeared, as quietly as she had gone. "They're only doping off," she said. "Two of them, parked just inside the gate. They could be there for hours—till their tour's over, for all I know."

Gillian, who had been listening impatiently, turned to Barr: "Can you launch her without the engine?"

"I don't know. Once I release the brake, she'll start to

run. She'll either derail—those tracks are pretty lumpy—
or hit the water hard."

"We can't brake her by hand?" Patrick asked.

"*Glory* weighs twenty-seven tons," Barr said slowly,
"and that grade looks to be nearly ten degrees. I can't do
the physics, but it doesn't inspire confidence."

"Well, we can't just sit here," said Gillian, irritably.
"It'll be light in a few hours, and they'll come back." She
paused, and Patrick knew she was feeling the same ebb of
adrenaline that he was. The whole thing was like combat:
As long as Barr kept them moving, nothing could stop
them; as soon as he dropped the reins, they began to see
how impossible everything was. Patrick was on the point
of stepping forward when Gillian spoke: "Will she go off
the tracks, if you let her roll?"

"How can I answer that?" There was a faint edge of
exasperation in Barr's voice. "I did the shoring myself,
and that'll hold, but I can't answer for the roadbed."

"If the boat did fall off," said Emerald, "what would
happen?"

"Oh, she'd go over on her side—break some ribs," said
Barr cautiously. "If the cars separated, though, she could
break her back."

Patrick felt Gillian stiffen beside him. They looked at
her. "She's your boat," said Barr, his face like stone.
Patrick felt anger pumping through him. It was unfair of
Barr to dump it all on Gillian. A man just didn't do that
to a girl, no matter how much he disliked her.

"What if . . ." she began, and then her voice hardened.
"There's no choice. Here's what we'll do: Barr, you cast
off the cable. Everybody but you climbs aboard. We'll put
the rope ladder over the side—you knock the wedges out,
climb aboard and we'll ride her down."

"You want the engine going—in *Glory*, I mean?" asked
Patrick.

"No," she answered immediately. "Too noisy—the
sound'll carry over the water. We'll just glide out into the
Sound, out of the light."

"There's six or eight boats on moorings out there," Barr
offered mildly.

"I know. That's why Patrick and Emerald and Troiano
are going to be standing by with fenders."

"And where will you be?" Emerald asked.

"At the helm," said Gillian. "Where else?"

She looked absurdly small behind *Glory*'s massive mahogany wheel, her face calm except for the muscle twitching in her cheek. At that moment, Patrick decided, he would die for her. And it occurred to him, a second later, that he might have to do just that.

Barr removed the heavy iron hook from the forward carriage, and knocked away all but the last two wooden wedges. His voice ghosted up to those waiting on deck: "We've got a problem, Gillian."

"What, for God's sake?"

"If I knock out just one of these blocks, she might start to skew off to one side before I can get to the other."

"You mean they both have to go at once?" Gillian was still at the wheel, her small grubby hands locked on the gleaming wooden rim.

"Afraid so," Barr called softly.

"How can two people get back on the boat?"

"A knotted rope'll do for me," said Barr.

"Okay." Gillian looked around at her three crew members.

"I'll try it," Patrick said.

"One-handed? Don't be a fool," she said, her smile—a surprisingly sweet smile—taking the edge off the words. Her eyes went to Troiano, and down to his gloved hands..

"Sorry," he said, and Gillian colored.

"Leaves me, I guess," said Emerald. She set down the fat white rubber fender she was holding. From the pocket of her slacks she produced a pair of black leather gloves and pulled them on.

"Are you sure . . ." Gillian began.

"If Barr shows me what he wants, I'll do it," she replied confidently. Swinging herself easily over the side, she slipped down the rope ladder.

A brief mutter of inaudible instructions drifted up from the ground below, and then Barr's voice: "Ready on deck?"

"Ready," said Gillian.

"One, two, three!" A double thump, felt as well as heard. Barr's urgent "Again, quick!" and *Glory* began, jerkily, to slide backward. Before they had gone ten feet, Barr was on deck, scrambling awkwardly over the gunwale. He had taken two steps toward the far side when Emerald's copper-red hair appeared, and Patrick pulled her up over the rail.

Glory was moving surprisingly fast, rocking badly. "Hold onto something," said Barr. "If she goes over, try to jump clear."

"She won't go over!" cried Gillian. She had one hand on the wheel and had turned to face the stern, exultation on her face. "We're going to make it!"

Barr caught Patrick's eye and shrugged. Each lurch was worse than the one before, and the big yacht was gaining speed as she swung from side to side. The rumbling of metal on metal rose to a crescendo, ended with a crash of spray and a three-foot wave that broke over the yacht's transom. But *Glory* was afloat, shooting back into the black water in a gentle arc. "Helm over to port, Gillian," said Barr quietly.

She was already spinning the wheel. "I see it. Patrick, fender on the port quarter—fast. Make that two." A ghostly shape, seemingly as high as a cliff, loomed out of the gloom. Rubber squealed as *Glory*'s stern ground into planking, then bounced free.

"Look back there," said Emerald, pointing toward the pier behind them. Two lights were visible, bobbing erratically among the stored boats, pausing at the water's edge. The lights played out toward where *Glory* slipped backward, more slowly now, but the beams faded far short of where the mastless yacht bobbed uneasily.

"We're clear," said Gillian calmly. "I think we'll wait a couple of minutes and then start up the engine."

"Perhaps we ought to decide where we're going," Barr remarked. In the scramble of departure, Patrick realized, the subject had never come up—anyplace was clearly better than being trapped in Tremaine's. But *Glory*'s launching had added a dizzying range of possibilities.

"They'll be after us as soon as somebody notices we're gone," Patrick said, thinking aloud. "Not long after first light, unless I miss my guess. And I bet Visconti puts a chopper up, first thing."

"I suppose you're right," said Barr reluctantly. In the

moonlight, he looked drained. "Let's see—Norwalk's out: it's too far . . ."

"And too obvious," Gillian put in, impatiently. "What we need is someplace close by that nobody's ever heard of."

"With a roof," Patrick added.

"Anybody here know Snapper Cove?" asked Emerald.

"Not really," Barr replied. "It's in Oyster Bay, isn't it?"

"Tucked up in a corner," Emerald said. "It's got big trees right at the water's edge. Best of all, I own it."

"You own it?" Gillian's voice was incredulous.

"Me and the bank. It's the back edge of the property my place is on."

"I don't suppose you know how deep the water is, alongside those trees," Barr said dubiously.

"Seven feet, at low tide: the guy I bought it from had it dredged last year."

Barr was looking thoughtful. "Let's see," he said. "Tide's just turned to ebb, and we need ten feet to float— probably the bottom of that cove is mud, so we can just let her sink in . . ." He looked at Gillian. "We can do it. Barely."

"Then let's go. Captain," she said.

Barr looked narrowly at her. After a moment a smile flicked across his face, and he nodded.

11

SNAPPER COVE
SATURDAY, MAY 11
ELEVEN-THIRTY
A.M.

Barr climbed fuzzily out of sleep to the sound of voices from outside the fo'c'sle. Two voices—Gillian's and Emerald's. He could not make out the words, but the tone was intransigence on Gillian's part and urgency on Emerald's. The sun, dappled by leaves, was streaming straight down through the deck prism: it must be nearly midday, and he had slept for eight hours. They had hit bottom twice getting into the cove, but on soft mud each time. Now *Glory* lay utterly immobile, and Barr's interior gyroscope told him that the floorboards were a degree or so off horizontal—she was definitely aground.

A crackling sound and the smell of bacon was coming from the galley adjoining the fo'c'sle. Barr rolled out of the bunk. He had pulled a muscle climbing aboard as the boat slid down the ways, and he was sore as well as stiff. He tugged a T-shirt over his head and opened the door. In the galley, O'Mara was standing over *Glory*'s big old kerosene stove, wielding a spatula and looking well in control. He had tied a towel around his waist by way of an apron, and glanced up as Barr came through the door. "Morning," he said. As Barr had expected, he was freshly shaved, and his clean shirt—how many did he have, anyway?—made Barr feel frowsty as well as ancient. "Scrambled okay?"

Barr grunted. Normally, the thought of food first thing in the morning was repellent, but after a moment he decided he was actually hungry.

"Five minutes," O'Mara said.

Through the bulkhead, Gillian's raised voice cut like a hacksaw: "I'm not discussing it any more. I don't care what you say; it's Uncle Dennis's funeral, and I'll be there."

O'Mara rolled his eyes at the overhead and whispered, "They've been at it for half an hour. Emerald's saying that Visconti and this General Hals are bound to be at the funeral, and it'd be crazy for Gillian to go. You just heard what Gillian says."

Barr did not want to discuss Gillian with this excessively handsome young man. He grunted again, and opened the door into the saloon. The two women were sitting almost nose to nose, with an array of tiny pots and jars on the tabletop beside them. Gillian, swathed in a huge beach towel, had her back to Barr, and Emerald was leaning toward her, doing something with a small brush. She looked up at Barr. "Stay right there," she commanded. "I'm almost done. Don't move, Gillian." A long silence, and then Emerald leaned back with a sigh of satisfaction. "Well, Cleo would've done it better, but it ain't bad, if I say so myself."

"Cleo?" asked Barr.

"One of my girls," Emerald said, examining Gillian's face. "You'd like her, Barr. Beautiful beyond belief and can't say a word. There, honey: you're finished."

"Barr would like the last part, anyway," said Gillian. She turned to him as she spoke, and he heard himself gasp. It was essentially the same woman, but subtly changed— her eyebrows had a new shape and there was a tint of something around her eyes that made them look bigger and brighter. Her mouth was different, too—softer and fuller—and her hair . . . "You like?" Gillian asked.

"It's amazing," he said. "Emerald, you're a genius."

"Thanks a lot," said Gillian, and Emerald replied, "It's easy when you've got good material to work with."

O'Mara appeared, holding a plate of scrambled eggs and bacon. He gave a low whistle. Gillian smiled at him, and he set down the plate and dropped easily onto the settee.

Barr took a tentative bite, and then a second. His mouth

still filled with the third, he said, "Is there anything you can't do, O'Mara?"

The large young man smiled politely. Emerald, still arranging stray wisps of Gillian's hair, said, "I need you to straighten this kid out, Barr. I've been telling her . . ."

"I heard," Barr put in, as Gillian opened her mouth to protest. "I agree with you completely, and there's no way on earth you can change her mind. End of discussion."

Gillian's mouth closed, and Emerald spoke again. "All right—I give up: you know her a lot better than I do. But it's still suicide. And she's risking everybody's investment."

"How's that?" Barr asked.

"While you were asleep, we had a little talk," Emerald said, glancing sidelong at Gillian. "We agreed that we have to stick together, if we're going to get anything out of this. And we decided to split whatever it is that's aboard."

"We decided to go shares, the way they used to do in whaling ships," Gillian broke in. "After we set aside enough money to fix up *Glory*, the rest gets divided among us—I get two shares, Emerald and Johnny Troiano get two shares, Patrick gets one . . ." she paused, not meeting his eye. "And there's one for you."

"Have we got articles to sign, too?" he asked. "Hell, Gillian, this all seems kind of premature." She looked defensive, and he added, "Generous, but premature."

"Baloney," said Emerald firmly. "This way we all know where we stand. As far as I'm concerned, a piece of the action is the best way to keep everybody honest." She looked directly at Barr as she spoke, but her expression was unreadable. He raised his eyebrows in a question, but she went on: "That's what I mean about Gillian risking our shares with this crazy idea—even if they don't scoop her right off the street, they'll tag her back here, sure as hell, and then we're behind the eight ball again."

Barr pushed his plate away. "You can talk till you're blue in the face, Emerald, but I know Gillian. Unless you tie her down, she's going."

"Don't try it," Gillian said. She got to her feet, grabbed the towel as it started to slip. "I've got to hurry," she said, walking back toward the aft cabin.

Emerald, an almost proprietary look on her face,

watched Gillian leave. When the door had closed, she turned to Barr. "It's funny—she reminds me of me when I was a kid. I didn't really expect her to give in."

"Then why . . ."

"It's kind of a negotiation," Emerald went on. "I have an idea; not a great one, but better than nothing. I needed Gillian softened up a little—and I need you."

"There's the car," said Barr. "The light-brown Oldsmobile, on the left."

"It's a Buick," Gillian replied. "Lurlene must be inside the funeral parlor." With an assurance Barr found himself envying, she slipped the red sports car around a double-parked delivery truck. "See anybody we know?"

"The guy standing on the near corner—staring in the window? He looks kind of familiar."

Her glance flickered across the street. "Not to me," she said. Then, her voice tight, "There's Bellairs, in that tan Ford, parked right across from the funeral parlor."

"Hals must be inside, in the chapel. We ought to park: the service starts in fifteen minutes." They made another right turn, off Madison and onto the side street, and a car pulled out from the curb in front of them.

"That's luck . . . uh-oh."

"Right," said Barr gloomily. "Come into my parlor."

"In Manhattan, a parking space is a parking space," Gillian replied, dropping the Mazda neatly next to the curb. "Even if it's Visconti's tame captain who hands it to you." She got out, locked the door. She was wearing a restrained black dress and a small round hat, and she looked, even to the slightly distracted Barr, wholly delectable.

"You'd better put on the raincoat," he said. She raised an eyebrow at him, and he added: "It's part of the profile—get them used to seeing a hat and a raincoat."

"I see. Have you done this before, by any chance?" The bland innocence in her voice told him he was being baited, and he ignored it. Side by side, they walked into the funeral parlor's entrance hall. A young man in a blue suit sidled up to them.

"Miss Verdean? We've been waiting for you," he said, his voice oozing disapproval. "We expected you yesterday," he continued, taking Gillian's arm. "Great-uncle is right in here."

She bestowed an icy smile, and let him lead her. They entered a smallish room hung with neutral drapes that made it seem even smaller. About twenty chairs were grouped before a modest-looking open casket. The muscles stood out along Gillian's jaw as she let the young man guide her forward. Hitchcock was in the front row of chairs, sitting alone. Behind him, Matt Visconti, in discreetly double-breasted charcoal gray, was flanked by anonymous bodyguards. General Hals, wearing a lightweight tropical suit with a black band around his left arm, sat alone, at the end of Visconti's row. Behind them was a solid detachment from Carey & Willard, led by a red-eyed Mrs. Mulvey.

Barr and Gillian stared down into the coffin. "It doesn't look like him at all," Gillian said.

Their escort obviously mistook her emotion. "Our people had to use more cosmetics than usual," he said. "Great-uncle's face was quite bruised on the far side."

Gillian looked at him, her lips quivering. Barr was not sure if she was going to laugh or cry, and perhaps neither was she. "Maybe we could be private for a couple of minutes," she said. This was a request the young man was accustomed to, and he led them through a door behind where the coffin stood. The room was windowless, with a couch along one wall, a couple of chairs, a side table with ashtrays. Barr, lighting a cigarette, was relieved to see a plain young woman with an unlikely wave of platinum-blonde hair.

"Glad you're here, Lurlene," he said. "Any problems?"

"No sweat," said the young woman. "Here you go," she said to Gillian, handing her a pair of car keys on a chain. "Tan Buick, Ohio plates; it's parked right on Madison, half a block down." She looked back at Barr. "Where's the Mazda?"

Barr found himself disoriented by the absence of windows. "Where does that door go to?" he asked the young man, who was hovering nervously.

"The street," he replied. "Your secretary said Miss Verdean wanted to leave by a private exit."

Barr turned to Lurlene: "The Mazda's right outside this

door, on the same side of the street, parked next to a tree. We've got company, though."

Lurlene shifted her chewing gum. "I wondered about that. How many?"

"One guy, very skinny and tall, in a light-brown sedan parked on Madison, right behind where the hearse will go. Another, a green four-door that's probably circling the block, unless he found a parking place. And there's got to be at least one more. You sure you can handle it?"

"Shit, yes," Lurlene said. "When I put the hammer down, I'll just blow their doors off." She seemed unworried—not surprising, considering that her last driving assignment had aborted (according to Emerald) in a hail of bullets outside a suburban bank.

The funeral director was beginning to look nervous. "I hope there's not going to be any trouble," he said.

Gillian, who had been watching Barr and Lurlene intently, let out a small, stifled sound. "So do I," she said.

The young man eyed her dubiously. "Then I suppose we may as well start. Doctor Carrigan is right outside— did you want to speak with him?" Gillian looked blank, and the young man, putting it down to shock, prompted, "Your minister."

"Oh," Gillian said. She was looking around for moral support, but Barr, avoiding her eye, slipped from the room.

The service was as bad as might have been expected. The minister, a well-preserved Presbyterian, kept referring to the deceased as "Dennis," and each time he did, Barr saw Gillian, in the pew immediately ahead of his, stiffen. At the end, the undertaker's men moved toward the coffin on cue, and Barr stepped forward and took Gillian's arm. "When I die," she muttered, "just chuck me over the side."

"Come on," Barr said. They were through the small door, Gillian shrugging out of her raincoat. As Lurlene pulled it on over her nondescript dress, Barr said, "But what about her hair?"

Lurlene grinned at him—she was missing a canine—and lifted off her wig. Under it, her hair was a brown not too unlike Gillian's own. She held the wig out to Gillian, who shook her head. "Up to you," Lurlene said, stuffing it into her purse and settling the small round hat on her head.

"I don't see why you have to do this," said Gillian. "I can take my own chances."

"We'll be all right," Barr said. "You just stay put till everybody's gone. Come on, Lurlene—let's blow their doors down." He opened the door to the street. There were few passersby, but signs of activity down by the corner, where the casket must be coming out, on its way to the crematorium. "Let's go," he said.

They darted from the door, running hard for the red car. Behind him, he heard Gillian's voice calling "Good luck!"

Lurlene had the car door open and was sliding behind the wheel, and from the corner of his eye Barr saw figures running down the sidewalk toward them. The engine roared. "Get in!" Lurlene cried, pulling at the wheel. It was Captain Arrow and another man, and Arrow had a gun in his hand. Lurlene looked at Barr, and he shook his head. "Go," he mouthed at her. The door handle was torn from his grasp as she floored the accelerator and the little red car leaped ahead like a deer.

Barr turned to meet Arrow. The revolver looked like a toy in Arrow's hand, but it was real enough and aimed right at Barr. "Take him," said the big man.

"What about the Verdean kid?" the bodyguard said, pointing to where a screech of brakes marked Lurlene's passage through the red light at the corner of Madison.

"We only need one of them," said Arrow, with heavy satisfaction. "He'll do."

The slap threw Barr back against the metal bulkhead hard enough so that he felt each rivet-head through his shirt. With his hands secured behind his back, he was off-balance, and the next blow knocked him to the deck. There was no animosity in the two men who were methodically working him over—who had been beating him for an hour or so, ever since he had been frog-marched, with a hood to blind him, up what felt like the gangway of a fair-sized vessel and then dragged down an echoing flight of metal steps to this cabin whose only porthole was painted out.

"Come on, sport," said the shorter of the two, a man in his middle twenties who affected a world-weary air. "Just tell us where you hid the boat and we can all take a break." On his knees, Barr watched the thick red drops fall one by one from the cut on his forehead to the scuffed gray metal. In the toe of his right shoe he could feel the lump that represented three tightly wadded pages from Dennis Falk's logbook. The first cursory search that had cost him his knife and wallet had missed the papers, but sooner or later they would find them, unless he could get away. Abruptly, a hand grabbed his collar and dragged him upright. It was, of course, the second man—bigger, older, and more powerful—who seemed to have a better idea of where a blow would hurt without leaving a mark. As if to prove it, he drove a short punch to Barr's kidney, folding his victim at the waist.

He grabbed Barr's hair, wet with sweat, and paused. Outside, shod feet clashed on a metal ladder, and the door swung open. One of Barr's eyes was nearly closed, but he could see Captain Arrow too well with the other. The heavy-jowled face was a deep red, as if with suppressed rage. "I thought I told you guys not to mark him up," said Arrow, his voice angry. "Get that blood off him—the man wants to see him."

The corridor was like a warship's—of course, it would be: he must be on Visconti's motor yacht. Up the ladder, and the gray-paint-and-steel-hatches decor abruptly gave way to carpet underfoot and exquisite paneling in some blond wood Barr did not recognize. Arrow was on one side of him and the larger of his tormenters on the other, hustling him along, but he caught a quick glimpse out a passageway porthole of a high cliff, about a mile away across the water, with huge apartment towers on the top and the sun red behind them—it could only be the Palisades, on the Jersey side of the Hudson, and that meant they were tied up on Manhattan's West Side, at one of the abandoned city piers.

They came to a heavy wooden door, more elegantly carved than the paneling, and a sentry holding a submachine gun standing in front of it. Like the rest of the men Barr had seen, he was young, blank-faced, dressed in neat khaki. He stood aside, and Arrow knocked.

"Come."

Arrow opened the door and pushed Barr through. A narrow passageway with a door on one side led into a large, airy cabin at least twenty feet wide, with curtained portholes to port and starboard. The rug was ankle-deep, of some off-white, fur-like material, and the bulkheads were teak, oiled to a maple-syrup glow. The room was dominated by a huge desk made from a single slab of steel that had been tricked out with heavy turned-wood legs. Behind the desk, in his shirtsleeves, sat Matt Visconti, his bright red suspenders incongruous against his somber necktie. His glance took in Barr's appearance and his face hardened. "Get out," he said to Arrow.

Barr heard the door close behind him, and the metallic echo of the bolt sliding home. Visconti indicated the chair in front of the desk. "Sit down, Captain Barr."

There seemed no reason not to, and Barr sank gratefully into the upholstery. Visconti grinned at him. "I'm sorry to leave you tied up like that, but the plain fact is that you and your friends have scared the daylights out of my employees." He held out a cigarette; Barr took it between his lips and drew in deeply as a heavy silver lighter was extended to him. "And I'm sorry about your face," he continued amiably. "I'm afraid Captain Arrow is angry. He's in disgrace, you see. Not to put too fine a point on it, he fucked up last night. Being who he is, he took it out on you."

The smoke swirling in Barr's lungs was making him light-headed. Or maybe it was the beating. He sat quietly, watching the man opposite him. He had the feeling that Visconti was feeling his way. After a long minute, Visconti took the cigarette from Barr's mouth and set it in an ashtray. "Look," he said. "I'll be straight with you. Last night we should have had you on toast— If that big oaf had waited a few more hours, we could have grabbed *Glory* and had . . . what we're looking for. But Captain Arrow jumped the gun, and what happens? By some prodigy of energy and skill you launch the yacht and hide her." He paused for a moment, as if waiting for Barr to speak, then continued. "I was surprised when Gillian appeared this afternoon—but it was certainly in character. I expect you tried to talk her out of it. And because she's stubborn she got away, and we have you." Visconti offered Barr the cigarette, but he shook his head. "I admire your loyalty, Captain Barr. And I admire your skill." Visconti stubbed the butt out in a heavy crystal ashtray, talking all the while. "It never occurred to me that you could get *Glory* afloat last night. But it's all so unnecessary. I don't have to guess where Dennis's hoard is—if Gillian hadn't disappeared so quickly, I could have told her that it's no longer necessary even to scratch the boat's hull. The hiding place is marked right here, on Dennis's set of *Glory*'s plans." He tapped a flat pile of wrinkled, folded papers sitting on his desk.

"But that's only part of it." He was watching Barr intently, and now he sat on the edge of the desk and leaned forward, his voice more urgent: "I could get in a lot of trouble for what I'm about to tell you, but I'm going to take the chance. Because I trust you. I want the money—sure." A self-deprecating smile crossed his face. "Dennis screwed me out of a bundle. But what's really important is to keep that Kraut bastard Hals from getting it. Because if he does get it, that's the end of a plan that a lot of people have put a lot of time and blood into."

His eyes bored into Barr's. "You know whose agent General Hals is? You know who I'm building fast attack boats for? I won't say the name, but it's the same person. If Hals can get his boss's money back, he'll be able to get the contract transferred to another builder. But if I build those boats, they might be just a little slower, a little more predictable than what the U.S. Navy has. Or doesn't that mean anything to you? Really, Captain Barr, behaving like the sphinx accomplishes nothing."

He paused again. "Have it your way, then—but I think you should be fully aware of the consequences." He rose and looked out a porthole. "I've occasionally been threatened by terrorists—it goes with the territory, so to speak—and even attacked, right aboard this very vessel. So my people have no difficulty believing you're another terrorist assassin."

He swung back to Barr. "Think about it, Captain Barr. I have a dinner date ashore, but when I return I really must have your cooperation, one way or another." He pressed a button on the desk and the door behind Barr flew open. "Put this gentleman in the little cabin. And send in Captain Arrow."

The little cabin was right next to Visconti's suite, as bare and stark as the other was elegant. Its only porthole was small and shuttered with steel, and there was not a stick of furniture. Through a grilled opening in the bulkhead came the hum of the ship's machinery. A single overhead

bulb in a frosted globe lit the cabin, presumably for the
benefit of whoever might be using the peephole that was
set into the door. Barr allowed himself to sag to the deck,
his head against the bulkhead, and realized that he could
hear the voices in Visconti's cabin, first dimly, and then
quite clearly when he pressed one ear to the metal.

". . . Nothing," Visconti was saying firmly. "Absolutely
not a word. This is another man you cannot beat into
submission, Captain Arrow."

A protesting rumble, ridden down by Visconti: "Not till
I get back. I would rather have his willing help. Of course
the other way works, but when a man tells you whatever
comes into his head, just to stop the pain, you don't always
get reliable information. I shouldn't have to tell you that,
after the other night."

Barr felt a cold trickle run down his back, and he missed
the next few words. ". . . don't understand," Visconti was
saying, "is where Miss Verdean or Captain Barr hired the
five men who jumped you last night . . ."

Five men? What was he talking about? Barr pressed his
ear hard against the bulkhead, as Visconti continued:
"They looked like sailors, you said?"

"Yessir," Arrow agreed reluctantly. "Like that. Big
guys. I didn't see their faces." Arrow's excuses rambled
on, but Barr was no longer listening, his mind grappling
with the implications of what Visconti had just said—and
what Arrow clearly had not: Visconti didn't know Emerald
was involved. *Glory* and the others were safe from him,
at least for a while.

Barr wrenched at the ties on his wrists: not line, but
some kind of strong fabric, like sail ties. The knots were
wholly professional, pulled tight enough so that even if he
had been able to get at them with his fingernails, he would
have had little chance of loosening them. If anything were
to be done, the strap would have to be cut.

A few minutes later, he heard Visconti leave, with Arrow behind him. The outer door to the suite shut firmly,
and locked. After a waiting to make sure both men had
gone, Barr pushed off his shoes and worked his way to his
feet. A sybarite like Visconti might easily require as much
as an hour to eat dinner, plus the time to get wherever he
was going, and return. But that timing hardly applied to

Captain Arrow, who might look in for a kick or two as soon as his master's orders had worn off.

The only chance was the light, and there was only one way to get it. Standing directly beneath the globe, Barr flexed his knees and jumped. The first time he was a good six inches too low, and landed off-balance with a crash that seemed to jar the entire yacht. After five tries he decided that jumping straight up was not going to work—and that if anything else were to be successful, it would have to be quick: he could feel his strength ebbing. Backing to the cabin's far corner, he pushed off the bulkhead, took two long steps and leaped. The globe and the bulb inside it exploded with a loud pop, and the thump as he hit the deck did not quite drown out the tinkle of broken glass.

For a few moments he lay panting on the wood-planked deck. The cabin was inky, and anyone looking through the peephole would be alerted by the absence of light. His fingers found a piece of globe, thick yet sharp, and he began sawing awkwardly at the straps that held him. Four times the glass between his fingertips fractured as he put too much pressure on it, and each time he had to scrabble among the remaining shards to find a new piece. His pain-fully cramped fingers seemed to be sweaty, too, and some-times his wrists were so constricted that his hands went numb.

Something gave a bit, and he tensed his shoulders and pulled, ignoring the pain of the wrenched muscle in his arm. No good. He went back to his sawing, furiously rub-bing the bit of glass against the strap until, with no warning, it fell away from his wrists.

He had a surprising urge to cry, followed immediately by a stronger urge to laugh. He forced both impulses down and instead sat rubbing his numbed wrists until the cir-culation fully returned. His hands felt sticky, and his fin-gertips hurt. But so did his jaw, his cheekbone and assorted points around his midsection.

A faint glow he had not noticed earlier was coming from the grille on the bulkhead. Shaking himself, he got up, put on his deck shoes and went over to it. The grillwork pre-vented him from seeing more than a couple of feet down the shaft toward the source of the light and the hum of idling machinery. On one side of the shaft he could make out metal rungs set into the bulkhead. Of course: a ventilation tunnel that doubled as an emergency exit for the engine-room crew. Quickly, he took the cheap brass buckle from his web belt and attacked the screws that held the grille in place. By the time he had backed them off, the buckle was a twisted wreck. He pocketed the screws, eased the grille from the bulkhead. The aperture was just large enough for a skinny, undersized, desperate man.

Braced inside the duct, he paused to consider the next step. If this was an engine-room ventilator, it must lead on deck. Painfully, he pulled himself up the ladder. Just above the vent where he had climbed in, another tube branched off. Forward, if his sense of direction was not wholly turned around. He put his arm into it, felt what appeared to be a wire-mesh grating with something like insulating fiber woven into it. Probably vents Visconti's cabin, he thought. The mesh would be sound shielding. He continued climbing up the main duct, and then it took a right-angle turn that almost defeated him.

He saw specks of light above and in front of him, realized that they were stars. With almost his last strength he pulled himself to the lip of a horn-shaped ventilator whose mouth was some six feet above the yacht's wheelhouse. Below him the whole vessel was spread out. The wheelhouse and bridge were her highest point, with a row of cabins—Visconti's office was probably one of them—below, on the main deck. As he had guessed, the yacht was lying alongside a crumbling pier, her gleaming paint and metalwork in stark contrast to the rusting cast-iron roof, almost more holes than surface, and the decaying concrete from which the rusty bones of reinforcing rods protruded.

There was a guard at the gangway, not visibly armed, but Barr knew there would be a weapon within easy reach. No one else could be seen, at least not from his constricted vantage point, but a vessel this big would have a crew of six at least, not counting Visconti's bodyguards. Slowly, Barr extracted himself from the ventilator, dropped to the deck, and froze there, as he caught the wink of a cigarette from up forward, where another man leaned on the rail and watched the Hudson River go by. Barr knelt on the roof of the bridge, bracing himself with one hand.

Above him, on the yacht's signal mast, a bright white light went on, and he dropped flat. No cries of alarm, no shots—apparently someone down in the wheelhouse had merely turned on the yacht's running lights. Barr's pounding heart slowed, then skipped a beat as he glanced at the gleaming white surface on which he lay: he'd left a trail of smudgy, reddish marks, like the paw prints of some wounded animal. In a sense, that was what they were. His fingertips, now that he could see them, were sliced in half-a-dozen places from the shards he had been clutching; anyone who wanted to track him had an easy task, at least this far. Or maybe a little farther. Moving carefully, he extended the trail of bloody smudges to the edge of the wheelhouse roof, from which a steel ladder led down to the main deck.

Lying flat on his belly, he peered over. Just below, in a recess of the wheelhouse bulkhead, something that resembled a small movie camera was mounted on a bracket. As Barr watched, it panned slowly across the deck, halted and panned back. He shrugged off his shirt and tore two strips from the back, for improvised bandages, after which he dropped the shredded garment to the foot of the ladder. It was surprising how much his fingertips had begun to hurt, now that he knew they were cut. He was awkwardly tucking the end of the second bandage under itself when a pair of plain four-door sedans pulled into the covered pier and stopped. Down below, a voice called and was answered, and the watching figure at the gangway surreptitiously straightened his shirt.

Visconti, bracketed by bodyguards, got out of the second car, as Captain Arrow, in a double-breasted navy-style uniform, clambered out of the leading vehicle. Barr knew he now had a couple of minutes at most. There was no chance of getting off the yacht—certainly not while dressed in a ragged pair of gray flannel pants and a shirt with half its back torn out. From where he was, in fact, there was only one place to go—back where he had come from.

The rungs of the shaft ladder had not been designed for someone with bandaged hands, and once he nearly lost his grasp entirely. Down he went and down, listening for the shouts from below that would announce the discovery of his escape. There was the duct that led forward to Visconti's office. Might as well try it; at this point there was less than nothing to lose. Without the use of fingertips, it was simply impossible to remove the sound screen quietly. Barr braced his back against the duct and lashed out with both feet. Inside the metal cylinder, the noise was cataclysmic, but there was no time to listen for sounds of alarm. Clutching a rung with one hand, he managed to get his padded fingers around the wire frame and wrench it free. The aperture was only barely wide enough for his hips, as he slid in feet first, and he had to round his shoulders painfully to wedge them inside. He pulled the screen to behind him; it would hardly stand a moment's close inspection, but he refused to think about that.

Wriggling, he forced his way along the duct. His feet hit a grating, and he slid over it until he found himself looking down, through a grilled aperture in the overhead. Visconti's great steel desk was immediately below him; on it, in an envelope, were the plans Visconti had mentioned. If only he could look at them, even for a minute . . . A foolish thought; they might as well have been on Mars.

The outer door to the office crashed open, and Barr was treated to a view of the top of Visconti's head, a foot below. Barr pulled back until he was pressed against the far side of the duct, but he knew that anyone who even glanced upward could not fail to see him. Visconti came around the desk and hurled himself into his chair. When he spoke, to someone outside Barr's range of vision, his voice was irritated: "You covered the whole western end of the Sound, you say?"

"Yessir." Barr had been expecting Captain Arrow's low rumble, but this was a new man. "We took the chopper east as far as New Haven, like you said. And west all the way to the Throgs Neck."

"And down both rivers," Visconti said.

"Yessir. Not a sign of them anyplace—we were out right at first light: they couldn't possibly have got more than fifteen miles. And the current in the East River and Hell Gate was dead on the nose. They wouldn't hardly have been moving against it." He paused. "You don't suppose they sank the old tub, do you, sir?"

"No," Visconti replied instantly. "Not with Gillian Verdean in it. . . . But how do you cause sixty-five feet of boat to vanish like that?"

"Well, they could be under one of these old covered piers, sir—could be right near us, for that matter. Or hauled out in some other boatyard, with a tarp over them. Lots of places."

"Too many places," said Visconti coldly.

"You want us to try again in the morning, sir?"

"I trust that won't be necessary," Visconti replied. "Tell Captain Arrow I want to see him."

"Yessir." The door closed behind the man and almost immediately reopened.

"You've talked to Murdoch," said Visconti.

"He told me, sir," said the well-remembered voice of Arrow. "No luck."

"Luck, indeed," Visconti repeated acidly. "So now it's up to you, Captain Arrow. You made this mess—you clean it up."

"Yes, sir," said Arrow stolidly. "Anything goes?"

Visconti straightened in his chair, apparently staring down the man who must be standing at the desk before him. "Remember what happened to the old man, Captain. It cost me some trouble to repair that error. This time, be more careful. Don't start enjoying yourself too much." Visconti leaned forward. "I want information—one piece of information. After that, I'm not interested in him."

"You're not going to let him go!" Arrow sounded appalled.

"Don't be absurd," Visconti replied. "It's a great waste—I tell you frankly, I'd rather have him in my employ than you. But we can't have him running around loose."

"No, sir," Arrow said, relief in his voice. "Shall I get him now?"

"Do so," Visconti replied with a sigh. "We'll see if the appeal to patriotism has worked."

"Just so we kill him afterward. Sir," Arrow said composedly.

"Get out," Visconti snapped. As the door closed, he sighed again and said something under his breath. Slowly he pulled *Glory*'s plans from the envelope, unfolded the top sheet of the stack, as if caressing it, and for a long moment Barr had a clear view of it—so clear a view that Dennis Falk's elaborate plan was suddenly clear as daylight in his mind, and he gasped aloud.

The only thing that saved him from discovery was the simultaneous, bull-like bellow from just outside the cabin. Visconti leaped to his feet, tipping over the chair, and then grabbed up the papers and stuffed them into a drawer in the desk as the office door crashed open.

Two men, and then three, all shouting at once, each trying to drown out the others, until Visconti cut them off with a gesture. Strangely, he seemed wholly calm, not even annoyed. The four swept out of the office, and a moment later Barr heard their voices again—they were in the little cabin, and the sounds were coming up the duct.

"Shine that flash up here," Visconti was saying. "Of course: the grating. Why didn't you leave him a screwdriver, too? You might have saved him a little trouble."

An embarrassed mutter answered him, with the word "blood" audible at the end of it.

"Of course there's blood," said Visconti, annoyance showing now. "He cut his fingers on the glass." Twisting his neck, Barr could see a beam of light darting up the main vent tube.

"There's blood in here, too," said Arrow, his voice echoing hollowly. "He must be in here. How about we send Grimes up. With a gun."

"Don't be an ass," Visconti replied. "A boathook will do just as well—I want Barr alive. And while you're at it, I want someone up on deck, or wherever this comes out."

"Aye, aye, sir," said Arrow. Now they were bound to find him, Barr thought. The boathook was the final touch; they could prod at him safely for as long as they liked.

He heard the audibly unhappy Grimes climb into the vent shaft, and the clatter of the long-shafted hook being passed up to him. "Check every cross-duct," Arrow was saying, "but look for the bloodstains—that's your trail."

Grimes's boot thudded on the first rung, and Barr tensed as an echoing cry came down the ventilator shaft. "Up here! Up here! There's blood all over the place, you guys— he must have come out the top."

Visconti now, his voice booming up the tubing. "Where does the blood go?"

"Right to the edge, sir." A murmuring from topside that echoed sepulchrally down the ventilator, and then the crewman called down again: "The blood ends here, sir. But he left part of his shirt. He must've bandaged his hands. He's got away, sir. Maybe jumped overboard."

"And nobody heard him?" Visconti sounded dubious and impatient. "Well, there's no time for a proper search, not if *Tiamat*'s to be in Norwalk by dawn. What I really want to find is in Long Island Sound, anyway. Grimes, get out of there. Captain Arrow, we have a considerable distance to go: Have the men continue looking, while we run downriver. But I want the yacht under way immediately."

12

MANHATTAN
EIGHT P.M.

Gillian waited for hours, pacing from room to beige-curtained room, peering cautiously through the windows at the anonymous street below. The staff of the funeral parlor had obviously decided she was more than a little odd—very possibly dangerous—and they stayed out of her way. At last, an attendant hurried up to say that she had a telephone call.

She reached for the instrument and her hand stopped in midair. What if it was Visconti? Or Bellairs? Well, only one way to find out.

"Hello?"

"It's Emerald."

Something in her voice made Gillian say, "What's wrong?"

"They picked up Barr," said Emerald. She sounded cool and unruffled. "They were waiting right outside. He held them off for a minute, so Lurlene could get away. She thinks they didn't notice it wasn't you, and she's sure she wasn't followed."

"Who got Barr?" Gillian demanded. "Is he all right?"

"Visconti's men, I think. Anyway, there were several, and at least two cars, according to Lurlene." She hesitated, then went on: "He was still on his feet when Lurlene lit out of there, but that's all we know."

It's my fault. Why doesn't Emerald say so? Gillian heard the other woman's matter-of-fact tone, as she went on:

"Barr's probably safe until he tells them where the boat is."

"What do you mean?"

"You think they're going to leave him walking around? Sweetie, this is the big league. I think you'd better get your little tail back here. Quick."

"What about the others—Hals and Bellairs?"

"I was going to ask you," said Emerald.

"I haven't seen anyone on the street. But this isn't a great place to watch from—there's too many doorways someone could be standing in."

"How about the Buick? Is it still where Lurlene parked it?"

"Yes. I can see it from here."

"Anybody hanging around it?"

"Not that I can tell," Gillian said uncertainly. "I wish I knew more about this kind of thing."

Emerald sounded amused: "Be glad you haven't had to." Then, briskly: "Come on, Gillian—get going. The longer you hang around there, the scareder you're going to get."

"I couldn't get more scared," said Gillian. "If you want to know, I'm petrified."

"Fair enough," Emerald replied. "You'll be okay once you're moving. Take it slow, and make sure you're not followed—for some reason, no one's tumbled to this place yet, but once they do we're in real trouble."

"The trouble we're in is plenty real enough for me," Gillian said. "I'm on my way."

Even so, it was another five minutes before she could force herself to step out the front door, following a small group of mourners who had come to pay their respects to someone who was being buried the following day. Only when she was on the street and the chill evening breeze swept around a corner and ambushed her did she realize that everyone in the party was wearing coats—that virtually everyone else on the street was, too. It hardly made for the kind of unobtrusiveness she wanted.

Ahead on Madison was Lurlene's car, and its keys were clutched in Gillian's wet palm. Slow and easy, she told herself. Just walking up to my own car. Perfectly natural . . . What's that on the windshield? A parking ticket, what else? She took it from beneath the wiper blade and stared at it, unseeing. Who was that very tall figure looking in the restaurant window? She folded the ticket in half and put it into her purse. The key in her hand didn't fit the door lock, and she nearly broke it off trying to force it in, before taking a grip on her nerves and trying the other key on the ring. She slid behind the wheel, thankful that the seat was already pulled all the way forward. The Buick felt immense after her little Mazda. It was a four-door sedan, several years old, but obviously well kept.

The engine started right away, smooth and powerful. The man across the street had disappeared, and Gillian felt a moment's panic. She began to pull out into traffic, checked herself at the bleat of a horn and a cabdriver's curse. Just a touch on the power brakes almost put her through the windshield.

This thing is going to take some getting used to. Headlights. Turn signal. Check the cars . . . Now. The big car eased out smoothly, and she felt her jaws begin to unclench.

By the time she had worked her way over to Second Avenue and swung into the southbound traffic stream, the Buick was hers. The brakes were all right—she would hate to try stopping a couple of tons of Detroit iron without them—but the steering was vague and sloppy, and the ride was like a waterbed. Still, the car's acceleration canceled out its defects: Gillian had no idea how many horses might be champing under the hood, but when she'd put her size-7 down hard, just once, she'd nearly gone through the back of a bus that had seemed a block ahead.

At Sixty-second Street, she lined up behind the other cars waiting to get on the northbound FDR Drive. Through the underpass ahead was a glimpse of the East River, and as she watched, a forty-foot sloop whipped by, borne on the current. For some reason, it put Barr into her head. Where was he now? She had forced herself not to think of him, but she knew that some part of her mind had been worrying about him ever since she had spoken to Emerald. Surely Visconti wouldn't . . . She could not allow herself even to put words to her fear. Irritably, she wrenched the wheel and jumped the car into the middle lane, which was moving fractionally faster than the other two.

Suppose something had happened to him, though. What would she do? Maybe she could call Visconti and arrange a trade. But would the others—her new partners—stand for it? Patrick would be no problem: she could handle him easily enough; but Emerald's pet toad . . . that was a question. She was driving by instinct now, letting the car out a little as the traffic thinned. She slid over into the left lane to avoid the upcoming knot at the drive's Ninety-sixth Street entrance, and noticed a car two vehicles back doing the same thing. It was too dark to see anything except its lights, but these were unusual—a slight, continuous flicker in the parking light on the driver's side.

Above Ninety-sixth the traffic stream went through a brief clonic spasm, and she changed lanes twice again— easily, but at moments that had nothing to do with the logic of the other cars' movement, and each time the anonymous follower emulated her. She floated in the middle lane as the Triboro turnoff approached, free to go either way, letting the faster cars slide past. A hundred yards before the bridge ramp she saw her slot. Flicking the turn indicator, she swung into the right lane, as if for the toll-free Willis Avenue Bridge. She waited for the following car to do the same, then with only feet to spare tramped down on the gas and cut left across two lanes onto the Triboro approach ramp.

Horns went off all around, and behind her she distinctly heard a rending, metallic crash, but she kept her foot down and skidded the Buick around the tight turns and into the right lane of toll booths.

Safe. Not a sign of a pursuer—in fact, the traffic coming up from the drive seemed to have stopped; maybe they were unbending some fenders back there. She allowed herself a tight smile as she fumbled in her purse. Her heart was beating fast and hard, but her hands were steady and reasonably dry. You could get to like this kind of thing, she thought, and her mind flashed back to Lurlene, and from Lurlene to Emerald.

Buddies with a porno queen? It was crazy on the face of it. But shielded behind years of scar tissue, Emerald was the kind of friend you could really count on—Gillian was sure of that. It was hard to appreciate that they were the same age . . . Well, maybe they weren't, when you came right down to it; if you counted experience, Emerald was a couple of centuries older.

She eased at last onto the Long Island Expressway,

crowded as it always was with bad drivers alternately as-
serting themselves and losing their nerve. Gillian moved
the Buick into the left lane, ahead of a motorcycle—no,
a car with only one headlight. Abruptly, her pulse started
racing again. Could be the same car. Hard to tell, when
it was lit only by the wash of headlights from oncoming
vehicles, but its whole left front seemed to be crumpled.
She changed lanes once and then again, and this time the
other car stayed put—but stayed put at the same distance
back, close enough so she could never manage a quick
escape off the expressway. There was no reason for her
pursuers to close with her, certainly not here, and probably
not at all. They knew—they must finally have figured out—
where she had to go, and all they needed was patience.
Oddly enough, she felt quite calm. Calm and absolutely
determined.

The exit for Glen Cove flashed by; she would have to
make a choice soon: Take 106 toward Oyster Bay and lose
them on the back roads? Or lead them out someplace into
Suffolk County and try to outlast them? The Buick's tank
was nearly empty, and time itself was in short supply. She
moved into the right lane, with the one-eyed car tight on
her tail. No one was fooling anyone now, or trying to.
They were ready for her to do something dramatic, but
she clicked her turn indicator properly and slid off the
Expressway, up to the traffic light, turned left on 106
North.

What if I just drove into Oyster Bay and stopped in
front of the police station? Officer, these men are following
me. She could hear the condescending little speech from
the desk sergeant. Forget it.

The car behind her had dropped back slightly as she
dipped off 106 onto a quiet, deserted road. Gillian pushed
the speed up, taking the Buick through screeching turns
that led them through a small housing development and
out the other side.

It was maddening—the car behind had reasonable acceleration, but nothing to match hers; yet even with its
crumpled front it was more maneuverable than the big
Buick, which wanted to take flight at every sharp corner.
Forcing herself to think while her hands drove the car,
Gillian added up her assets: she knew where they were
going, and her car was faster on a straightaway; as against

that, it was clumsier, heavier, and probably had less fuel.

To her horror, she saw that her subconscious had put her onto the long, winding, empty road that led directly to Emerald's estate. Big houses set back in the scrubby trees, and not a person in sight. Instinctively, she floored the accelerator and the Buick leaped ahead. There were just enough twists and turns and side roads so the following car picked up to close the gap. They rounded an S-turn doing eighty, and Gillian stabbed the brakes. With the power assist, it was enough to lock them, and her car began a series of tight skids, tires squealing. She heard the car behind braking, too, but the driver was an instant too slow, and she felt the Buick lurch heavily as it was struck at the left rear wheel.

In the mirror, the car behind, lightless now, end-for-ended twice and hurtled into a tight grove of man-high pines. Gillian, battling the Buick's swerves, brought the big car down to a semblance of control and sped along the darkened road, hearing over the engine an increasingly unnerving ratcheting noise from the rear axle. She nearly missed the unmarked turn into Emerald's long dirt driveway, but she could not miss the blaze of windows that confronted her beyond the last stand of trees. On the dash a red light, two red lights, winked on as her car swung into the turnaround. The ratcheting changed suddenly to a series of grinding thumps, and the left rear corner of the car sagged to the ground, dragging the Buick to a sliding stop. As she looked over her shoulder, she had a quick glimpse of the rear wheel, released from its axle, bounding away to freedom.

A young woman she didn't recognize helped her out of the Buick. Smoke or steam was coming from under the car's rear, and she saw the bright, metallic gash where her pursuers had rammed her. The house in front of her was immense, with a pillared front porch and a knot of men and women, most of them wearing evening clothes, gabbling at the top of the steps. Emerald, in a vivid green dress that was cut to show off every curve of her magnificent body, stepped forward.

"Take her to my office," she said, before Gillian could force herself to speak. "Call Charlie's in town and get a tow truck out here. Now." She turned to the crowd. "Okay, folks—someone wanted to get to the party a little too fast. Excitement's over out here, but there's lots more in the reception room."

The door to Emerald's office closed behind Gillian, who slumped into a chair. Seconds later, it opened and Emerald herself came in. She seemed more angry than afraid. "What happened? Somebody followed you, right? Where are they?"

Gillian started to laugh, saw Emerald's hand poised ready for the slap and took a quick grip on herself. She was sitting in an oversize leather chair that matched the big mahogany turn-of-the-century desk. Overhead, a small chandelier that was missing half its bulbs. Stacks of lacy clothing and bills and builders' plans covered every surface.

"I put them off the road," Gillian said slowly. "Into some trees. I'm sorry about Lurlene's car, but it was the only thing I could do."

"How far back?" Emerald picked up a cut-glass decanter, blew the dust from a cheap tumbler and filled it with something thick and colorless.

"Maybe three miles." Gillian took a long swallow. "Whoof! What's this?"

"Aquavit. Finish it," Emerald said absently. "We haven't got much time."

Gillian drained the glass. A tide of molten licorice coursed down her throat and detonated in her stomach. "Ohmigod," she gasped. She cleared her throat with an effort. "I can hide aboard *Glory*—they don't know she's here."

"She isn't here," Emerald replied. She stabbed at a button on her desk. "When Lurlene told me about Barr, I got to thinking. This guy I know has a dock across the harbor. A lot of barges, dredging equipment, that kind of thing. I got him to tuck the boat up with some of his stuff— you'd go right by it without noticing. Patrick and Johnny are aboard, but it's five miles by road from here. I'm afraid you're stuck . . . What's up?" A blonde in a low-cut black dress had stuck her nose in the door.

"Charlie says he can't come till the morning," she reported nervously. "Without that wheel, I guess the car has to stay where it is, Em."

"Just shove it into the bushes," said Emerald. "Find

Cleo—she's in Suite A with the Great Man. Tell her I need her in my room, right now."

"You got it." The door closed, and Emerald rose to her feet. "Come on," she said, her voice quiet but urgent. "We've only got a few minutes."

Gillian stood and almost collapsed. Her legs were trembling violently; her balance seemed to have disappeared. Emerald took her briskly by the arm and led her to a second door, set unobtrusively in the paneling. "Trouble with this place," she said, as they half ran down a long, unpainted corridor stacked with ladders and cans of paint, "is that it's only half done. I had just enough cash to finance the front and a few bedrooms, and the rest is bare-ass naked." They came to a door, which Emerald unlocked. "This is where I live," Emerald explained. It was a big, cluttered room, with stacks of books on the floor and clothing everywhere.

Gillian was dragged into a large and beautifully appointed bathroom. Beautifully appointed, anyway, if you wanted to be able to examine every inch of yourself, pore by pore. Impatiently, Emerald thrust her into what looked like a barber's chair, surrounded on three sides by mirrors with lights over them. "The problem is, there's no place to hide," Emerald was saying. "So we've got to hide you the Edgar Allan Poe way."

"What?" Gillian shook her head, trying to clear it. "Oh, you mean in plain sight. . . . Hey, what're you doing?"

"Getting you out of that stuff." Emerald took Gillian's dress in her two hands and ripped it to the waist. "Come in, Cleo." The woman behind her had the placid, regal, Nilotic features of Nefertiti, and she was dressed and made up to emphasize the resemblance, except for a jarringly brassy choker necklace. Her smile was the smile of a happy five-year-old. "Help me take this shit off her," Emerald ordered. For all her languor, Cleo was quick and her slender fingers amazingly powerful. Gillian squirmed and squealed and finally fought in earnest, but inside of a minute she was completely naked, cruelly illuminated, reflections of her slender back and small breasts and bright-red face endlessly repeated.

"Now calm down," said Emerald, as Cleo took Gillian's upper arms in an iron grip. "We're going to drop you into a scene we're staging upstairs." Emerald was rummaging through a box of alarming-looking lingerie that sat under the dressing table.

"What?" Gillian demanded.

"Relax, you'll be one girl among about twenty. Here, stand up. This should fit," said Emerald to Cleo, tossing her a black corselet picked out with red ribbons. Wordlessly, Cleo began to strap it around Gillian's torso, to the accompaniment of a stream of pleas and imprecations from the victim. When she was done, Cleo grinned and pointed to her own striking, barely veiled bosom, shaking her head.

"Too small. I know," said Emerald. "Here, stuff these in underneath." She handed the other woman Gillian's discarded stockings. Balled up and strategically wedged in place, they thrust Gillian's own small breasts up and out, making them seem at least twice their real size.

Her outrage had ebbed, Gillian noted, as from a distance, to be replaced by a kind of woozy interest. "My nipples show," she observed solemnly. Her lips felt as if they were turning to wood, and it was increasingly hard to form words.

"They're supposed to," Emerald replied, standing back with her hands on her hips and surveying Gillian. "Cleo, the black stockings with the clocks—third drawer from the top. And spike heels. I'll start on her face."

The two women spilled Gillian unceremoniously into the barber's chair. As Cleo pulled the long stockings up Gillian's legs, Emerald bent over her with a steaming washcloth. "What's that for?" Gillian demanded. Her fuzzed voice—and Emerald's—seemed to be coming from a considerable distance.

"Get this morning's gunk off before we put on the next layer," Emerald said. At her elbow a phone rang and she picked it up. "Yes? Stall them as long as you can. I'll be down in a couple of minutes." And to Gillian: "They're here already—that old general and his weirdo buddy. The young guy has some kind of rifle."

"Don't you have bouncers or something?" Gillian asked. "Ouch—that hurt."

"Sorry. Yes, Johnny's my bouncer, and he can handle most things. But even if he was—were—here, guns are bad for business. This is a whorehouse, not a pistol range." She put down the washcloth and addressed Cleo, who had risen to her feet and was waiting: "Big eyes, red mouth, forget the base—we haven't got time."

Cleo raised her eyebrows questioningly and tapped the top of her own head.

"Black," said Emerald. "Bangs, shoulder length. I've got to run."

Cleo nodded and held up a device Gillian recognized: A man's electric shaver, just like her father's.

"Good idea," Emerald said, opening the door. "Gillian, you just do what the other girls tell you, and stay in the background. We'll shove so much tits and ass at those two they'll be dizzy for a week." The door slammed shut behind her, but Cleo was already working furiously. The eye makeup was two slashes of black filled in with electric blue, and a pair of absurd false eyelashes. From a drawer below the counter, Cleo produced elbow-length black gloves and handed them to Gillian, who began to tug them on, and then sat up with a yell of pain.

"What in hell are you doing down there?" she cried. Cleo, on her knees, was brandishing the shaver for another sweep. "Are you crazy?" Gillian said. "I'll look like a plucked chicken." It was too late. Gillian staggered to her feet, and Cleo pulled a black wig from a rack and jammed it down on her head, tucking Gillian's own mouse-brown locks up under it. As Gillian opened her mouth to protest, Cleo stepped from in front of her, and the protest died. Looking back at her from the mirror was a slender, high-breasted, long-legged woman with a wasp waist and huge, knowing eyes. Between the stocking tops and the lower edge of the corselet, which ended halfway up her belly in a froth of black lace, her skin was creamy white and as bare as a newborn's.

Gillian stood for a moment, stunned, and then began to laugh helplessly. "Well," she said, between giggles, "I've got to give it to you, Cleo—it does attract the eye." The phone on the counter rang twice, and then stopped. Cleo took Gillian's bare arm. "Okay, I get it. We're onstage."

Down another hall, this one carpeted, paneled and hung with oil paintings of a remarkably explicit nature. From behind one door came noises that sounded like someone beating a rug, except that each blow was punctuated by a man's cry. The door they came to was at the end of the hall, and Cleo put her finger to her lips. Behind them somewhere Gillian could hear voices, male and female, raised in argument and coming nearer.

Inside, the room was dimly lit and full of smoke—pot overlaid with incense—and half-naked people. To one side was an immense four-poster bed like a throne, piled so high with pillows and young women that Gillian for a moment missed the small, fat old man in the middle of it all. His face was that of a baby's—tight features and a mean little mouth. He was nearly bald, and the long hairs that normally ran across his scalp now stood grotesquely askew. Amid the firm, smooth young bodies, his skin was drooping, marbled, crepey. Although a young blonde of startling beauty was energetically working between his legs with lips and tongue and fingertips, he was quite limp.

When he saw Cleo, his small, deep-set eyes lit up. "There's my baby," he called, in a surprisingly deep voice with a syrup-thick accent. "Takes a little nigger gal to satisfy an old country boy." Cleo smiled dazzlingly and moved forward, dropping her snowy linen dress to the floor. Naked, she was even more ravishingly beautiful than Gillian had imagined—a skin the color of milk chocolate and the texture of silk, and a full, soft body. The blonde who had been servicing the old man slipped off the bed with no reluctance. She took Gillian by the arm and pulled her to one side. "Here," she whispered, giving Gillian a six-foot-long feathered fan. "Just wave it at them once in a while." Gillian obeyed, but she was swaying with alcohol and fatigue, and the shoes were at once too small and terribly unsteady. She felt another nearly naked body next to her. It was a young black woman about her own size, but wearing only a white garter belt and stockings. "You stoned, baby?" she asked. "Just lean on me."

Anonymous, saccharine music began to ooze down from a speaker high up in the wall, and Gillian realized, in a flash of awareness, that the black girl, who looked to be about sixteen, was holding a complicated electronic control at the end of a heavy cable. She noticed Gillian's look and grinned, which made her seem momentarily even younger. "Special effects," she whispered. "Wait till the old bastard gets it up. If he ever . . ."

The door at the end of the room was flung open, silhouetting Emerald and Hals, with the tall figure of Bellairs

looming behind them. One of Emerald's arms seemed to
be twisted behind her back, but her face was coldly calm.
As the three moved into the room, lit now from overhead
by a blue spotlight, Gillian could see that Bellairs had a
raw bruise on his temple. He blinked rapidly as if he was
having trouble with his vision, and Gillian felt a sudden
stab of fierce joy, until she saw the ugly-looking shotgun
in his free hand.

"Steady," whispered the black girl. "Eyes on the bed."

The old man had not even noticed the intrusion. He was
staring down at Cleo, who was crouched before him in a
way that was at once submissive and intensely sensual.
"That's it," he was saying, in a low, crooning rhythm.
"That's the way, honey."

Gillian wielded her fan languidly, trying to force her
painted features into an expression of boredom. She was
getting a cramp in one thigh, and she shifted her weight,
drawing Hals's eyes to her. She ignored him, feeling the
sweat cold on her spine, the supports of the corselet digging
into her ribcage, the ache that seemed to be rising up from
her feet like a tide. She moved again, to ease the stab of
the cramp, and saw Hals's eyes run over her shaved body,
blink twice and then dart away.

The black girl had turned up the electronic music
slightly, and now there was a perceptible beat behind it.
Gillian saw Emerald mouth the words, "Seen enough?"

Hals started to turn away, but Bellairs checked him, and
the two whispered angrily. Gillian felt her heart sink. Naked women would not divert Bellairs; he would see right
through her disguise once he got close enough. What he
would do to her if he had the chance was written on his
face, and she felt herself begin to tremble.

On the bed, the old man was moving, pumping, as Cleo
worked over him, and then suddenly he cried out wordlessly. An expression of intense disgust creased Hals's
leathery face, and he flung out of the room, with Bellairs
unwillingly in his wake. "Hey, baby—take it easy with that
fan," said the black girl. "You'll blow the old bugger
away."

She was drifting in a warm, scented haze, thinking about
nothing except the residual tingle from the hot bath and
the eerie caress, over her bare skin, of the first silk sheets

she had ever lain between. The door opened and Emerald entered, glancing quickly at the big bed. She still carried herself like a dancer, but when she turned on the bathroom light, her face was drawn. The door closed quietly behind her, and Gillian heard the sound of running water. She stretched her legs, acutely aware of the slippery coolness of the sheets. At the same time, there seemed to be a kind of screen between her emotions and the shambles of the day. She could feel only a detached remorse over the funeral—she had not even seen Uncle Dennis to his grave—and over the other results of her own pigheadedness: what had she accomplished, except to reveal a safe hiding place to her enemies, and get Barr kidnapped?

Barr. He might be dead by now. Sudden apprehension made a fist-sized lump just under her ribs. She knew she wanted him, could admit it to herself, even if he gave less than a damn for her. If he was alive.

The bathroom door opened, framing Emerald. She had a big white towel wrapped around her, and her strong legs and shoulders were silhouetted in the light behind her. She stood nearly still, only her right hand moving, massaging her left bicep, her eyes appraising. Gillian realized she had sat bolt upright in the bed, was bare to the waist. She made a motion to pull the sheet up over her breasts, then realized how silly it was—what was left for her to conceal? For some reason, she felt an urgent need to break into Emerald's silence. "Did he hurt your arm? Bellairs, I mean?" Gillian asked.

Emerald flicked a wall switch. Without makeup, her face was much older, though not lined at all. "Nothing serious," Emerald replied. "I just bruise easy. Like a peach." The mark was visible now, an angry purple-red against the perfect creamy white. "Someday I'm going to kill him," she added, not so much a threat as an observation, delivered so matter-of-factly that it carried absolute conviction.

Gillian shivered, and now, as Emerald came over to the bed and sat down on the edge, she did pull the sheet up and tuck it around herself. Emerald smelled of soap and skin cream, and warmth came off her damp skin in waves. "You okay, kid?" she asked. "A few minutes ago I thought you were going to fade out of the picture."

"I was a little zonked," said Gillian. "It's not been my best day ever."

Emerald's chuckle came from deep down. "Not just for you and me. You should've seen Lurlene's face when she got a load of the one-time Buick."

"Oh, God, I forgot about that," Gillian moaned. "I'll pay her back." Without warning, she found herself laughing at the edge of tears. "Pay her: with what?" she said.

"Don't worry about Lurlene. The car wasn't exactly hers." Emerald's hand was warm on Gillian's shoulder, almost a caress, pressing her back down in the bed. "You were just fine tonight," she said. "If you ever decide to give up boats, you've got a job with me."

"It was a change of pace, all right," Gillian replied, forcing a smile that turned into a grimace, as memory flooded in. "That kind of thing could put you off sex permanently," she added, responding to Emerald's quizzical stare. "Though I expect you've had enough sex to last you for a couple of centuries."

Emerald seemed to be weighing her response. "Nothing wrong with sex," she said slowly. "But I've sure had enough men for one lifetime." She interlaced her fingers and stretched her arms until Gillian heard the sinews crack. "Jesus, I'm tired. Spent the last couple of hours fending off some guy with a breath on him like the morgue."

The bedroom door opened quickly, and Cleo looked around it. She was swaddled in an oversize terrycloth robe, and without her Egyptian headdress looked like an ordinary teenager, if one could ignore the streak of scar tissue, shiny white across her brown skin, that zigzagged down her throat. She smiled and held up a big key.

Emerald nodded. "All locked up? Thanks, Cleo. You can go to bed."

Cleo smiled again—a different, oddly knowing smile—and closed the door.

"Her neck . . ." Gillian began.

"That's why she can't talk, of course. Her pimp tried to cut her throat, but all he did was tear up her voice box."

"That's awful," said Gillian, reflexively. "No, it's vile."

Emerald shrugged. "Like I said: Men."

"But is she all right . . . otherwise?" Gillian persisted.

"You mean a little extraterrestrial? It comes and goes.

You should've seen her when I first met her. Her big sister worked for me in a couple of movies. Cleo must've been about fourteen, all eyes and bones. And this dirty bandage around her throat."

"She was a prostitute? At fourteen?"

"Twelve," Emerald replied. "She started back home—Alabama, Mississippi, one of those places. She ran away to the big city to make her fortune. Kind of like me."

"But you weren't twelve."

"Sixteen. And I'd had an abortion and been on the street and in the slammer. So I knew what was going down. And what I wanted."

"I wish I did," Gillian said. "If we ever get out of all this, I mean."

Emerald took a silver-backed brush from the night table and attacked her copper-red hair with long, powerful strokes. "You don't look like the husband-and-kiddies type," she offered. "That's a compliment, by the way."

"Accepted," Gillian replied. "Kids? I don't know . . . I just don't think of them much. A husband?" The silence dragged out, and she felt Emerald watching her.

"Well, you're tangled up with one guy even I might make an exception for," Emerald observed, shifting the brush to her other hand.

"Patrick? He's okay, I guess, but . . ."

"Crap. When I was doing porno, I used to hire Patrick O'Maras by the gross. He's better than most of them—at least he doesn't worry about getting it up. No, the one I meant was Barr."

Gillian was astonished. "Jeremy Barr? You?"

"Just a manner of speaking," Emerald said. "But how could you even look at an O'Mara with Barr around?"

"After what I did today, we don't even know if he *is* around," Gillian said, trying to keep the anguish from her voice.

The brush crackled through Emerald's hair. "Don't write him off. He's a lot tougher than he makes out."

Reassurance flooded through Gillian's veins. "You're right," she said, sitting up and wrapping her arms around her knees. "I ought to know just how tough he is." She paused. "But he's never thought much of me, even before today."

Emerald put the brush down and turned to her. "Maybe

you ought to lighten up on the Captain Bligh act," she said. Her smile drew a wry grin from Gillian. "You're so busy playing bossy broad you've probably got him believing it. Guys like Barr don't know how to handle that kind of thing. They were brought up to treat women like ladies. The thing about Barr is that he really *sees* women as ladies. And as whole people, too—which is one of the things I like about him."

"Bossy broad," Gillian said slowly. "It's funny. You never met my father, but I was the man around our house from the time I was sixteen . . ." She let the thought trail off. "I guess I am bossy. Bitchy, too, sometimes."

Emerald put her arm around Gillian's shoulders, her fingertips gently touching Gillian's bicep. "Don't get me wrong," she said. "You've got whatever it is that counts. Brains. Nerve. You bounce back."

Gillian looked into Emerald's face, turned quickly away from the glowing green eyes. "I think I used up my year's quota of bounce this evening, Em—do you mind if I call you that? I feel as if I'd known you forever. Like an . . . like a sister, sort of."

Emerald's voice, from six inches distant, was a vibrant undertone: "I had four sisters and hated all of them. Anyway, I'm not feeling sisterly right now."

Awareness clicked like a circuit-breaker in Gillian's head. "I know," she said, trying not to stiffen, afraid to look around. "The thing is, I'm not ready for . . . I just don't know. I like you a lot, Em—more than I can say. I owe you my life . . ."

"This isn't about owing," Emerald said. "Turn around and look at me, Gillian."

She did, though it took more will than she thought was left in her. The towel had fallen away from Emerald's body. For a long moment, Gillian could not tear her eyes away. "You're the most beautiful woman I've ever seen," she said at last.

"But not for you," Emerald added, reading Gillian's tone.

"But not for me," Gillian said. "Not that way. Could you believe I love you other ways, Em? Just love you?"

Slowly, very slowly, a smile spread over Emerald's face and her laugh, when it came, was rich and real.

"What's so funny?" Gillian demanded, suddenly weak with relief.

"You love me for my mind, right?" Emerald managed, and giggled. "Nobody ever tried *that* one on me before."

It was, Gillian thought, an almost perfect performance. "I love you for a lot of reasons, Em," she said. "And if you'll put some goddam clothes on, I'd like to give you a hug."

13

For more than an hour, Patrick lay on the settee in *Glory*'s saloon, listening to the awful sound of Troiano snoring through his broken nose, before he dragged himself up on deck. *Glory* was lashed alongside a barge, shielded from any observer ashore; an artfully arranged mass of tarps, empty barrels and scrap lumber camouflaged her deck from the air. The labor involved had flattened Troiano, and Patrick himself felt as if every muscle in his body had been stretched past its limit. But his brain was still racing, circling around one concern he could not suppress.

Did Bellairs and the General have Gillian? Emerald had told Patrick and Troiano about the kidnapping from the funeral parlor, and Patrick was sure, from the operation's style, that it was Visconti's men. And Gillian: she'd escaped Visconti, but was she still safe? Had Bellairs been drawn off by the decoy car? Patrick had a bitter respect for the tall Englishman—it would take a lot to fool him, and the plan had been harebrained to start with. But not knowing drove you crazy. On shore, just a few yards away, was a pay phone. The photo with Hals's phone number on the back was in Patrick's pocket. A call would settle it, one way or the other.

If Gillian was in the clear, now might be the chance to get her and Tracy out of this nightmare. It was so obvious. Turn the damn boat over to Bellairs and it'd be done.

Patrick's fingers groped for the photo. . . . But what if they had Gillian already? Would they let her go, knowing what she did? Patrick could make himself believe the General would do it, but Bellairs?

He had to find out. Without information, he was helpless; with it, there might be something he could do. He dialed the number automatically, his mind scrabbling through alternatives, and was caught aback when the line clicked alive on the third ring and he heard the softly grating "*Ja?*" at the other end. He had not expected the old man himself to answer, and he was too paralyzed to say anything more than, "Sir? It's me. O'Mara."

"Report, please."

"Sir, I couldn't get to a phone before this. There was somebody watching me all . . ."

"Never mind that," said the General. He was speaking so softly that Patrick could barely hear him. "Where are you now? And where is the boat?"

"She's tied up at a place called the Oyster Bay Gravel and Dredging Company, sir. It's up at the head end—the south end—of Oyster Bay, but I don't know how to get there by car. There is a mark, though. A white water tower with a red aero light, about a hundred yards southwest of the pier. I'm calling from outside the office."

"So." There was a pause. "Who is on the boat with you?"

"Just Troiano, sir. Emerald's bodyguard. He's asleep."

"Not the girl—Miss Verdean?" The general sounded exhausted, and a little woolly. Patrick wondered where Bellairs was; the Englishman had always handled debriefings.

"Gillian?" Patrick's attention was suddenly razoredged. "No, sir. I don't know where she is. We moved *Glory* over here about eighteen hundred, after we heard that somebody snatched—kidnapped—Barr from the funeral. I thought maybe it was you, sir."

A snort came back over the phone, followed by General Hals's voice, angry as well as tired. "It was Visconti's men who got Captain Barr. We followed the Verdean girl out to Long Island—near, I think, to where you are now."

"Sir, I don't understand," Patrick replied, trying to keep the excitement out of his voice. "You don't have her, then?"

"No, O'Mara, we do not have her. She went into the brothel of the woman Emerald, but we could not find her."

She was safe, then. Let them have the damn boat and anything on it.

"What now?" asked Patrick cautiously.

A silence of several seconds, marked by the sound of the old man's breathing.

"Wait there," he said at last. "We shall join you, soon after daybreak."

"Yes, sir. But the longer you delay . . ." He was speaking to a dead line. Slowly he replaced the receiver. Just let them come before Gillian does. I'll give them the goddamn boat. Barr was probably done for—Patrick felt a pang of real grief that surprised him. He shook his head, bewildered at his own feelings.

Better get back aboard. Troiano was still asleep, with a liter of cheap red wine inside him, but there was no telling how long he would be out. Troiano: Patrick had had a bellyful of him, knew the type too well. Always doping off when he could, and ready to frag you if you crossed him. Troiano and Bellairs could shoot it out, and screw the both of them.

The night sky, which had been completely clear a few hours before, had begun to fuzz around the edges. Some stars overhead were still sharp, but there were streaks of high cloud, and the horizon was blurred. If Hals and Bellairs wanted him to move the boat, it would be a real pain in the ass to get anyplace with that sick little engine as the only power.

Patrick stuck his head down the companionway hatch. Troiano's wheezing snores echoed through the main cabin, and Patrick stretched out on the wooden cockpit seat, with his windbreaker jacket balled up under the back of his head, his hands in his armpits for warmth. From the shore road he heard the sound of someone taking a sports car up through the gears, and it made him think of Gillian.

But it was Gillian and Emerald, not the General, who came aboard first, at about eight in the morning. The boat was wrapped in a fog so thick Patrick could barely see the bow from the stern; Troiano was slumped in the cockpit, too hung over even to snarl.

Gillian was wearing a pair of jeans that were slightly too

large for her and a man's dress shirt, a combination that made her look like a teenager. Emerald, of course, was dressed to kill: green slacks, a white blouse with a green kerchief at the throat, oversize sunglasses. Patrick, stiff from his night on the cockpit seat, felt grubby and muddleheaded, consumed by anxiety. Emerald seemed not to notice. There was something between the two women, an electric tension that was very familiar to Patrick, but he was strung too high to identify it.

"You look terrible, Patrick," Gillian said, her voice bright and slightly harsh. "This is the first time I've seen you without a shave."

He passed his hand over the lower part of his face without really feeling it. "Sorry," he said. "I didn't know it was an inspection day."

"Well, it's not," said Emerald. "We've got to get this boat out of here. Farther away from my place."

Gillian rounded on the tall woman. "What about Barr?" she demanded. "We can't just throw him away."

"We already had this discussion," Emerald said, strain audible in her voice. "There's nothing we can do, except make sure Visconti doesn't scoop us up, too. If Barr's still alive, maybe we can make a deal for him later."

"Emerald's right," Patrick put in. "We'd better get *Glory* someplace else, as quick as we can. This fog's too good to waste—nobody's going to be able to find us from the air, and they won't have a much better chance on the water." Emerald looked at him with surprise, but Patrick's sudden new decision had made itself. Bellairs and Hals might turn up at any moment. He had to get Gillian out of this place, and he knew she'd never leave *Glory* behind. The fog was not only good luck but an omen, and if there was one thing he was sure of, it was that you had to pay attention to omens. The danger to Tracy and Joanie remained, but the first danger was to Gillian, and it was blindingly clear to Patrick that Gillian now meant too much to him to risk her life. One thing at a time. It was the best he could do.

Gillian started to say something, but Emerald interrupted her. "You're sure we can get the boat out of here?"

He did not feel as confident as he hoped he sounded. "No problem, as long as we're careful."

"How long to get going?" Emerald demanded. Gillian looked rebellious, but she said nothing.

"A few minutes, if we get our tails in gear," he replied. "You guys want to start casting off from that barge, I'll get the engine started." The more he thought about it, the surer he was. This was their chance to ditch all their opponents at once. He would just have to hope—to pray— that the kid would be all right, at least until there was time to square things. But he would have more leverage dealing with Bellairs and Hals if they didn't know where he was. It had been a mistake to call them at all, last night . . . He cursed and took his finger off the starter button. Not even one cylinder was firing. Maybe the fuel line, he thought.

Gillian, up at the bow, had *Glory*'s forward lines off and was looking back at him. "What's up?" she called.

"No fuel getting through," he said. "You two walk her out from between the pier and the barge. I'll check the gas line." He dived below, pulled out *Glory*'s huge tool chest. As always, what he wanted—the rusty set of wrenches and the vice-grips—were at the very bottom.

He threw the engine hatch open and dropped into the bilge. The filter bowl was full, so the gas was getting that far. He selected a small wrench for the first connection, when he sensed someone standing over him in the companionway. He looked up, and into Bellairs's face. The Englishman's mouth was smiling, but his red-rimmed eyes were deadly. A solidly purple bruise covered most of the left side of his forehead, and his left forearm was wrapped in a crude bandage. Even so, his hands were steady, holding a pump-action shotgun pointed right at Patrick's chest.

"Leave it, Mister O'Mara," he said. "Climb up out of there and get in the cabin."

Next to Bellairs stood the General, looking a dozen years older in the daylight. He was holding a pistol, his old Walther PPK that Patrick remembered from the desert. Emerald, Gillian and Troiano had already been searched—Emerald's neat revolver was in the old man's left hand and Troiano's big automatic was jammed in his waistband—and Bellairs went rapidly and expertly over Patrick. "Nothing," he said. "Mister O'Mara still doesn't bother with handguns."

"Sit over there," the General commanded. "On that couch. Not so close to each other. Leave your hands where I can see them." He sat down heavily, facing them. Bellairs, holding the shotgun with exaggerated carelessness, lounged against the handsomely restored locker at the after end of the cabin. Patrick sat very still, knowing that Bellairs wanted only to have one of them go for him.

"So," said General Hals. "You were planning to leave, O'Mara. A double cross?"

Patrick met the General's hard stare and said nothing. There was nothing to say—he had gambled and lost.

"What do you mean, 'double cross?' " Gillian demanded.

Patrick shrugged. He felt drained. "I was working for the General when you hired me."

"Why?" Gillian asked.

"Reasons," he said helplessly. Something kept him from saying more, though the stunned look on Gillian's face was tearing him apart.

"You were working for them the whole time," she said slowly, trying to assimilate the idea.

"Not, alas, the whole time," said Bellairs. "And not, I think, with his whole heart," he added, looking at Hals.

"You may be correct," the General conceded. He turned his attention to Patrick: "You are aware of the penalty, O'Mara?"

He felt a trickle of sweat run down his backbone. Somehow, he had to arrange his swirling thoughts. "Sir," he began, "there's no point . . ."

To his astonishment, it was Bellairs who came to his aid: "The child is safe, O'Mara—at least for a while."

"What . . . ?"

"I will not lie to you," said Hals slowly. "You have betrayed me, and you will be executed for it." Gillian gave an audible cry, and Hals pressed on, not looking at her. "But you may still save the child. If you show me where it is hidden—what we seek—you shall have a single bullet. If not, we shall bring the child here, and I shall turn her over to Major Bellairs."

"What about them?" said Patrick. "The women and Troiano."

"I am sorry," Hals replied.

"The fact is, we're simply too thin on the ground," Bellairs added cheerfully. "Too many of you to watch."

"At least her—Miss Verdean," said Patrick. "She's not dangerous . . ."

Bellairs whinnied. "Not dangerous, indeed. She damned near killed us both last night." He turned to Gillian: "By the way, just to satisfy my curiosity: you were in the room with that dreadful old creature, weren't you?" She nodded. "Which one were you?"

"With the fan," she said dully. "What's this about a child?"

"Mister O'Mara didn't tell you?" Bellairs said, smiling. "No, I don't suppose he did. Well, Mister O'Mara has a daughter, who lives with her mother and stepfather in a gray little town not far from here. Mister O'Mara left General Hals's employ somewhat abruptly, a year or so ago, but we knew we could track him through his little by-blow."

"And that was why you worked for them," she said to Patrick. He nodded. "But this morning you were trying to help us get away," she went on. "What made you change your mind?"

"I don't know," he said. "What difference does it make?"

"Quite right," Bellairs said. "None whatever. Sir, I think . . ."

Troiano, who had not moved a muscle since he sat down, suddenly slumped forward and Bellairs swung and fired in a single motion, the hoarse roar of the shotgun deafening in the confined space of the cabin. The charge of shot took the burly man high in the back, folding him even further forward for a second. With a hoarse yell, he straightened, his mouth working, and then sagged down in a heap, the back of his sweater a torn and bloody horror. Something clattered to the deck and Bellairs bent to scoop it up. "A gun in his sock!" He exclaimed with delight. "How American!"

Gillian, her face spattered with Troiano's blood, leaned forward and vomited on the deck. Emerald, expressionless, sat without moving. Bellairs turned to Hals: "As I was starting to say, sir, I think there is no point in putting things off."

"Yes," Hals said. "You may shoot the women, Major."

14

LONG ISLAND SOUND
EIGHT-THIRTY A.M.

The rowboat's bow pushed its way into a curling white-cap, the wake from an invisible vessel whose engine noise came blurrily through the fog. A bucketful of spray splashed over the gunwales. Most of it landed in the bilges, but a cupful or so struck Barr full in the face. The small outboard behind him raced momentarily as the stern rose and lifted the propeller from the water, then dropped back to a querulous whine. The visibility was much better—a quarter of a mile or so—here in open water. Back in Norwalk harbor it had been more like a hundred feet.

A shiver ran through Barr's body, and his gashed fingers stung under the wet wrappings. Without a compass, he had been steering by the wavelets that were pushed toward him by the light southeasterly. The mouth of Oyster Bay should be dead ahead of him, an opening a good mile wide, with bluffs on either side. The fog was thickening again and the easterly wind had become lighter, both of which suggested he was near shore. When he had gone a little farther than wishful thinking told him was correct, he shut off the motor and let the rowboat drift. Behind him, out on the Sound, he could hear the deep mechanical hoot of a tug's foghorn, blowing one long and two shorts. He waited for half a minute, then heard over his left shoulder four faint notes in a ragged sequence—a gong buoy.

Up ahead a different sound, the repeated single tone of a bell. Straining his eyes to pierce the fog, he made out what looked like a fat cylinder sitting on the water. So the harbor entrance he wanted was half a mile ahead and to starboard.

He tugged the outboard's starter cord and the motor, still warm, caught immediately. This fog was a godsend: no helicopter pilot would fly in it, but *Glory* could pick her way through, and a couple of hours' running could get her out of what yesterday had looked like a trap. Fog was an untrustworthy ally, though: it could burn off or blow away by noon, leaving *Glory* wholly exposed. Still, it didn't feel as if it would burn off, not for several hours at least. And unless his weather sense had completely deserted him, there were clouds above the fog, and a change of weather behind them.

But the tide of things was running his way at last—had been doing so since the night before—and Barr felt a confidence he had not known in years. The ventilator tunnel just over Visconti's cabin had been a crazy place to hide, and yet it had turned out to be the safest spot aboard. Once the crew were convinced that Barr had indeed escaped over the side, their search for him flagged, in spite of Captain Arrow's increasingly furious urging.

A little before dawn, the sound of reversing engines and the rattle of anchor chain had awakened Barr. He pulled himself back to the main ventilator shaft and climbed silently up to the wind scoop atop the bridge. The yacht's foghorn stopped, and was replaced by the rapid ringing of her bell. Above him, on the mast, the anchor light was on and the radar antenna was still turning, but no one was visible on deck: Captain Arrow might order the anchor watch to stay alert for the escaped prisoner, but the crew clearly felt they had already done their duty. Barr allowed a half hour for the crew to settle down before he crept from the bridge to the main deck, edging past the swiveling TV camera, and lowered himself, hand over still-bloody hand, down the anchor chain and into the icy water. At first, he had not been sure precisely where he was—the scattering of mooring buoys just at the limit of visibility could have been anywhere, but the battered little rowboat secured to one of the floats was exactly what he needed. He was in the act of pulling himself over the gunwale when he saw the stenciled lettering on the buoy itself: "C&W"

it read, and as the buoy swung, "23." Carey & Willard.
Of course—Visconti had dropped anchor in the deepest,
widest part of the lower Norwalk River. Barr did not need
to be able to see the shore; he knew, having placed them
himself, just how Carey & Willard's moorings were set
out: 23 would be at the south end of the westernmost line,
on the edge of the entrance channel. He hooked a leg over
the rowboat's gunwale and eased himself over the side.
Better and better—a dented three-horsepower outboard
lay on the floorboards, alongside a single oar. A rusty one-
gallon gas can was wedged behind the thwart.

Ahead of Barr a black, cagelike shape loomed suddenly
out of the fog and winked its white light at him. So far so
good. A spasm of shivering reminded him that he had been
soaked for several hours now, and he was ravenous as well
as nearly frozen. Never mind—they would have something
hot, and some dry clothes, aboard *Glory*. He was just
coming to the obstacle course of moored boats that marked
the anchorage off Oyster Bay when the engine, which had
been running evenly all the way across, slowed, coughed
twice and died. The manner of its death told him what had
happened, but he unscrewed the gasoline filler cap and
looked in the tank anyway; as he had expected, it was dry.
  There was no more fuel in the boat—she was used, he
guessed, strictly to scuttle about the harbor, and had probably never had so long a run before. Unhappily, he hefted
the single oar. It was going to be a long and painful paddle.
With Barr kneeling uncomfortably in the eyes of the boat,
she was nose down and unstable. He found himself cursing
under his breath at her maddening desire to move any way
but forward. At least he was getting warm, he told himself.
Five minutes later, the sweat was coursing down his torso,
and he was grinding his teeth in frustration.
  Yet he was making progress. The buoys ahead thinned
out, and up ahead, though he could not see its entrance,
should be the creek where *Glory* lay hidden. He stopped
paddling for a moment, to wipe the sweat from his eyes,
and heard, over the lapping ripples, the muffled blast of
a shotgun, from off to port. Through the haze he could
see a pier, where a barge too loosely made fast swung with
the wind out into the channel. As it swung, it revealed a

low, gleaming hull, painted an unmistakable deep green. The gunshot had come from there. In an instant, he was paddling again, desperately now.

He eased his stroke as he drew alongside the silent hull. Why was *Glory* here? Something told him not to pause, and he swung himself silently up on deck, confronting a litter of crates and drums. He picked his way carefully among them. The skylight over the saloon was wide open, and the unmistakable smell of gunpowder smoke stung his nostrils.

He crouched by the skylight. From the cabin below he heard a Germanic voice, heavy with fatigue, saying, "You may shoot the women, Major."

There was no time to think, no time for anything but a blind, feet-first leap through the skylight. Something ripped at his forearm as he fell, in a shower of broken glass and rending woodwork, to land squarely on the huge saloon table, right in front of General Hals, who was holding a revolver in one hand and an automatic in the other. From the corner of Barr's eye he saw a flash of movement as Bellairs, cradling a shotgun in his arms, spun around. The gun crashed and shot stung Barr's leg, as the gimbaled table tipped him into Hals's lap.

The old man was surprisingly strong, but his reactions were slowed by age and fatigue. He got off one shot from the automatic—Barr felt it pluck at his shirt—and then Barr managed to brace one leg and kick hard with the other. His foot caught Hals's right wrist, and the automatic clattered to the deck. Barr grabbed for the revolver, hearing from behind him a confusion of shouts, grunts and crashes.

Hals kicked out and Barr, dodging back, hit his head a shattering crack against the table stanchion. He seemed to be moving underwater, unbelievably slowly. Hals, grimacing, was bringing the revolver to bear, when suddenly two small, muscular hands appeared from above and gripped his wrist. As the old man wrenched furiously to pull free, Barr felt the automatic on the deck under his hip. He snatched it up and jammed the muzzle in Hals's face. The old man winced, opened his hand and let his gun drop, then sagged back gasping.

With infinite care Barr wormed backward until he could

stand. Kneeling on the settee, her hands still locked around Hals's wrist, Gillian was staring at him. On the deck across the cabin Bellairs was on his back, snarling up at Patrick O'Mara, who was sitting on his chest, holding the shotgun. Emerald was bent over a slumped figure on the far settee and, as Barr watched, she straightened up, her hands bloody and her face like chalk.

"Get up," said Barr to Hals. "Very slowly—Gillian, you stand clear of him."

Hals dragged himself back up on the seat. His chest was heaving, his face purple. Barr took a step backward, his heel crunching broken glass. The sound seemed to release the others from a spell. "They were going to kill us," said Gillian tonelessly.

"They did kill Johnnie," said Emerald. Her eyes were green ice and with her bloodied hands she looked like Lady Macbeth. Except that her hand held a stubby revolver. "Get out of my way, Patrick," she said quietly.

Without a word, the big young man rose and moved to the side, but the shotgun's muzzle remained pointed at Bellairs's chest.

"You're going to shoot him," Gillian said. She had begun to tremble.

Emerald's face softened as she glanced at the girl. "This isn't your kind of fight, love. Don't look."

Hals moved as if to object, then fell back helplessly as he saw Barr's gun come up. Behind him, Barr heard two pistol shots, close together. He turned back. Bellairs, bent nearly double, was writhing on the deck, his legs jerking uncontrollably. Emerald stood over him, the revolver in her right hand, with her left bracing the wrist. Bellairs's heels beat against the wooden facing of the settee, and the whole front of his shirt seemed to be a dark and dripping red. His bulging eyes were locked on Emerald. His teeth were fixed so hard in his lower lip that blood ran from the corners of his mouth. As Barr watched, he shuddered violently, his back straightened and he gave a gurgling cry, then slumped to his side on the deck.

Patrick dropped easily to one knee and took the Englishman's wrist in his fingers. He looked up at Emerald and nodded.

"Johnnie was no prize," said Emerald calmly, "but I owed him that." She set the gun down on the table.

"What about him?" asked Patrick, gesturing at Hals, who stared back at them expressionlessly.

"Kill him yourself," said Emerald. "He's not my problem."

"No!" cried Gillian. "No more!"

"That's right," Barr echoed. He felt a million years old. "In that locker behind you, there should be a bottle," he said to Emerald.

She watched him as he put the neck to his lips and swallowed a long gulp. "What now?" she asked.

He held the bottle out to her and, when she shook her head, set it down on the table. "Not in front of the General," he said.

"Of course," she replied. "Stupid of me."

"Could we do something about them?" asked Gillian quietly, nodding at the two bodies. She seemed quite calm, but Barr heard a strain in her voice that told him she was barely in control of herself.

"Yes," he replied. "Patrick, why don't you and Gillian go up on deck and get some line and a couple of pieces of canvas. Big pieces."

"Right, Skip," said Patrick. He set down the shotgun and raced up the companionway ladder, followed, more slowly, by Gillian. A few moments later a coil of line sailed down and landed with a splat, followed by Patrick, his arms full of canvas. "I told Gillian to stay on deck," he said to Barr. "She's a little green."

Barr glanced at Emerald, whose face looked carved from marble. "I'll help Patrick," he said to her.

Her smile was real, if bitter. "You think I've never seen a stiff before?" she said. "You keep an eye on the General; I'll clean up."

Patrick unfolded a square of filthy canvas and unceremoniously rolled Bellairs over on it. He folded it to make an untidy parcel with a spreading red stain in the center, then lashed it tightly. "More than you deserve," he said. "I hope you rot in hell."

In the meantime, Emerald had managed to stretch Troiano's body out on the second piece of cloth. In death, his face wore a surprised, angry expression. Without a word, Emerald covered him and let Patrick lash the canvas around him. "Patrick," said Emerald, "why don't you tie up the General and put him in the back seat of my car.

On the floor." She turned to Barr. "My friend who owns this place tells me nobody comes near it all day on Sundays, so we're safe for a while."

"Really?" said Barr, his mind working rapidly. He watched as Patrick heaved Hals to his feet, hands pinioned behind his back.

The younger man paused. "You sure you trust me with him—out of your sight?"

"We'll know when you come back, won't we?" Emerald said. She watched them climb the companionway ladder, then swung back to Barr. In the thin light that streamed down into the cabin her face was gray and tired. She managed a smile. "I didn't thank you," she said. "Another minute, we'd've been dead." She sat down across from Barr. "What are you going to do with *Glory*?"

"Get her rigged, if we can—they've got a derrick here, I see—and then get out of the Sound. Visconti's yacht is just over on the other side, in Norwalk, and he'll have his helicopters out looking for *Glory* as soon as the fog lifts."

"And then?"

"Visconti brought *Tiamat* up the East River and through Hell Gate last night. Out to Norwalk," said Barr slowly. "I'm betting he won't think we'd double back past him— at least not right away. We need to find someplace where we can count on being undisturbed for maybe a day."

"So you do know where Dennis's stuff is," Emerald interrupted.

"I'm pretty sure," Barr replied. "Trouble is, so does Visconti."

She waited for him to continue, and when he didn't she said, indicating the two canvas-wrapped bundles, "What about them?"

"Well . . ." he began.

"Over the side, right?" He forced himself to look at her stony face. "That's the traditional way, isn't it?" she demanded. "And what difference does it make?"

"It's not my traditional way," Barr said mildly. "I expect you want to make some arrangements about Troiano . . ."

"Christ, where do you come from, anyway?" she blazed at him, then sank back, shaking her head. "I'm sorry, Barr. I didn't have to yell at you. But there's not too many arrangements you can make for a body with a load of buckshot in it."

"Oh," he said. "Of course." He thought for a minute. "The trouble with bodies," he continued, "is that they float. Even if you weight them down, they come to the top sooner or later."

"What about if you put them in a car and sank the whole thing?" she asked.

This is the strangest conversation I've ever had, Barr thought. Aloud, he said, "Oh, that would be fine. If you . . ."

"I have friends who'll take care of it. They've done it before. Besides, who's going to miss Bellairs or Johnny? You just leave it to me," Emerald said, getting to her feet. "I'll take care of them, and I can keep the old guy on ice in my place. Now, let's see about getting our boat out of here."

"Where will I meet you?" Emerald asked him, three hours later. She was standing on the pier, and Barr, holding a dock line, was a few feet away from her on *Glory*'s bow. The old boat's engine coughed uncertainly in the background. At the helm, Gillian looked pale and strained. She had not said a word to Emerald or Patrick beyond what was absolutely necessary, but had dogged Barr's every step.

Barr cast off the bow line. "I don't know where we'll be able to stop—Twenty-third Street marina, maybe, or Sheepshead Bay. We'll call you as soon as we can."

"I guess you don't want to tell me what it is we're looking for," Emerald said quietly. "I don't blame you, under the circumstances."

"It's not that," Barr replied, as the bow began to swing out. "Let go aft, Patrick. Gillian—dead slow forward, please." The engine staggered and then rallied as Gillian edged it into gear successfully, and a tentative smile appeared on her tired face. "Good going," Barr called to her. "It's not that," he said to Emerald, as the yacht began to slide past the pier. "I just don't like to cluck before I see the egg."

She looked at him steadily. "I trust you, Barr."

He gave her a small, embarrassed wave, then hurried back to the helm.

15

~~~~~~

LONG ISLAND SOUND
THREE P.M.

The fog on the water seemed to have crept into Gillian's head. She supposed it was something to do with fatigue. Her attention, such as it was, locked on the compass card in front of her; there was a bubble in the fluid, and its motion, darting from side to side under the flat glass surface, had nearly hypnotized her. On another level, she was dimly aware of the two men moving about—Barr on deck tuning the rigging, and Patrick below, doing something that involved a seemingly endless train of buckets dumped surreptitiously over the side. Her mind fled back into its sheltering daze, from which it did not completely emerge until Barr, at her side, asked, "Are you all right?" for the second time.

All at once she was conscious of the cold, damp, surprisingly strong breeze on her face, of the stuttering vibration of the engine coming up through the soles of her deck shoes, of the hazy outlines of the shore on either side. She glanced down at the compass. "I'm on course," she replied.

"I know you are," Barr replied. He was wearing his revolting old foul-weather jacket that had once been yellow and that left a trail of brownish-yellow fragments to mark its wearer's track. The wind was blowing his straw-colored hair straight back from his forehead. There were smudges under his eyes and his face was puffy and discolored. She was almost sure she loved him. "It's not the course," he went on. "Have you noticed the wind's coming up fast? The fog'll be gone in an hour."

"Oh," she said. She had not noticed. "Do you want to put some sail up?"

"We'd better. I don't remember how much fuel we have, but it can't be a lot."

Like a genie, Patrick appeared in the companionway. His foul-weather suit was, of course, immaculate—snowy white, with a blue stripe. "Did somebody say something about fuel?" he asked. "Because when I tap the tank, it sure sounds empty."

"Right," Barr said. "We'll make sail, starting with the mizzen—you want to give me a hand, Patrick?"

"Sure, if you tell me what to do." As the sails inched up their tracks, Gillian's trained eye began to take over. Working with sailmakers had given her a solid armory of information, but Barr was purely maddening. He claimed to have no idea why he did what he did, but he would float about the decks, apparently lost in thought, taking in a sheet here or easing a halyard there, and before you knew it, *Glory* would pick up a knot at least. When Gillian attempted to force an explanation out of him he just shrugged. Pressed too hard, he would retreat to his favorite perch, astride the main lower spreaders, thirty feet above the deck, where conversation was impossible.

For some reason, the recollection made her smile and Barr, who had just finished retrimming the mainsheet, saw her. "Feeling better?" he asked.

"I'm okay."

"Glad to hear it," he said. To her surprise and pleasure, he sounded as if he meant it. He called to Patrick, who was waiting forward at the halyard: "Okay, take her up. Hand over hand till you get to the wire, then four turns around the winch." The working jib, thundering like an artillery barrage, crept up its stay. Patrick was fighting the halyard, out of rhythm with the puffs that bellied the sail and then emptied it. At last he had the luff taut and Barr called to him to cleat it off.

Gillian turned the big wheel and *Glory* fell off the wind, her sails filling. As she heeled, Patrick, bounding aft, lost his footing and slid into the leeward scuppers, to be sluiced by a rush of white water tumbling aft. He was clearly annoyed with himself as he stood up on the windward side, glancing nervously at the water that rushed along the lee rail.

Gillian laughed aloud as *Glory* put her shoulder into a sea and cut through it easily. A gust laid the yacht over, and for a moment the white water swirled around the turnbuckles. "A little too much sail?" she asked. "Maybe the staysail would be better than the big jib."

Barr, swaying easily on the balls of his feet, shook his head. "She's all right," he said. "Let me know if she starts to get hard-mouthed." He paused. "But I think she might take a spoke more off the wind."

For the life of her, Gillian could not see why—*Glory* was in full stride, eating her way through the small, steep-sided waves. But she moved the helm slightly and, sure enough, the old ketch sat up five degrees. Gillian's eyes went to the speedometer, dead for two seasons now, and Barr noticed. "Just as fast," he said. "Less fuss, is all." He looked up at the towering mainmast. "She can't point up with the forestay soft like that," he observed. "But I don't have a lot of faith in the portside backstay chain plate."

She looked back and down at the heavy bronze strap. "It looks solid enough to me," she said.

"The plate's fine—it's the hull that's a problem. Watch when we hit the next swell . . . Now: See the gunwale flex?"

She shook her head. "Can't say I do. How bad is it?"

"I don't know, really," Barr replied. "But when the wind gets up a little more, we may have to take a reef. Oh, and keep an eye on that rowboat we're towing; if it starts taking water, let out some more towline. I'm going below: I've got to get some sleep." At the companionway he paused as if he wanted to say something else, then obviously changed his mind.

Alone together on deck, Gillian and Patrick were silent. *Glory* rolled on, closing the reef-studded shore of Larchmont at an alarming rate. At last she said, "We're going to tack—can you handle the jib sheet?"

"This line? I suppose so. What do I do?"

"I'll talk you through it." He looked dubious, but Gillian had seen Barr tack *Glory* singlehanded, and she was not about to call for his assistance. "Ready?" she asked.

He was poised over the leeward winch, the sheet held easily in his powerful hands. "Ready."

She spun the wheel and *Glory* began to round up into the wind. "Cast off," she called. "Good. Grab that lever on the deck and throw it all the way forward . . . Right." *Glory*'s bow was just coming through the wind's eye. "Now, pull back the lever on the other side. That's it. Grab the sheet . . . No, not around the winch yet. No, you can't pull . . . it'll take a riding turn. Oh, shit."

"I guess that's a riding turn," said Patrick unhappily, staring down at the snarl of line around the winch drum.

"That's what they call it," she said through gritted teeth. But already she had the wheel turning back, and *Glory*, balked, headed up until the sails thundered. Patrick did not need to be told what to do. He clawed the twisted line off the winch—cursed under his breath as a fingernail snapped down to the quick—and Gillian spun the helm again. *Glory* was still edging forward, and her bow fell slowly, slowly away from the wind.

"Now," Gillian called. "Hand over hand. Good. Three quick turns on the winch and take up the slack. Use the winch handle the rest of the way. Okay—cleat it off."

He was looking at her with admiration in his eyes, the effect slightly marred as he sucked his injured finger. "You were great," he said.

"*She*'s great," Gillian corrected him, patting the binnacle.

He shook his head. "Listen," he said, abruptly, "about what I was doing for Hals and Bellairs . . ."

"It doesn't matter," she said. "No, that's not what I mean. I understand why you did it. You didn't have any choice. And you tried to get me out of it. That's something I'll remember. Maybe someday you'll let me meet your kid—you must love her a lot."

He looked, if anything, slightly puzzled. "I guess so," he said slowly. "I don't even know her, but it doesn't seem to make any difference; she's still my kid."

Glory's bow had steadied on the new heading. "How's that?" Gillian said. "I mean, how come you've never met your own daughter?"

"It was when I was in high school. My senior year. Everything just seemed to come apart: Joseph, my younger brother, was killed in a car crash, and then Joanie—this girl I was going with—told me she was pregnant."

"She wanted you to marry her?" Gillian asked.

"Of course. But when I said I wouldn't, she told me she was going to have the baby anyway."

"What's she like?" asked Gillian.

"Joanie? Gorgeous—she was a cheerleader. Tall and blonde. Smart, too."

"But she wanted to keep the baby."

"Yeah." He hesitated. "Her father would've killed me —I guess I must have panicked. It was crazy. Bay Shore's a small town, and the high school isn't big. Joanie and I were going together, and everybody would've known . . ." He shrugged. "I wanted her to get rid of it, have an abortion. She said no. I thought she was just trying to lean on me: If I wasn't there, she'd come to her senses. So I took off. Went to New York City and joined the army. I figured nobody would be able to trace me. What I didn't count on"—he smiled wryly—"was that nobody'd bother. It was my kid sister who wrote me when the baby was born, and when Joanie got married. At first it didn't make a difference to me, not really. I felt bad about running out. Took a while before I figured it was me I let down, not them. The army sent me to Salvador as an advisor. When I got down there, I started wondering what the kid was like. If I would ever see her. It's funny, the things that get to be important when people are shooting at you."

Gillian murmured something vaguely encouraging. He looked at her, as if seeing her for the first time. "I wanted to help out, send some money. But Joanie said she'd only take it if I stayed away, let them live their lives. So I did. Played soldier, right up to the hilt. Finished my tour in Salvador, and when it was over I went to Bay Shore and saw the kid, without Joanie knowing it. She'd got married to a skinny little guy who was in the class ahead of ours. They were happy, the three of them; you could see it. So I took off again, back to soldiering, but I was thinking of the kid—her name's Tracy—all the time. When I got near the end of my second hitch, I was recruited by one of Hals's agents. He had 'em in several of the big U.S. posts, to pick up guys like me, who were fed up with the peacetime army."

"Salvador wasn't exciting enough for you?" asked Gillian.

He laughed. "Hell, yes. But it was enough to drive you buggy. We were supposed to be advising, not shooting back. And they—Washington—meant it. I got in trouble that way more than once. So I was sent home, and the first thing I knew, some dude in a beer hall at Fort Dix had talked me into Hals's private army. Biggest mistake of my life. We wound up in the desert, in northern Chad, up against Egyptian regulars, plus some real mean French paras. I don't even know who was paying us. I can guess, but we weren't ever told."

"What's-his-name, the Libyan?" said Gillian.

"Him. Who else would want that terrible place? Anyway, the General—Hals—got us into a tight corner, and it looked like it was all over, so I took off, me and another American, in a light plane. The thing was, Hals—or maybe Bellairs—knew about me sending money back home, and that was how they could trace Joanie's address. I suppose it wasn't real hard to track me, either, once I got a job and began to send Joanie money again. Then when they wanted me, I was right there, ready to be scared shitless."

"Listen," she said firmly, "you weren't doing it for yourself. If you were scared, it was for your child. I met Bellairs, remember? I'd say you had no choice at all."

"Nice of you to think so," Patrick replied, looking quickly away from her. "Don't you think we'd better tack again, pretty soon?"

"Another few minutes," she replied, glancing at the Long Island shore ahead of them. "I mean it, Patrick— you had those two come out of your past, and you managed to face them down at the end."

"And if it wasn't for Barr, it would've been the end— and for you, too," Patrick replied bitterly.

"Well, Barr's something else," Gillian said.

Patrick was looking at her hard. "He is that," he said. For a moment the only sound was the hiss and crash of *Glory* moving through the water. "You like him a lot, don't you?"

She was ready for it. "I admire the things he can do," she said carefully. "I wanted him to like me when he first started working for Uncle Dennis, but right from Day One he's treated me like a child, and an annoying child at that."

"So how do you feel about him now?"

"Now?" She nodded pointedly at the shore. "Now I think we'd better tack."

The wind was noticeably stronger as *Glory* came out from behind the lee of Hart Island. Ahead, where Long Island Sound narrowed to its close, the lights that picked out the cables of the Throgs Neck Bridge had just been turned on. One more tack and they would be headed right for the channel entrance that would take *Glory* into the East River. Gillian sensed that Patrick, at her elbow, wanted to talk, but she had seldom had so strong an urge to keep silent. Without warning, the sight of his powerful, well-kept hands cupped around the winch drum, easing the sheet during the last tack, had put into her head a tightly focused image of another pair of hands—equally big, but with broken fingernails and scarred knuckles. In her mind, the hands were not on the winch but on her body, handling her with the same expertness they brought to every job they touched. It was so real that for a moment she could feel Barr's blunt, callused fingers on her skin, under her coarse sweater, a perfect tactile mirage . . .

"A what?" said Patrick.

The word must have escaped her. "Never mind," she said quickly. "I was just thinking about something."

"Oh. I was thinking, too. About what we do next . . . or is that up to Captain Barr?"

"No, it's not," Gillian said automatically. "We're all in this up to our necks, so we all get to decide."

Patrick, back in the cockpit, glanced down the companionway. "I hear him stirring down there. Are you going to tell him about this group decision, or do I?"

Barr's head appeared in the companionway hatch, his strawlike hair every which way. He still looked tired, but not as flat-out exhausted as he had before. In his free hand, his bandaged forefinger looped through the handles, he held three steaming mugs of black coffee, which he extended to Patrick. "Here," he said. "Clear away the cobwebs. The one with the chipped rim is mine."

The coffee smelled wonderful but strange, and Gillian realized that one cup at least was heavily laced with rum. She took hers and sniffed at it. Barr drank his off as he always did, in a sustained gulp, and then set the mug down. "I'll take her, if you like," he said.

"That's all right," Gillian replied, sipping at the too-hot liquid. As always, the taste was a distant second to the smell, but it was the first thing to go down her throat since . . . She forced her mind to the present. "Barr, Patrick and I figured it was time you told us about Uncle Dennis's stash and where it is." Damn it, why do I always sound like a prosecuting attorney when I want something from him?

"All right," said Barr mildly. Patrick's eyebrows shot up, but his face remained expressionless. "Let's tack— you're lined up for the bridge—and then I'll bring you up to date."

When *Glory* was settled on the new heading, Barr sat down in the cockpit and, to Gillian's utter surprise, began taking off one of his shoes. Probing into the toe, he extracted a lumpy, sodden wad of paper. "Pages from Dennis's logbook," he said.

"So you did take the logs," Gillian exclaimed.

"I guess I ought to apologize," said Barr, carefully unfolding the papers. "But I won't. These are still wet— thank God the ink didn't run. Now, why don't you let me take the helm while you read this entry here?"

She moved from behind the wheel and crouched down below the coaming, spreading the damp paper out on the seat. " '. . . from 88s to 88—safely accomplished.' I don't get it."

"Now the next page," Barr said. "About halfway down."

" 'A letter from João. He has been very sick'? That part?"

"Yes. And then the last one—nearly a year later, by the way. Written when Dennis was back in the States."

"João—whoever he was—is dead," Gillian said. From the writing, it had hit Uncle Dennis hard. She looked up at Barr, who was watching an advancing tug with a barge lashed to its side. After a long moment, he turned to her.

"Do you still have that dictionary down below? The one Dennis used for crossword puzzles?"

"I think so. Why?"

"Would you get it? In the meantime, Patrick and I have to do a couple of quick tacks."

Fumbling through the bookshelf, Gillian felt the yacht come about smartly. Patrick had gotten the hang of the sheets, and Barr's tacking was invariably precisely timed and smooth as glass. She took down the red-covered dictionary; it had been a gift from her, when Uncle Dennis could no longer get out of bed.

As she climbed the companionway ladder, Barr was tacking *Glory* again—they were off LaGuardia airport, in a narrow part of the East River, and the rising wind was right on the bow. Ahead lay Hell Gate, a stretch of water that was narrower still, where the current ran fast and turbulent.

"Tide's just about slack," Barr said, answering her thought. "But we'll have to fight the current going past Welfare Island, and the river's goddamn narrow there."

"I know," she agreed. "Here's the book."

"Good. Now, look up radium."

"Radium?" She turned pages swiftly. "Okay . . . here we are: 'an intensely radioactive shining white metallic element that resembles barium chemically, occurs in combination in minute quantities (as pitchblende or carnotite), emits alpha particles and gamma rays to form radon, and is used chiefly in luminous materials and in the treatment of cancer—see element table.' "

"That's all?"

"That's it. So what?"

"Damn," Barr said. "Well, see 'element table.' "

"Anything you say," Gillian replied. If only she were not so knocked out, maybe some of what Barr was up to would make sense. "Here it is—Chemical Elements. Listed alphabetically."

"All right—Patrick, stand by to tack. Here we go." *Glory* swung up into the wind's eye and through it, losing scarcely a knot before she was on the new tack. "What does it say next to 'radium'?"

"Um . . . 'radium (Ra)' . . ."

"Is there an atomic number?" he interrupted.

"Next column. Ninety-one—no that's something called protactinium. Eighty-eight. I'll be damned." Barr's thin face was creased by a satisfied grin. "How'd you guess?"

"I didn't, for a long time. But that sentence about 88s was so typical of Dennis being cute and cryptic. It just had to mean something. Since he was writing right after the war, the eighty-eight that jumps to mind is the famous German field gun, but what was the other? And João: He was Dennis's friend, and the manager of the boatyard where *Glory* was laid up during the war. Anyway, João helped Dennis stow the treasure, whatever it was—in fact, he was the one who handled it. And then he got sick. Not right away, but fatally—which is typical of radiation sickness. And his getting sick didn't seem to surprise Dennis all that much."

"And Uncle Dennis's bone cancer?" Gillian asked.

"From radiation, but it can take years to develop," said Barr. "Maybe Dennis was too close when João was shifting the stuff from container to container. Or maybe somewhere along the line he got up the nerve to make a withdrawal from his hiding place. Took precautions, but not enough of them."

She shivered, but it was Patrick who spoke: "You mean we're sitting on top of a bunch of radioactive stuff? You're goddamn calm about it."

"If I'm right about where and how it's hidden, we're perfectly safe as long as we don't disturb it," Barr said.

"Then where is it?" Gillian demanded.

"What do you shield radioactive material with?" Barr asked.

"Christ, I don't know," Gillian said. "A vault, I suppose."

"Lead," said Patrick suddenly. "The keel's lead, isn't it?"

"Give the man a Kewpie doll," Barr said. "It was right in front of me—a log entry I didn't take in, because I didn't see its importance: When *Glory* was overhauled, after the war, new holes were drilled for keel bolts, among other things. Reading the entry, I figured the old bolts—they're really steel rods, several feet long—had rusted, and what Dennis meant was that he'd had them drilled out. But he didn't. He meant what he wrote: he had new holes drilled, to put the radium in."

"And then capped, to look like bolts with nuts and washers," said Gillian.

"Sure. I finally got it when I was hiding in that air vent in Visconti's yacht. I could look down at his desk, and there was this one sheet of *Glory*'s plans. Someone had drawn in two extra keel-bolt holes, and someone else—

Visconti himself, I expect—had circled them in red. I mean, *Glory* was built by the Herreshoffs: she wouldn't need extra keel bolts. But what a perfect place to hide something small."

"Small," Gillian said slowly, "and—what was that term?—'intensely radioactive.' "

"What's radium worth, anyway?" Patrick put in.

"There you've got me," Barr said. "It used to be fantastically valuable. Thousands of dollars an ounce. No, thousands of dollars a gram. I have no idea what it goes for now."

"And we have to get it out first. Without frying ourselves," Patrick went on.

"Right." He hesitated. "Oh, there's something else I heard," he said, and Gillian somehow knew what he was going to say.

"Which of them was it?" she asked. "Which of them killed Uncle Dennis?"

"Arrow, I'm pretty sure. But from what I overheard, it was a mistake. He got carried away."

She felt nothing. Not even surprise. It was like news from another world. Barr spoke again, his eyes on her: "New tack coming up, Patrick."

16

❧

EAST RIVER
ELEVEN P.M.

One more goddamn tack, Patrick thought, and my arms are going to come right out of their sockets. He had lost count at fifteen, and that had been half an hour ago, back before Hell Gate. The current turned against them early—pushed, Barr had explained, by the rising southerly wind that funneled up the river. "We ought to reef," Barr said at one point, as *Glory* staggered under an exceptionally heavy gust. "You ever reef a sail?"

Draped numbly over a cockpit seat, feeling only the smarting pain in his hands, Patrick shook his head. "I could wake Gillian up," Barr said tentatively, then, "No. She's had it."

Patrick agreed. When Gillian had gone below, her eyes had been glazed. Patrick had seen just that look on faces of men who'd been in combat too long, and it shocked him to see it on this young and lovely woman. Even so, he told himself, she had held up damn well. Better than most men would have. He was jarred from his daze by Barr's crisp voice. "Ready about."

Jesus God . . . He got to his feet, feeling the throb of sore muscle down one bicep, and uncleated the sheet, flipping two of its three turns off the winch drum. "Ready," he said.

"Hard alee." He waited till the jib began to ripple and then threw the remaining turn off the winch. Not ripple, he reminded himself. Luff: that's when the sail hasn't got

enough wind to fill it, and it flutters. But it's also the name
of the leading edge of the goddamn sail. . . . He found
himself at the other side of the cockpit, with no recollection
of how he had got there, the limp sheet in his hands. Barr
had said something—what was it?

"Windward runner," Barr repeated, a snap in his voice.
"Move it."

"Right." Patrick turned back, slapped the heavy bronze
lever forward. Quickly, he spun around, set his feet, and
began to take the sheet in hand over hand. He felt the
heavy line come taut, tossed three coils over the winch,
slapped the handle into its slot and threw his weight against
it while pulling in the slack with his free hand.

"You really need two people on the winch," said Barr.
"One to crank and one to tail." Patrick grunted. His right
hand—his tailing hand on this tack—felt as if there was
no more skin on its palm. He gave one final heave on the
winch handle and bent to cleat the line.

"Don't bother," Barr said. "We'll tack again as soon as
we pick up speed."

They were in the narrow slot between the FDR Drive
and Roosevelt Island. The river here was no more than a
couple of hundred yards wide, running fast between the
steep concrete abutment on the Manhattan side, behind
which the stream of traffic on the drive beeped and gasped,
and the jagged boulders on the Roosevelt Island shore,
with the towering new apartment buildings over them.

"Hard alee," Barr said, his voice tense. Casting off the
sheet, Patrick risked a look over the bow and caught his
breath. For a moment he thought *Glory*'s long bowsprit
was going right into the concrete. From just above them,
as the yacht pivoted, Patrick caught a sharp tang of exhaust
from the traffic, and then he was releasing the one lever,
setting up the other and yanking the sheet.

"I figure we're making about fifty yards a tack in here,"
Barr observed, as *Glory* stretched out toward Roosevelt
Island, already close. "The current's going to get worse
for the next couple of hours, but there's no place to stop
and park."

Patrick groaned inwardly. He stretched his aching back
and reached for the line. "After the next tack," said Barr,
looking over the bow, "we'll change over: You take the
helm for a while." Patrick looked up, jolted out of his

timing. "There's nothing to it," Barr continued. "I'll talk you through the first two or three tacks. Ready about."

"Ready."

"Hard alee." They were around again, and Patrick found himself standing behind the big wheel. "Hold her like that," Barr said, one hand on the sheet. "I'll give you the timing."

The Manhattan shore was coming at them fast. Entirely too goddamn fast.

"Ready about," Barr said. "Now: wheel to port, not so quickly. That's it . . . steady up—center the wheel. Okay, meet her; wheel to starboard a little, not quite so high. A little more to port. Good enough." It was easy to surrender himself to Barr's orders, to the tone of absolute assurance. He became aware that the slender man had moved from one side of the cockpit to the other, had worked the heavy bronze levers, had taken in the sheet, all without visible effort.

"What about the bridge up there?" Patrick asked, inclining his head toward the gleaming string of lights that arched over the river at Fifty-ninth Street. He had discovered that if he kept his eye on the leading edge of the jib—the luff—he could see the curve of the fabric begin to soften when the boat was too close to the wind.

"No problem," Barr said. "There's a tide rip under it, but let her fall off a little just before you hit the standing wave, and she'll drive right through."

"Anything you say." It was fully dark now, but the lights all around reflected off the fast-moving river's surface so that the center of the stream was brightly lit. Only at the banks or directly under the bridge was the water obscured. Patrick could see the turbulence Barr had mentioned: just north of the bridge, it caused a steep wave to form, breaking in place but not moving. At Barr's quiet command, Patrick eased the helm slightly and felt *Glory* heel to the added thrust of the wind. She put her high, sharp bow through the breaking sea like a knife going through cottage cheese. Spray flew back over them, but the narrow, heavy hull barely trembled as it carved through the water.

Glory tacked as she slipped into the shadow under the bridge; her sails were blanketed momentarily and she came upright, sails volleying, then abruptly heeled again as the wind picked up. Patrick caught the wind change neatly and was looking to see if Barr had noticed, when a bank of lights, like an apartment building come adrift, loomed up ahead around a bend in the river. He could make out an immense bow that seemed to fill the channel from side to side. "Oh, Jesus," he said softly.

Barr, following his look, said, "Relax," but his voice did not sound relaxed. A long, echoing bellow rolled up the river, but the ship—a big tanker, riding high and light—held her course and speed. She could, Patrick knew, do nothing else. Barr was at the forward end of the cockpit, watching intently. "Okay," he said, almost to himself. "Ready about."

They were in the middle of the river, and Patrick opened his mouth to object, then closed it.

"Hard alee," Barr said. "Really hard, this time." Patrick spun the wheel and *Glory* came around fast. Barr's hands moved like lightning as he took in the sheet. "Head up a little," Barr said. "Into . . ." His voice was drowned out by five stabbing blasts from the tanker's horn, but Patrick had guessed what Barr wanted and edged *Glory* up into the wind, watching the luff of her jib shiver. He felt her slow beneath him, as the huge bulk of the tanker bore down irresistibly. "Like that," Barr was saying. "Hold her so." Patrick could feel *Glory* losing way—in a moment she would be dead in the water, right under the tanker's bow, from which, he could now see, someone was frantically waving a light.

"Okay," said Barr quietly. "Hard over to starboard."

Patrick spun the wheel. "I don't think . . ." he began, but then he felt the yacht begin to respond. "Come *on*, baby," he said, under his breath. Barr was hauling fiercely at the jib sheet, keeping the sail from going across the boat, and the wind in it pushed the bow around.

"Helm amidships," Barr said, letting the sheet run. He darted across the cockpit and took in the other end. *Glory* began to move, picking up speed, as the tanker's high, rivet-studded side slid past, almost near enough to touch. From high up on her bridge, a foreign voice roared down a few words that needed no translation, and the ship was past, her immense screw thumping the water.

Barr laughed quietly. "This is what you might call the crash course. Mostly, things are more peaceful. I wasn't expecting traffic—not at this time of night, and certainly not on a Sunday. That was a dangerous thing for us to do," he added. "The pilot on that tanker must've been terrified."

"Fuck the pilot," said Patrick.

Barr laughed again and pulled out a crumpled pack of Camels. He lit one, cupping his hands around the match. In the reflected glow, the lines in his face looked gouged, but his eyes gleamed. He took a deep puff, exhaled the smoke. "As soon as we get below the end of the island, we can tack clear across the river—almost a mile on a straight run."

When *Glory* was cutting silently across the deserted river, Patrick broke the silence again. "What are you going to do about Emerald?" he asked.

"I've been thinking," Barr said. "We'll give her a call and set a rendezvous to pick her up."

"You mean we'll land and find a phone?" Patrick asked.

"Hell, no," Barr replied. "We'll use the ship-to-shore."

Patrick was astounded. "You mean through the marine operator? What makes you think Visconti won't have somebody monitoring the VHF?"

"I'm counting on him doing just that," Barr replied. He was standing halfway down the companionway steps, groping behind the antiquated transceiver that comprised *Glory*'s link with the outside world. A switch clicked. "New York marine operator," Barr said into the microphone. "This is Whiskey Sierra Victor Eight Five Seven Niner, yacht *Glory*."

The reply came right back. "*Glory*, this is New York Marine."

"New York Marine, I want to make a collect call," Barr said. "To—wait one, please—" he pulled a matchbook from his shirt pocket, opened it, and read off a number with a Long Island area code.

"Speak to anyone there, sir?" said the operator.

"Miss Emerald," Barr replied. Over the air they could hear the burr of the ring. Seeing Patrick staring down into the lighted companionway, Barr held up the matchbook. The cover was a deep green, without lettering. Inside was nothing but the phone number. "Discreet, isn't it?" Barr said.

Emerald came on almost immediately. Her voice was toneless and harsh. She must, Patrick thought, be as tired as the rest of them. "Where are you, Barr?" she asked.

"Going down the East River," he replied. "Can you come to meet us?"

There was a pause at the other end, and when Emerald spoke, she sounded hurried. "Sure. Where's it to be?"

"Do you know Brooklyn? Down below the Navy Yard?"

"Only the dead know Brooklyn," she replied. "You tell me where to go, and I'll find it."

"At the end of Van Brunt Street," Barr said. "There's some derelict piers. Right across Buttermilk Channel from the Coast Guard base on Governors Island. It's not a great neighborhood; is there someone you can bring?"

Her laugh was unnatural, and abruptly cut off. "Oh, sure," she said. "I'll bring somebody. When will you be there?"

"Two—three hours at least," Barr replied.

"I'll be waiting," she said.

"What I wonder," said Patrick, staring up the river, "is who's going to be waiting with her." He and Barr were crouched in the stolen rowboat, which was tied alongside *Glory*; the yacht was in a slip large enough for an ocean liner and shielded by huge covered piers on either side. Rain spattered down in halfhearted little bursts, driven by a wind that whistled past the end of the wharf.

Barr, who was whittling a piece of spare planking into a crude paddle with the aid of a murderous-looking sailor's knife, glanced up from his work. "You heard it, too, then," he said. "At first I thought she was just tired. But now I think she was trying to warn us."

"Visconti's people?"

"Most likely. The only reason Visconti hasn't checked Emerald out already was that his skipper, Arrow, didn't tell him it was Emerald who ruined his first attempt on *Glory*. But Emerald was a loose end—Visconti was bound to look her up sooner or later."

Patrick wished he were a little less tired. "So if you figured Visconti was right there, listening," he said slowly, working it out, "then you were bluffing."

"Double bluff," Barr said. He folded the clasp knife and slipped it into his pocket. "There. Not much of a paddle, but it'll have to do. Emerald must've thought I'd lost my

mind, calling on the VHF like that—it's nothing but a huge
party line. I'm betting Visconti will assume I meant him
to overhear, and that I'm not on the river at all."

"Couldn't he DF your transmission?" Patrick asked, and
then answered himself: "No, I guess not—if his yacht's
still in Norwalk, there's too much in the way of her direction finder. All he'll get is the booster signal from the
phone company's antenna." He looked hard at the wiry
man sitting opposite him. "So what happens? If he thinks
you aren't where you say you are, he sure won't let Emerald come to find out."

"Maybe," Barr replied. "He won't let her come alone,
of course. But I hope he'll send her just in case, as bait."

"Okay," Patrick replied. "And we jump them, is that
it?"

"More or less. But we don't stick our heads right into
it. Van Brunt Street, where I told Emerald to go, is a
quarter-mile up the shore from here. If anyone's there at
all, they'll be looking for us to come from upstream. Instead, we'll paddle along the piers and take them from
behind."

"This sounds crummy to ask," said Patrick. "But why
don't we just keep going? Emerald can take care of
herself."

"I don't know, exactly," Barr said. "But I gave her my
word I'd stop for her."

Patrick heard himself say "yes," as if Barr's answer had
been in his own mind. And then he knew that it had been.
He rose cautiously to his feet and reached up to *Glory*'s
gunwale.

"Where you going?"

"Be back in a minute." He swung himself aboard the
yacht and slipped quietly down the companionway, intent
on not waking Gillian. She lay on her back, sprawled across
the berth in the aft guest cabin—the same berth Patrick
had occupied his first night aboard. Her face was pale and
there was a smear of makeup behind her ear. As he
watched, she smiled in her sleep. He had to force himself
to turn away. Moving quickly, Patrick felt under the settee
cushions in the saloon and came up with Bellairs's pump-
action shotgun. Nearly new, Patrick decided. He was not
familiar with shotguns, but he had a vivid picture of it in

Bellairs's hands. He worked the action once and a shell popped out and clattered to the deck. Behind him, he heard Gillian stir.

I guess we ought to tell her something—but what? She had rolled on her side, and he had the almost overpowering temptation to kiss her. He paused, looking down, and heard a gentle rapping on the deck overhead. Barr. Time to go. So long, kid.

"I'd have brought one for you," Patrick said, when he was back in the rowboat, "but Emerald waltzed off with the rest of the armory."

"That's all right." Barr was untying the bow line that held the little boat to *Glory*. "I'd just shoot off my foot." Outside the shelter of the slip, the wind and current snatched up the skiff, whirled it northward past the wharves.

Patrick, at the stern, put his back into paddling with the boat's only oar. Forward, Barr plied the shaped plank, but all they needed to do was guide the boat as the wind and current swept it on. "Going to be a bitch getting back," said Patrick, raising his voice over the wind and splashing whitecaps.

"Tide's only got an hour more to run," Barr said. "It'll carry us back."

"If we're around to enjoy it," Patrick said, under his breath.

"Steer us closer to the piers," Barr called softly. "We don't want to be out in the stream where they might see us."

"Right," said Patrick. The little skiff wanted to spin, not steer. Even though they were going with the wind, splashes of spray were coming over the transom and soaking his back. The salt water on his scored palms stung him awake, and then, up ahead, he saw broken pilings, like snaggleteeth, and a tumbledown pier, outlined in black against the distant lights of Manhattan, across the river, and a figure—no, two—looking upstream.

Barr glanced back and nodded. They were right among the rotten pilings, working the boat along by hand. Patrick reached out to grasp a big timber and felt it move; it was rotten at the base, ready to topple at a touch. They had stopped moving forward, and the rowboat swung around with the current. Barr crept aft. "Up here," he whispered, pointing to a hole in the pier flooring through which the night sky was a shade lighter than the rotten wood.

"Wait a minute," Patrick whispered, tugging Barr's sleeve.

"What?"

"I'll go first—I used to do this for a living."

Barr nodded. "Okay."

"Hold this till I get up, then pass it to me." Barr took the shotgun gingerly. Patrick got to his feet, balancing against the boat's motion as it jerked against its painter. He put his foot on a crossbeam and slowly let his weight come onto it. Then he reached up and grasped the jagged edges of the gap in the pier flooring and lifted himself, groping with his foot until it found a bent spike that protruded from a piling. With infinite care he pushed himself up until his head emerged through the hole. The pier had been planked and then patched with asphalt, and the tar gleamed damp in the light from a streetlamp at its shore end. The two figures were just visible, standing side by side with their backs to him, looking out over the water.

Patrick hoisted himself through the gap and crouched motionless on the pier. There were sodden heaps of trash here and there, but nothing you could call cover between himself and the two figures—nothing, anyway, except a huge old bollard, half the height of a man, fixed into the heavy timbers that formed the pier's lip. Patrick looked into the hole and caught a gleam of metal. He put his hand down and Barr placed the shotgun in his grasp. The metal was cold against his lacerated palm.

The figures were definitely facing away from him; he was sure of it. He slipped the shotgun down the back of his sweater so that it lay along his spine, and began to work his way, on his belly, across the pier surface toward the edge. The wet ground's chill came right through his sweater and trousers, but he was barely aware of it.

Now he was level with the bollard, no more than ten feet away from the standing figures. One of them was heavy and tall, and he stamped his feet every few seconds. City shoes, from the rasping sound, and probably soaked through. The other person was slender and straight, standing awkwardly with hands clasped behind its back. No, not clasped—bound. Emerald, of course. There was something funny about the lower part of her face, but as she turned, he recognized the straight line of her nose, silhouetted against the lights of Manhattan.

What's wrong with this picture? Of course—Visconti would never send one man by himself: there must be another, keeping dry in a car, most likely. Probably they change off. He worked the shotgun down his back and extracted it, then settled down in the shadow of the bollard to wait.

Fifteen minutes later the drizzle changed suddenly to a downpour, a wind-driven sheet of rain that marched across the pier. The heavy-set figure at the pier edge turned toward the streetlamp and called out, waving. A minute or so later, a second man appeared, scuttling head down across the driving rain. He was clutching something—probably a coat—and the first man stepped toward him, reaching for it.

"Freeze! Both of you!" Patrick's parade-ground roar cut through the whistle of the wind. The heavy-set man skidded to a halt, turning and reaching into his jacket until he saw the metallic glitter in Patrick's hands. The other figure, caught running, lost his footing and fell full-length in a puddle. At the corner of his eye, Patrick saw Emerald spin about, totter for a second and then regain her balance.

"You—on your belly!" Patrick snapped, waving the shotgun at the standing man, who was frozen in a half crouch, his hands well away from his body. "Right there. Arms out—I don't care if you drown." He turned his head to call Barr, saw him scrambling out of the hole in the planking. "Search them," Patrick ordered. "But don't get in my line of fire." He stepped to one side, watched as Barr pulled a revolver from the heavy-set man's shoulder holster and tossed it over the pier's edge into the river.

Emerald was at his side, making strange moaning sounds. Patrick risked a quick look and saw that she had been gagged, was desperately trying to say something. Barr had found the other man's gun. "Don't . . ." Patrick began, but it was too late: the gun glittered as it spun through the air. Barr's knife gleamed wet, and he slashed Emerald's gag. She gasped and coughed, spitting pieces of cloth.

"Watch out, Patrick," she managed, faintly. "There's another . . ."

At the shore end of the pier, an engine roared into life and headlights stabbed through the murk, swung around

and fixed them in blinding light. Over the sound of the
engine came a rapid *pop-popping* noise. Whack-and-
screech of a ricochet, and Patrick's left leg was wiped out
from under him. He crashed heavily to the asphalt, bringing the shotgun around as he fell. The first blast was wild—
off into the night—but with the second, the car's headlights
went abruptly dark.

Through the hiss of the rain, Patrick heard the rasping
clatter of footsteps. Running away. To hell with them. The
car engine had died to a mutter, but then it burped and
slowed. In gear, Patrick thought. He'll use it for cover.
Barr and Emerald were flat on the rainswept pier a few
feet away. "Move it!" Patrick called softly to them. "Back
to the rowboat!"

He saw them begin to crawl toward the hole. His whole
left leg was numb. Suddenly a glint of metal caught his
eye—a sedan, rolling slowly onto the pier, light reflecting
off its wet windshield. He raised the shotgun, took careful
aim, fired. The windshield vanished in the gun's roar, and
the car leaped ahead, straight at him. Desperately, he
rolled to one side, clutching the shotgun, until he rolled
right into the gaping hole. He heard Barr call out from
below. Patrick was hanging by his good leg, his foot caught
between two planks. His hands grabbed, found a piece of
timber that tore away like wet cardboard. Over him, the
car's left front wheel ran square into the hole, and the tire,
ripped by a projection, exploded. The force of it shook
Patrick free and he began to fall, but something struck the
back of his head and he never felt himself hit the water.

17

N E W   Y O R K   H A R B O R
M O N D A Y ,   M A Y   1 3
F I V E - T H I R T Y A . M .

Glory put her bow into a sea, and a bucketful of spray shot back over the deck, rattling off the cockpit dodger, which looked like an oversize baby-carriage hood with a clear plastic window. Barr, moving with the boat's motion, ducked and then straightened up again. The wheel turned under his hands, and the big old boat corkscrewed easily over a second sea. Somewhere just below the hard edge of concentration, Barr's mind was appraising the rising wind and lowering cloud: this storm was coming on faster and stronger than he had expected. He saw Emerald's bare head in the companionway. "How's Patrick?" he asked.

Stiffly, she climbed out on deck and sagged against the cockpit coaming, under the shelter of the dodger. In the washed-out light of dawn her face had a greenish tinge and sweat—or spray or rain—made it gleam. "He's conscious," she replied, her eyes closed.

"How's his head?"

"You can't hurt an Irishman by hitting him on the head. It looked worse than it was—his scalp's torn." She pulled herself upright with an effort. "What I'm worried about is the leg," she continued. "The entry's a nice small-caliber hole, but the exit is a mess. I think the bullet must've ticked the femur and bounced off. The bone's not broken, but I'll bet there's splinters and torn muscles and Christ knows what all in there."

"You know bullet wounds," Barr observed, his eye on the luff of the mainsail.

"I've seen a few," she replied. "And abortions. And a lot of cuts and gashes. Speaking of which, your little sailmaker friend is stitching up Patrick's scalp right now. She's tougher than I'd have thought—I had to come up here. I chucked my cookies twice already, the way the boat's bouncing around."

"Gillian's all right as long as she's busy," said Barr, ducking behind the dodger as another cloud of spray hurtled over the bow. "You just have to give her something to do."

"Um," Emerald murmured, clearly disinclined to open her mouth. She took several deep breaths and a little color came back to her face. "Got a lot of guts, anyway," she offered.

"Doesn't she, though?" Barr was surprised at the warmth in his own voice. "I thought she was just bossy, but I was wrong." He pulled himself back. "She's brave *and* bossy."

"Well, she's got a crush on you," Emerald said. "An old-fashioned crush."

"She's a kid—what do you expect?" he said.

"Nothing, I guess." She sounded disappointed. "Say, where are we, anyway?"

"Entrance to New York harbor, though you might not think so with these seas. The lights back there are the Verrazano Bridge," said Barr, nodding over his shoulder. "We're going to change course in a minute or two, as soon as we're a little further past Coney Island—those lights over there to port."

"I see," Emerald replied, looking under the main boom at the gray, wave-washed beach. "Where are we going?"

"That's what we have to decide. I think we need a quorum. Would you get Gillian up here, please?"

Emerald looked at the companionway hatch, then put her head into it and called. From below, Gillian's voice floated up: "Be right there."

As they waited, Barr looked at Emerald, whose eyes had closed again. Her face still had the pallor of seasickness, and the bruise where the tape had torn her lip was clear against her skin. Aside from that, she was immaculate—her blouse's rolled-up sleeves showed her slender forearms and hid the fact that one of the sleeves was torn, and she had somehow managed to wash or scrape away the dirt and slime from the pier. By contrast, Gillian's face, when it appeared, was stained with dirt as well as blood—Patrick's, he supposed—and there were other spots on the too-large gray sweatshirt that hung about her. She looked alert enough, though, for which Barr was grateful.

"Here's the situation," he began. "First, the weather. The forecast on VHF is for a southeasterly gale by tonight, but I'll bet it's here a lot sooner." And stronger, too, he thought, if it keeps making up at this rate. "Next, where can we go? As you can see, we're in the Lower Bay. New York harbor widens out here, and there's several possible courses. Off there to starboard—you can't see it through this rain—is Sandy Hook. We could sail inside it, up Barnegat Bay all the way to Red Bank; or we could go outside Sandy Hook, down the Jersey coast; or we could turn east, past Coney Island, along the South Shore of Long Island. We could even double back and go up the Hudson. The question is, what will Visconti do?"

"He's probably already doing it," Gillian said. She was standing on the companionway ladder, her elbows resting on the sill of the hatch. Her wool watch cap was cocked back on her head. "The two guys who got away must've found a phone by now."

Emerald, her eyes open, was watching Gillian intently. "Emerald, you said that Visconti and three of his hoods came to your place, right?" asked Barr.

"Right. They were waiting when I got back from getting rid of . . . Hals's car," she replied, her eyes flicking to Gillian. "They'd forced their way in, and they had the General."

"Did they say where *Tiamat*—Visconti's yacht—was?"

"No," said Emerald slowly. "Not that I remember. They came by car. Two cars, actually. Visconti drove off in one when his thugs took me away in the other."

"We've got to assume Visconti is bringing *Tiamat* down the East River by now," Barr went on. He eased the helm to miss a breaking sea and heard an unpleasant creak from the rigging behind him. "So we have to figure out what he expects us to do."

"You've been working on it," said Emerald wearily. "Just give us the answer."

"Okay. Barnegat Bay is a dead end: once in it, we're trapped. The same is true of the Hudson. This wind's already east of south, which means if we head east—along the South Shore of Long Island—a hard beat to windward with the beach under our lee. So going down the Jersey coast is the logical route. There's several inlets, and the wind would be more or less abeam. It'd be a fast passage, besides being easier on the boat."

"And that means you're not going to do it," said Gillian.

"We bluffed Visconti once, doing the obvious," Barr said. "I don't think we can do it again. It would have my vote—going east. What do you say, Emerald?"

Emerald leaned around the dodger's side curtains and threw up, with neat economy, over the leeward rail. She wiped her mouth with the back of her hand and said, "Frankly, sweetheart, I don't give a damn."

He looked at Gillian, who was watching Emerald with an affectionate grin. She reached under her sweatshirt and produced a crumpled paper towel. "Here," she said, extending it to Emerald.

"Thanks." She wiped her mouth fastidiously. "Really," she said after a moment. "I don't know enough to have an opinion. What do you think, Gillian?"

"The only thing that worries me is the weather," Gillian said slowly. "The barometer's dropped eight millibars since we left."

Nearly a quarter of an inch, Barr thought. Even worse than I'd figured. "I'm worried, too," he admitted. "But I still think east is the best choice. If we can make it around Montauk Point, we're home free."

"There's only one skipper on a boat," Gillian said firmly. "The skipper wants to go east—we go east."

"Let's come about, then," said Barr.

"Soup," called Gillian, an hour later. "It's only out of a package, but it'll make you feel better." She passed up a steaming mug and Barr caught a quick, meaty whiff. Emerald took it from her reluctantly. Patrick O'Mara, gray-white as old canvas, sat beside her huddled in a blanket, with a foul-weather jacket thrown over it. A bandage cov-

ered most of the top of his head and another swaddled his
right thigh, below where the leg of his khaki trousers had
been hacked off. Sitting on the weather side of the cockpit,
he braced himself against the yacht's heel with his good
leg, grimacing every time *Glory* fell off a wave.

The yacht was bashing along, close-hauled on the starboard tack. The gray, cresting seas came on from the
southeast, row upon row, whipping sheets of cold spray
over *Glory*'s bow. She was about a quarter of a mile off
a flat beach on which the waves were breaking with increasing force, collapsing explosively on the sand, hurling
white water high into the air. Behind the beach, big new
apartment buildings stood in blank-eyed rows. Barr had
dropped and furled *Glory*'s mizzen, with Emerald's help,
and had replaced the jib with the staysail. The main needed
a reef—he could feel the yacht heeling too much, throwing
more spray, fighting the waves. Gillian had reported, a
few minutes earlier, that there was a good foot of water
in the bilge. But to heave to and reef meant losing precious
yards toward the beach, already closer than he liked. Once
in the surf, *Glory* would be lost, and once on the hard
sand shore, she would break up in minutes.

"There's soup down below for you, Barr. And I made
a sandwich. Why don't I take her while you eat?"

"We'll come about first," he said. It was easier than he
had feared. Gillian took the helm while he tended the
sheets, and Emerald assisted Patrick in a combined heave
and lurch that carried the pair of them across the cockpit
to the new high side. Patrick's face was wet with sweat
when he was done, and Barr intercepted a meaningful look
from Emerald. He nodded—Patrick was clearly near the
end of his strength; the only wonder was that he was still
conscious.

When *Glory* was on the new tack, pointed straight out
to sea, Barr fought his way forward to put a reef in the
main. It was a brutal business: solid water was coming over
the foredeck every few minutes, drenching him as he stood
by the main halyard winch. Fortunately, Gillian's sailmaking associates had set up *Glory*'s mainsail for jiffy reef-
ing, one of the very few innovations that Barr would sit
still for, and he was able to get the reef tack and clew
socked down without assistance.

By the time he had worked his way back along the boom,

tying in the reef points, his foul-weather gear was soaked through and his fingertips were bleeding badly. Even so, he stood for a moment at the windward backstay, his hand resting on the thick wire. Every time the yacht crashed through a wave, the backstay chain plate moved, just slightly, as the load from the mainmast came on it. He saw Gillian watching him and shook his head: there was no point in alarming the others. "Don't try to point too high," he said at last. "Ease her as much as you can."

"Right," she said. Her eyes told him she understood completely: in *Glory*'s present state, she could not sustain too many blows from the sea, especially on port tack. A really bad one could knock the mainmast right out of her.

Barr ducked under the shelter of the dodger and marveled, for perhaps the hundredth time, how the fabric hood cut the force of the wind. In the open cockpit, he'd had to pitch his voice up to be heard over the seas. Here, a couple of feet away, he could speak in nearly normal tones. He pulled his sodden foul-weather jacket off, tossed it in a corner of the cockpit and went below. The saloon, where the two women had worked on Patrick's injuries, was a moderate shambles—a blood-soaked trouser leg on the wet cabin floor, where glass shards still crunched underfoot; sticky bloodstains on the settee; and on the gimbaled table a metal bowl with pink water, scraps of blond hair and a soapy froth, all sloshing back and forth at an angle of thirty degrees to the cabin floor, as the table responded to the heavy counterweights below it. Overhead, spray and rainwater dripped steadily from the bedding that was stuffed in the broken skylight.

He paused, sorting out the chorus of creaks and groans that came from the hull and rigging. Most of them were familiar enough, and of the others only one—an intermittent series of sharp cracks, coming apparently from the mainmast step—gave him serious qualms.

He picked up the bowl of bloodstained water and took it forward to the galley, poured it down the sink. The yacht was heeled far enough so that an inch or so was unable to drain out. On the counter, a sandwich had been wedged between the freshwater pump and its handle; the bread was stale, the ham stiff at the edges, the lettuce limp and brown-spotted—it tasted delicious. On the stove, a blackened pot, kept in place by metal arms, held about a quart

of still-steaming oxtail soup. He dipped up a mug of it and
went back to the saloon. Swaying easily to the boat's motion, he drank off the soup without waiting for it to cool,
extracted the least soggy of his Camels and lit it. There
seemed, to his tuned ear, an addition to the barrage of
sound—a deep, skeletal creak that came from right aft
every time the yacht's bow dipped. The backstay, he
thought. Not a whole lot of time.

He lifted the hatch to the bilge and listened to the water
sloshing back and forth—sloshing, if he was correct, over
the false keel bolts that concealed Dennis Falk's legacy.
Oh, for an electric bilge pump. He got wearily to his feet
and took out from its recess the four-foot iron bar that
served as a handle to the main pump, which was under
the floorboards in the passage aft of the saloon, so a crew
member could brace himself against the chart table and
pump standing up. Barr worked the handle back and forth,
keeping his arm rigid and letting the yacht's motion sway
him. A hundred and forty-six strokes and the pump sucked
air.

At three quarts a stroke, he thought, that's a hundred
and ten gallons (the calculation was automatic) . . . so
she's making, say, twenty-five gallons an hour. Probably
be more, as it gets rougher. Time to tack again. He left
the pump handle in place—they would need it soon
enough—and tapped the big barometer over the chart table. 29.72, down from—he pulled the open logbook toward
him—29.77 an hour before. More wind soon. A lot more.
He entered the new reading, his lips pursed, and added
"Wind ESE Force 8 increasing. Continuing E under staysail and reefed main."

Glory rose to a wave, paused and kept rising. Barr
braced himself, heard the landslide sound of a breaking
sea—this was not a single wave but two, one mounting the
other. The yacht was taking it wrong, he felt, as he leaped
for the companionway. Gillian, biting her lip, was fighting
the wheel. *Glory's* stern sideslipped down as the breaker
passed under her, filling the cockpit with white water, and
hit the trough with a crash that shook the hull. Barr heard
the rending of wood behind him. "Hard alee," he snapped.
"Right now."

The wheel spun under Gillian's hands—her knuckles
were red-raw with the cold—and Barr leaped for the back-

stay levers. Reluctantly, *Glory* came about, pressed by the backwinded staysail. She seemed to have made it when an errant sea slapped her bow and she hesitated. Barr hauled on the sheet with all his strength, till he felt her fall away once more. He cast the sheet off, slapped the other backstay lever free, and threw himself across the cockpit, treading down a body that was struggling on the floorboards.

He heard Patrick's voice, faint with exhaustion, gasp out an agonized "Oh, God," and then he had the sheet in his hands and was hauling in on it.

"Ease her," he called to Gillian, as he groped desperately for the winch handle. From beneath him, Patrick's hand held it out. Barr snatched it, jammed it into the socket, and began to crank. He saw Emerald's pale face from the corner of his eye. "Tail off," he said; then, seeing her incomprehension: "Grab this rope and pull."

As the sheet came in, inch by protesting inch, he watched Gillian edge *Glory* up into the wind. "No more," he said at last. "You'll pinch her to death." She inclined her head toward the beach. "I see it," he said.

Emerald had managed to haul Patrick up on the seat. He was whiter than ever, his eyes tightly closed and his face drawn with pain. Suddenly, Emerald's eyes widened. "Oh, no," she said quietly.

Barr followed her look. Behind them by a mile or so was the dim, washed-out silhouette of a vessel. She was on the same course as *Glory*, pressing hard and throwing spray right over her high bows. "Oh, yes," he said. "That's her."

Gillian, her eye fixed on the luff of the staysail, had not turned. "*Tiamat?*" she asked. "What do we do now?"

"We keep sailing," Barr replied. "They can't board us in these seas, and I doubt he wants to sink us." He glanced at the beach, already closer than he liked to see it. "All this shore looks alike to me," he said. "I've got to pick a couple of landmarks off the chart."

"Long Beach," said Patrick faintly.

"What?"

"Long Beach." His eyes were open, and he forced a weak smile. "I grew up down here," he explained. "You should have Jones Inlet off the port bow."

"An inlet," Gillian said. "Any chance we can sail into it?"

Patrick shook his head. "Not a prayer. Not in this boat. What does she draw, anyway—ten feet?"

"Just about," Barr replied.

"Forget it," Patrick said. "You'd gut her. Besides, the inlet channel changes every week. You can't count on the buoys."

Barr looked back. Whoever was at the helm of Visconti's yacht was pushing her to the limit. She bucked and slammed through the cresting seas, but the powerful hull would handle it, he knew. "How far off do we have to be to clear the inlet?" he asked Patrick.

The wounded man dragged himself up. "Give me a hand so I can see over the dodger," he said. With Emerald and Barr supporting him, he peered forward. "We're not going straight," he said after a minute or so. "We're sliding off to port."

"About five degrees' leeway," Barr said.

"We should still be okay," Patrick said, and to Gillian, "Can you see the light—on the end of the breakwater?"

"I think so . . . Yes."

"How much will you clear it by?"

"Two hundred yards," she said. "An easy two hundred yards."

"That's good enough." He looked up at Barr. "After the inlet, you've got Jones Beach Island—thirteen miles of sand. And then Fire Island Inlet."

"I know," Barr said. "But the axis of Jones Island runs north of east. We ought to be able to hold a course along the beach, instead of sliding down on it."

"Yeah," Patrick agreed. "But remember you've got an outer bar most of the way, maybe a hundred yards offshore. And Democrat Point—the beginning of Fire Island—sticks out to the south a mile or so. You'll have to tack to clear it."

Barr shook his head. "Look." He pointed to the backstay chain plate on the port side. The stay flopped out to leeward and the metal plate was pulled six inches up, its topmost bolt torn free of the hull. "Another tack and we lose the mast." He looked at Gillian, whose jaw was set. "We could head up now," he said. "Drop the anchor and lower the sails. This is good holding ground—we could probably ride it out here."

"And as soon as it was calm enough, Visconti's people would come aboard," she said.

"Afraid so."

"What about Fire Island Inlet?" she demanded. "Can we sail in there?"

"I don't know," said Barr. "It's sand, like all the rest—the entrance channel isn't even charted, it shifts so often."

"You could do it," Patrick cut in. "It shifts, all right, but not that much. The main channel's been in the same place for years. More or less. You've got enough water, and I know it like the back of my hand."

"Will we have to tack?" asked Barr.

Patrick looked perplexed. "I don't know," he said at last. "I just don't know—but I don't think so. You'll have to get a little more offshore, though." He thought again. "Okay. If you can work her maybe a quarter-mile further out, you should be able to take her right on in. The approach is oh-four-five . . ."

"Magnetic?"

"Right. And there's a dogleg just short of the beach—you have to come up to about oh-nine-oh. In this kind of weather, there's breaking seas all across the entrance. But there's enough water, and I can guide you in."

"Can he follow?" asked Gillian, nodding back to where *Tiamat* was bashing through the seas, already visibly closer.

"If he has the nerve," Barr replied. "She draws less than we do, and he can control her better. But we might not make it, Gillian. These are big seas—if they're breaking in the inlet, we'll have to ride *Glory* through on the back of one of them. We could broach in a second."

She managed a tight smile. "Broached, knocked flat, sunk like a stone—isn't that how it goes?"

Did she know what she was saying? She made it sound like some kind of jingle. Broaching was unnerving enough: Barr knew, and hated, the feel of the dead helm as the boat swung uncontrollably up to windward, lying over until the lee rail disappeared in the exploding flurry of white water. And knocked flat was worse, with the hull on its side, the sails scooping up seawater, and everyone aboard scrambling for the windward rail until the boat responded—heavily, sullenly—to the downward pull of the lead keel and hauled herself upright, streaming water. Only this time there would be more breaking waves crashing clear over the hull and pressing *Glory* down until the water forced its way through the broken skylight and the hatchways, and she slipped beneath the surface.

Gillian looked him in the eye, and he realized that she knew exactly what was at risk: her life and his, and Emerald's and Patrick's. And *Glory*'s. "All right," he said. "We'll do it. But let's start edging offshore as much as we can."

"You take her, Barr," Gillian replied. "You can work her up to windward better than I can. I'll go get life jackets for Patrick and Emerald—you want one?"

"Not while I'm steering," Barr said, taking the helm as she relinquished it. "What's the matter?"

"It's *Tiamat*," Gillian said. "She's getting damn close."

Barr glanced over his shoulder. The power yacht was right on *Glory*'s starboard quarter, looming hugely over them. There was no one visible on deck, though he thought he could detect movement behind the glass of the pilothouse windows. As he watched, she headed up for an instant and slipped forward, edging alongside. The mainsail luffed, caught in the wind shadow of the high, sharp bow—the letters TIAMAT looked at least two feet tall.

"What's he doing?" Gillian demanded. "Is he going to board us?"

The sail flapped again, and as *Glory* wallowed, Barr drove her off to get clear air. "He doesn't have to," he said. "He's blanketing our sails—probably figures he'll force us down on the beach until we give up."

"I'm goddamned if he will," said Gillian, and darted down the main hatch.

18

OFF JONES BEACH
NINE A.M.

"Goddamned if he will," Gillian said again, under her breath, as she fumbled with desperate haste through the lockers in the after cabin. It had to be here—she remembered putting it back after the police had looked it over. Surely Barr would not have thrown it out. Or Patrick. Her heart was sinking, and then her fingers touched the familiar canvas wrapping lashed with tarred marline. Her knife was out and the line fell away. The canvas was stiff with age, the oiled butcher paper inside it had cracked and worn through in places, but the heavy metal pieces underneath were still slick with grease.

On deck, the mainsail thundered again, stilled as *Glory* fell off and caught free air. *Glory*'s helplessness was so maddening—*Tiamat* was just pressing her down. A metallic click under her fingers; her hands, with a memory of their own, had fitted the stock to the receiver. Now the trigger housing . . . There. She groped through the wrapping and came up with the clip. Eight rounds. The brass casings were green from the salt air. Or from age. Swaying, she braced the rifle against her thigh, slammed the bolt back with the heel of her right hand, pressed the clip into place, and let the slide crash forward. Clutching the rifle—slippery as well as heavy—she scrambled up the companionway.

"Holy Christ," said Patrick, who saw her first.

"What is it?" Emerald gasped, her eyes tightly closed, her ashen face wet.

"It's a fucking antique," Patrick replied. "An M-1, right?"

"It was Uncle Dennis's," she said. "You've been a soldier, Patrick—can you shoot it?"

He hefted the rifle with obvious effort. "I ran into a few of these in Africa," he said, his hands caressing the weapon. "They last forever." He drew the bolt partway back. "Eight rounds to a clip. This all we got?"

"That's it."

"I hope the ammo's newer than the piece," he muttered. "Somebody brace me." Silently, Emerald swiveled around to put her back against his. *Tiamat* was towering over them. The big yacht sank into a trough. In just the few minutes Gillian had been below, the troughs had become like canyons, and the offshore sandbar, where the waves towered and broke, seemed right under their lee. With what felt like an effort, *Glory* rose. As her deck came nearly level with *Tiamat*'s wheelhouse, Patrick brought the rifle up in a single clean, liquid sweep and squeezed the trigger. In the howl of wind, the click of the action was barely audible. Snarling, he yanked the bolt back and the round leaped clear. At his gesture, Gillian picked it up and handed it to him. "Bent," he said. "But at least the action works."

Tiamat seemed right on top of them, and for a second Gillian was sure her steel sides would tear into *Glory*'s gunwale, but her bow, hurtling down, missed by three feet, crashing into the water alongside and sending up a solid sheet that drenched *Glory*'s foredeck. Now *Glory* was rising as *Tiamat* subsided, and once again Patrick brought the rifle up—a little slower, a little less smoothly—and squeezed. The shattering, flat *whango!* echoed off *Tiamat*'s side, and one of the windows on her bridge exploded into fragments. As if by magic, the power yacht yawed up into the wind, then across it, and lay rolling horribly as a breaking sea slammed into her.

"Wonderful, Patrick!" Gillian cried, but he had fallen back into Emerald's arms, his face yellow-white. She thought he was unconscious, but after a long moment his eyes opened.

"I'm sorry," he whispered. "What a kick that bastard

has." He took a deep breath. "I don't know if I can do it again."

"You may not have to, at least for a while," said Barr, glancing over his shoulder. *Tiamat* was back on course, but running slowly and lying well astern. "I don't expect there's too many candidates for helmsman right now," he continued, with a tight smile. "It's not easy to steer lying flat on your face." He was balanced on the balls of his feet, his bloody fingertips just touching the rim of the wheel. As Gillian watched, *Glory*'s bow edged up toward the wind, then fell slightly off, edged up again—not quite so high this time—and fell away. She had seen Barr do this dozens of times, working the big old yacht to windward, riding every puff, and even with *Tiamat*'s bulk looming up astern she found herself transfixed. Gillian knew what he was doing—any sailor would—but it was still hard to believe that anybody could be so completely at one with a boat, the wind and the sea.

Barr did not seem to be aware of her, but she knew from experience that his senses were shaved raw. After a few minutes he said, without turning his head, "Maybe you'd better dog down the ports and vents, Gillian. See if we have a tarp you can lash over the skylight. And when you're done with that, it'd help if the bilge was dry."

"Seal her up and pump the bilge," Gillian repeated, and darted below, moving as gently as if her own hundred and five pounds would make a difference to *Glory*'s fifty-four thousand. And of course they did, even though the difference was undetectable, except maybe to Jeremy Barr.

She emptied the bilge first, remembering to count the pump strokes—thirty-seven—and to write the number in the log. Then she scrambled up on deck and unscrewed the big bronze ventilators, replacing them with flat plates. After stowing the ventilators below, she checked the ports and hatches from stem to stern, making sure each was dogged down tightly. Digging in a locker, she unearthed a paint-stiffened tarp and bundled it up on deck. As she spread it over the shattered glass of the skylight, the wind got under one edge of the cloth and whipped it free, sent it coasting over the wave tops to leeward. She looked up at Barr and he shrugged. If *Glory* were rolled and dismasted, nothing would keep her from going right down. Finally, she dug out a pair of the yacht's old life jackets—

cumbersome, kapok-filled vests, smelling strongly of mildew. On deck, she gave one to Emerald and helped Patrick into the other. He grinned at her, and she noticed the yellow bristles on his cheeks. "You need a shave," she said.

"And a shower," he agreed. She was shocked at the weakness of his voice. He was cradling the old rifle, one hand over the bolt mechanism to keep off the spray. "Did your uncle show you how to use this?" he asked.

"Tell me again," she said.

"Nothing to it," he answered. She bent lower: his voice seemed to come and go, like a radio with a dying battery. He raised the rifle, and she saw his arms tremble with the effort. "Sight like this, with your cheek right up here. Put your left hand under here. Brace your elbow on the gunwale." He lowered the weapon; his face was running with sweat. "Take a deep breath, let half of it out, and hold. Then take up the trigger slack and squeeze—don't pull. It'll cock itself for the next round." He paused to catch his breath. "It kicks like a mule, so make sure your face is tight up against the stock, or you'll wind up with a purple cheekbone."

"Okay," she said. "I can do it. You just sit back and relax."

"Yeah," he said. His eyes closed.

"Patrick," said Barr, his eyes still on the staysail luff, "we've gone about five miles and we're maybe a half mile off. How's that?"

"Eight miles to go," Patrick replied, without opening his eyes. "It'd be good if you could get offshore another half mile, too."

Crouching to shield the rifle from the rain and spray, Gillian saw that *Tiamat* was once again closing on them, and that there was something—someone—moving up at her bow, sheltered by the high steel gunwale. Gillian wedged herself against the mizzen, bracing the rifle as firmly as she could. It was amazingly heavy, when you had to try and hold it steady. Over the sights she could see a lump right at *Tiamat*'s bow, silhouetted against the sky. It had no particular shape, and she was wondering if it were a person when a loud *clang!* sounded next to her, followed an instant later by the crash of a gun on the other vessel.

She looked down at a bright, fresh gouge on the starboard winch drum, then up as a booming, electronic voice echoed over the water: "Heave to! Heave to! The next one will be to kill!"

Some part of her was standing to one side, seeing the four of them in *Glory*'s spray-swept cockpit—Barr, tensely focused on the trim of the sails; Emerald, white and sick and defiant; Patrick, drawn and barely conscious. And herself: a thin, tired-looking young woman holding a greasy old rifle more than half as tall as she was. From the same middle distance she watched herself kneel at the after end of the cockpit and bring the weapon up to her shoulder, bracing it as Patrick had told her to do. The indistinct figure at *Tiamat*'s bow wobbled in the sights, and she saw a tiny flash, heard the crash of breaking glass over her shoulder. She glanced around and saw Barr, his concentration momentarily broken, looking down at the wreck of the compass in the binnacle before him, then back up at *Glory*'s sails.

Now or never, she told herself. She steadied the rifle. Deep breath in; half of it out; take up the slack and . . . *crash!*, right in her ear, louder than anything she had ever heard. The recoil slammed the stock into her shoulder hard enough to send her sprawling. As she sat up, she saw something small and dark spin up from *Tiamat*'s bow and, caught by the wind, sail gracefully into the foaming sea. Of the silhouetted figure there was no sign at all.

Patrick was grinning weakly at her. "His hat, not his head. But he'll lie low for a while."

She managed to smile back. "I see what you mean about the kick," she said.

"Next time, wad something up and jam it between the butt and your shoulder," he said.

"Shall I put one into the wheelhouse?" she asked.

"Better not," said Barr, over his shoulder. "You've got five rounds left, remember—and some of them may be duds."

"Barr's right," said Patrick. "We may need them later."

Gillian's single shot had apparently discouraged their pursuers, at least for the moment. Plunging and throwing spray in all directions, *Tiamat* dropped back to her previous position, about two hundred yards behind *Glory* and slightly to seaward, as Barr continued to edge the old yacht further away from the shore. After a long while, he said, "I see a lot of breakers ahead. About a half mile."

"That should be the inlet," Patrick replied, pulling himself up. "Okay, see the land behind? That's the west end of Fire Island—Democrat Point. It overlaps the east end of Jones Beach."

"But the inlet doesn't run straight in, does it?" asked Barr.

"No. The end of the channel's just off the point. It goes from south to north, almost to the Jones Beach shore, then makes a sharp dogleg to the right. It's buoyed, but they'll be hard to see in these seas."

Barr was silent for several minutes, scanning the seas ahead. "Tide's ebbing," he said at last.

Patrick caught his meaning before Gillian did. "Wind's across the current, you mean? That's not good." Leaning on the dodger frame, he shielded his eyes from the flying spray. "I don't know," he said slowly. "I never tried to run the inlet in weather this bad. We ought to wait till the tide turns—till the seas lay down a little."

"We can't," Barr replied at once. "As soon as they"— a nod over his shoulder—"see what we're going to try, they'll move right in on us. Sink us if they have to." He caught Gillian's puzzled look from the corner of his eye. "They'd rather fish for Dennis's loot out here in open water than in the inlet itself, after we capsize."

"It's that risky?" she asked, surprised that her voice was controlled—that she herself was so calm.

"As a seaboat *Glory*'s wonderful," Barr said, moving his hands on the wheel in a gesture very like a caress. "But she's no surfboard . . ."

"Can you do it?" Gillian demanded. "Is there any chance at all?"

"It's a long shot," he replied, shrugging. "The thing is, if I broach her and she rolls, nobody has much chance of making it to shore, life jackets or no."

She looked back at *Tiamat*. Were they closing the gap again? "Speaking as the owner," Gillian said, "I'll take the chance with the boat, and with my own neck. But you're the captain."

"How about it, Patrick?"

"If we pass up the inlet," Patrick said, clearly thinking

as he spoke, "you've got maybe ten-twelve miles of towns along the beach, and then a bare stretch. No more usable inlets till Montauk Point, and they could nail us almost anywhere." He hesitated. "I vote we go. If we're voting."

"Emerald?"

"One question," she replied.

"Make it fast," Barr said. "We have to turn soon or not at all."

"Once we're inside," she said. "Then what? I mean, can they follow us?"

"If *Tiamat*'s skipper has the nerve—yes," Barr replied.

"Visconti's got the nerve," Gillian said.

"But Arrow's driving the boat," Barr said. "Anyway, there's a Coast Guard station in the inlet, plus a lot of small fishing boats. It may only be buying time . . ."

"Okay," Emerald interrupted. "Let's do it."

"Right," said Barr. "Patrick, I have to run that channel diagonally. If we go straight in, the wind'll be on our quarter. I don't think I can hold her that way. It has to be a reach, to keep our speed up."

Patrick's white face had a dubious expression as he surveyed the inlet—breaking seas from side to side, as nearly as Gillian could tell. "It'll be a damn tight squeeze, Skipper," he said. "Out at the channel entrance you're okay, but by the time you're halfway in, you've got to be right in the slot or you'll put her on the bricks."

A huge, steep sea, its crest toppling, lifted *Glory* up and up. Gillian could just make out what seemed to be tiny figures on the shore. "All right." Barr's calm tone cut through the shriek of the wind. "Next one is it. Gillian, ease the mainsheet as I head off—but not too much: I'd rather be a little overtrimmed. Patrick, I want your eyes on the channel. Emerald, can you do one thing?"

"Name it."

"Take the rifle. When I give you the word, let them have the rest of the clip. I just want their heads down for a couple of minutes, so they can't cut us off."

Silently, Emerald reached for the rifle, braced herself against the coaming. "Just keep pulling the trigger, right?"

"Right," said Gillian. On an impulse, she bent forward and kissed the other woman on the cheek, then turned and did the same for Patrick, who looked up at her and grinned feebly.

She was leaning toward Barr when he said, "Stand by the sheet."

"Right." She cast the mainsheet off its cleat and crouched ready, trying not to see the huge waves that mounted, like rank upon jagged rank of steep, moving hills, each one streaked with long lines of foam and crested with white.

A bigger wave than the rest began to bear down on their bow. "This one," Barr said quietly. "Emerald, you ready?"

"Ready."

"Let 'em have it," he called, spinning the wheel. Three quick shots cracked out, nearly in Gillian's ear. The intermittent background thunder of the seas was swallowed up by a hoarse rising roar that reminded her of an approaching train. She forced the sound from her mind, her entire attention on the luff of the mainsail. She felt *Glory* come around, quick and smooth, and eased the sheet swiftly. "Not too much," Barr called. Then: "Patrick, this is my course."

"Good luck. And nothing to port," the other man replied, his voice straining with the effort.

"Nothing to port," Barr echoed. *Glory* was sliding diagonally across the face of the wave, her stern rising as she did so. Gillian, tending the sheet, had a glimpse of Emerald, her jaw set, wrestling with the rifle's bolt and then slamming it open at last. A jammed round leaped free and she slapped the slide closed, raised the rifle, and fired, all in one motion. The flat *whango!* of the last round and the sharp *ting!* of the clip ejecting were simultaneous, as Barr called out, "Hold on!"

It was like a roller coaster, Gillian thought. A roller coaster running wild. At the last moment, Barr straightened *Glory* out to avoid a broach, just as the breaking crest exploded around them and the yacht sagged back into the trough. "Trim!" Barr snapped. "The staysail too!"

She horsed the mainsheet in, hand over hand, as Barr turned *Glory*'s bow up to a reach. Emerald, who had dropped the rifle, was fighting with the staysail sheet.

"That's enough," Barr snapped. "Ready for the next one."

"Ready." He must, Gillian thought, have eyes in the back of his head. Once again, *Glory*'s stern rose to meet the advancing wave, once again the yacht shot forward, her bow wave amidships, high as the spreaders, as she planed down the wave's face. Back at the inlet's mouth—already a quarter of a mile behind them—*Tiamat* had swung up into the wind and seemed to be holding her position.

"More to starboard!" Patrick was calling, his voice urgent. "See the nun and the can up ahead? You've got to be between them, in the slot."

"Here we go," said Barr, his voice taut, and *Glory* roared down the face of another wave. Off to the right, Gillian could see where the inlet doglegged east to reveal the bay entrance. As the wave ahead of them rolled forward, its back streaked with foam, the red nun buoy that marked the channel's turn popped to the surface. It looked to be right up on the beach—would there be enough water for *Glory*, in so close? Wouldn't she be dashed onto the shore?

"Still too far to port!" Patrick's voice was weak but it cut through the noise around them. "You've got to get her over, Skip—see where those seas are breaking, next to the can buoy? That's a shoal there."

Barr was looking astern, his mouth in a thin line. Gillian turned and felt her heart sink. The wave coming toward them from seaward was bigger than any they had yet seen, a deep-chested comber whose steep forward side was a dirty blue-green. Its crest was already toppling as it advanced, bearing down on *Glory* with a deafening roar. Barr's eye caught hers and, unbelievably, he winked. He had the old yacht on a screaming reach, making for the deep-water channel and heading diagonally across the wave's path.

"Hold on!" he called out, his voice almost drowned by the continuous rumble of the breaker and the steady shriek of the wind. They were going to be rolled—Gillian knew it: the breaking crest would catch *Glory*'s uptilted stern first, swing the yacht broadside-to and then crush her. Suddenly the wind on deck was gone as the sea blanketed the sails. Barr spun the wheel so fast the spokes blurred, and *Glory* turned away more quickly than Gillian would have imagined was possible.

Still, the ketch was losing speed, beginning to wallow, as her stern lifted to the oncoming hill of water. "Ease it!"

Barr yelled to her. "Ease the mainsheet!" His voice snapped her back to life, and she let the sheet burn through her hands until, at his signal, she cleated it off. *Glory* was still forging ahead, wind pressing the upper quarter of the mainsail, when her stern began lifting to the breaking crest. Gillian felt a mighty shove as the wave picked up twenty-seven tons of wood and metal and hurled it, like a stone from a slingshot, toward the shore.

It all depended on how well Barr had lined up the boat with the wave, and how well—in the first mad seconds of her rush—he could hold *Glory* on her course. As she plunged forward, her bows went down and down until she was ripping through the green water with the base of her bowsprit, her bow wave a double sheet of white going straight up into the air and whipping back along the deck. If her bow dug in any deeper it would catch, and the whole yacht might pitchpole, end-over-end. Gillian felt as if her heart had stopped, and then she heard Barr say, surely to the boat herself, "All right. Nicely done."

A moment later Gillian saw what Barr had sensed: *Glory*'s bow was lifting, her stern dropping until the rudder could bite and she could be steered again. Over his shoulder, Barr yelled, "Stand by the sheets! Trim them fast when I give the word!"

Of course: the turning buoy was just ahead, and beyond it the shore. Suddenly, as the water deepened, the surging crest lost its force and *Glory* dropped back, no longer riding the wave. "Now!" Barr snapped, and Gillian threw herself on the mainsheet. Behind her, Emerald was pulling, too. *Glory* rounded up as they trimmed in the staysail sheet. The force of the wind laid the big yacht over till her gunwale was level with the sea, but the low sandbar of Democrat Point was enough to break the waves' force. Ahead in the channel a scattering of anchored fishing boats bobbed in the more or less sheltered waters, their occupants waving and yelling and blowing air horns. "Be a while before they see that again," said Barr, grinning at her. Suddenly, the expression was wiped from his face. Following his look, Gillian saw *Tiamat*, poised at the inlet entrance. She glanced back at Barr, who nodded. "He's going to try it."

The thunder of the seas, breaking on the outer and inner bars and on the beach itself, was nearly continuous, under the pulsing shriek of the wind. Nearly half a mile to sea-ward, Visconti's big power yacht teetered in the crest of a breaker and then hurtled toward them. "He'll try and ride it all the way in," said Barr, in Gillian's ear. "Stay on its back, behind the crest."

The huge wave rolled inexorably toward them, with *Tiamat*'s bow right up in the breaking crest. "Too fast, too fast," said Barr, as if to himself. "He'll overrun it." He was right, Gillian saw: The breaking sea slowed for a moment, and *Tiamat* shot forward until half her hull was ahead of the roller. Gillian heard Barr suck in his breath with a hiss, and she half turned. His eyes were fixed, gleaming, on the oncoming yacht. The rain and spray streamed down his lean face, and his lips were blue with the cold. Abruptly, his narrowed eyes widened, and he cried out, "No!"

Tiamat was swinging sideways, ahead of the breaking wave. As Gillian watched, she heeled over and farther over, until her lee gunwale was underwater. The roller burst against her, a sudden tower of wind-driven spray. Still racing diagonally across the wave's path, *Tiamat* shuddered to a halt. As the backwash of the wave receded, Gillian could see the yacht was aground, her bow raised high.

Beside her, Patrick had somehow managed to pull himself up to the seat. "She ran out of the channel," he said. His face was bloodless white under the tan. "Right out of the goddamn channel. Now watch." As if she could have dragged her eyes away. There was a tremendous boil of water under *Tiamat*'s counter. "Full astern," Patrick said.

"Too late," Barr put in. "Here it comes." He spun the wheel and brought *Glory* up into the wind, her sails volleying.

The cresting wave bearing down on *Tiamat* was simply enormous—bigger far, Gillian thought, than the biggest roller *Glory* had ridden. As it felt the shoal, its foaming crest cascaded down ahead, exploding against the helpless vessel in its path. Gillian saw *Tiamat*'s funnel wrenched right off, white water shooting from the lee side bridge windows, a launch ripped from its davits and lost in the surging water.

And then the wave was past. *Tiamat* rolled sluggishly in the backwash, still hard aground forward. In one blow,

she had been transformed from a powerful living vessel
to a waterlogged wreck. On her afterdeck, a huddle of figures wrestled with an oversized metal drum. As Gillian
watched, the drum split apart lengthwise, and a rubbery
bulge appeared—a life raft, inflating itself from a com-
pressed-air bottle.

Gillian rummaged in a cockpit locker and pulled out the
yacht's binoculars. One lens was fogged, but through the
other she could suddenly see faces, real men struggling
and yelling red-faced at one another as they fought to get
the still-expanding raft clear of the rails and over the side.
As she watched, they straightened and turned to face forward. Gillian swung the binoculars, and the figure of Matt
Visconti leaped into view. Blood was streaming down his
face and one arm, and tatters from his suit flapped in the
wind, but the gun in his hand was steady.

"It's him, isn't it," said Barr, at her elbow.

"Yes. What . . ." The picture in the lens leaped, as
another breaker struck *Tiamat* broadside. Visconti stumbled, and his crew were on him. She could not tell what
was happening, but a crew member—Captain Arrow, from
his bulk—pulled free, and then another and another. She
swung the glasses back toward the stern, just in time to
see the empty raft, fully inflated now, snap free of its tether
and come skittering over the waves toward them like a
child's balloon. She saw the big wave towering behind
Tiamat and lowered the field glasses, unwilling to watch.
Barr's face was like stone, but then he winced. When she
forced herself to look back, *Tiamat* was over on her beam
ends, pushed off the bar into deeper water, but awash and
sinking fast. Of the cluster of men who had been on her
deck moments before, not one was visible.

19

SOUTH NORWALK
JUNE 3
TEN-THIRTY A.M.

The car jerked to a halt, and Patrick lifted his hands from his thighs; two damp stains remained on the khaki cloth. Emerald, at the wheel, looked down and laughed. "Am I that bad a driver?" she asked.

"Worse," he said.

"Well, we can't all be Lurlene," she replied, opening the door. "Come on—they're waiting for us."

Painfully, Patrick eased himself out the door and took the cane she handed him. He was supposed to still be on crutches, but he had forced the pace. He could walk—he *would* walk, even if it was only fifty yards across the boat-yard parking lot, to where *Glory* sat alongside the pier. The sun was hot on the top of his head and he felt unsteady on his feet, but it was good to be outdoors again.

"You're damn cheerful, I must say," Patrick gasped, stumping along in her wake. "Gillian said she had some real bad news for us."

Emerald turned. Her eyes were hidden behind the huge sunglasses. "Listen, are you coming or not?"

Gillian, a slight figure in skintight jeans and a sweatshirt, was standing on *Glory*'s gunwale, shielding her eyes with one hand. Slowly, she stepped ashore. "Hello, Em," she said, embracing the taller woman. "How's it going, Patrick? You look a lot better."

But you don't, he thought. "I'm fine. It's good to see you. Where's Barr?"

223

"Down in the bilge. I think he lives there," she replied, trying for a light tone and missing it. "Do you want to have our meeting here on the pier?"

The sun felt as if it was frying his brain. "Maybe not," he said. "I can get down below."

She looked worried. "I guess we should've come to Emerald's," she said. "I didn't know you . . ."

"He's all right," Emerald interrupted. "He's just worn out from corrupting my employees." She grinned at Gillian. "The girls are supposed to be selling it, not giving it away. But they can't keep their hands off him."

Gillian's smile was wan but genuine. "They'd better be careful. He's nothing but skin and bone."

"They're all over him anyway," Emerald replied. "Two at once, sometimes."

"Hey, come on . . ." Patrick began, feeling his cheeks go hot.

Barr's head appeared in the companionway. He looked worn but at peace. "Welcome," he said. "I rigged a bo-sun's chair on a tackle from the boom. I figured you might need an elevator."

Patrick felt a surge of gratitude; he was weaker than he had thought. He allowed the three of them to seat him in the chair and lower him down *Glory*'s companionway. In the saloon, half the floorboards were up; Patrick edged his way behind the big table and sat, letting the weakness wash over him.

"Been digging for treasure?" Emerald asked innocently. She cocked the sunglasses back on her head and put her elbows on the table.

"That's what I have to tell you," Gillian said. She slid in next to Patrick and he stole a glance at her. She looked drained. Not physically, but as if her spirit were nearly snuffed out. He wanted desperately to comfort her, but he had no idea how.

"I'll save you some trouble," Emerald said, into the gathering silence. "You can't sell the radium, right?"

Gillian looked astounded. "How . . . ?"

"You forget," Emerald replied. "I've got contacts everywhere."

"I guess you must," Gillian said. She pulled a folded, crumpled letter from the back pocket of her jeans and straightened it. "Here's the bad word," she said, tossing it to Emerald.

It was an old-fashioned letterhead, Patrick could see, a colored engraving of a building and lots of curlicues around the type. From where he sat, he could read only the company's name: *International Hospital Supply*. There were three long, single-spaced paragraphs below the salutation.

"What it boils down to," Barr said, after a quick look at Gillian, "is that hospitals don't use radium anymore. Neither does anybody else. There's better substances for radiation treatment. Radium is so scarce it still carries a big nominal value—anywhere from five hundred to twenty-six hundred dollars a gram—but nobody'll touch it. Too dangerous to handle."

Emerald looked up from the letter. "This guy says he's willing to send a truck to pick it up, and he won't charge you to haul it away."

Gillian nodded. "I'm going to call him back tomorrow," she said, and took a deep breath. "I'm sorry, Em. I'll pay you back somehow. You, too, Patrick."

"Pay me back for what?" Emerald demanded. "Listen, kiddo, we all gambled on Dennis's nest egg. We took a chance—we lost. End of story."

Nothing, Patrick told himself. All that effort and danger for nothing. Why did he feel so little surprise, so little disappointment? He looked up and saw Barr watching him and smiling. "You're taking the news very well, Patrick. Or did Emerald already break it to you?"

Patrick shook his head. "Hell, I'm just glad to be alive, after hanging out with a bunch of crazies like you. Besides, I got what I came for. Most of it, anyway. And what are you smiling about?"

"Nothing. Us, maybe." Barr chuckled. "You know, if Dennis was here, he'd be laughing his head off."

"He would, too," Emerald agreed. She turned to Gillian, and her smile turned to concern. "Cheer up, kid. I told you you didn't owe us anything."

"Money's the least of it," Gillian said. "You saved my life, Em." She was looking into Emerald's eyes with fierce concentration. "I'll never forget."

For once, Emerald seemed at a loss. "If it comes to lifesaving," she said, "seems to me that Barr gets the prize.

And Patrick saved my bacon, back on that pier. I'd say we're pretty much even." She looked around the table for help, then went on: "What're you going to do now?"

Gillian shrugged helplessly. "I'm not sure—I guess it's back to the sailmaking business: I'm broker than broke. And *Glory* needs so much work . . ."

Emerald snorted. "You don't have to tell me about that. I remember how Dennis used to moan when the boatyard bills came in. A five-bag habit's cheaper any day."

Alarmed by the naked despair on Gillian's face, Patrick blurted, "You're not going to sell her?"

"Not while I'm alive," Gillian replied evenly.

Her words hung in the air, until Emerald demanded, "Why in hell can't *Glory* bring some money *in*, for a change?" She turned to Barr. "Dennis used to talk about chartering her in the Caribbean. Or was that just talk?"

"Oh, it's possible," Barr said. "She'd need a lot of work—beyond repairs, that is. Fix up the sleeping cabins, overhaul the galley, replace the engine . . ." He stopped short, a wry smile twisting his lips. "Gillian and I were discussing it," he explained.

"So I see," said Emerald. "What would it cost?"

"To fit *Glory* out for charter service?" Barr shrugged helplessly. "Maybe twenty thousand."

"Ten," said Gillian quickly. Barr looked at her, his eyebrows shooting up in surprise. "I checked it all out," she went on, ignoring Barr and speaking to Emerald. "Carey & Willard say they'll let us haul her here at cost. And she can stay blocked up till September, for nothing. Well, for auld lang syne, actually. And I know where we can get a reconditioned diesel for three thousand, and a complete, all-electric galley for just the work of cutting it out of a wrecked Hatteras the owner walked away from." She was leaning forward, her eyes shining, her voice vibrating with eagerness. "And Manny Vargas will give me a whole truckload of mahogany planking, half off . . ." She became aware of Barr's sardonic smile, and her voice trailed off into silence.

"Last I heard," he said, "Carey & Willard was billing forty an hour for engine work. Wood joinery—when you can find a shipwright—that's even more."

Gillian shook her head angrily, unable to speak. Patrick, weak as he was, found himself wanting to take a swing at

Barr, when the older man added, "Unless, of course, you could con me into doing the work for free. Which is what you've been counting on."

Gillian's face was scarlet. "I never even . . ."

"I used to manage a boatyard, remember? Free labor's the only way those numbers of yours make sense." Gillian seemed ready to explode, but Barr held up his hand. "Just shut up for once. I've been reading your mind ever since that letter from the radium people came. The funny thing is"—his smile had become gently mocking—"you figured me right. I'd do the work. Hell, I'd even throw in what's left of the money you paid me. Which leaves us short only ninety-nine hundred and change."

Patrick saw Gillian's eyes fill, and Emerald cut in, her voice acerbic. "Ten thousand, is that it?" She had produced a checkbook and, as the other three watched in silent astonishment, she began to write.

"But you said you needed money as much as we did," Gillian finally managed.

"More than you do," Emerald corrected. She looked up, waving the check to dry it. "But then we were talking about real money. This," she let the check float to the table, "this is tips. Go on, Gillian—take it."

"What can I say?" Gillian's voice was unsteady. "Except that I really, truly will pay you back, Em."

"You bet you will," Emerald replied. "You're an investment. Diversification. You've got five years, ten percent interest a year. I'm not a charity."

"You want a second opinion on that?" Gillian said. "Never mind. This calls for a drink, Barr. What've we got?"

He reached back into the locker above the settee and came up with a nearly full bottle of rum. "The usual. But we only seem to have two glasses. You mind drinking out of the bottle, Patrick?"

Before he could answer, Gillian had turned to him. "What about you, Patrick? What're you going to do?"

"Here comes the knuckle ball," said Barr, not quite under his breath.

"Put a sock in it, Barr," Gillian said sweetly. "I'm serious." And to Patrick: "I guess you could go back to working for what's-his-name, with the daughter, once your leg's better."

"I've had enough of her," Patrick replied, as lightly as he could. "Just like I've had enough armies."

"I couldn't pay you anything, of course," Gillian continued, as if he had said something quite different. "Not till we had some money coming in. But it's a good place to convalesce, and healthy outdoor work when you're up to it."

He found himself wanting desperately to believe she meant it, but he heard himself say, "You don't need me. You and Barr can handle *Glory* together."

"Three could do it better," Gillian said.

"Even so . . ." Patrick began, but Barr interrupted, amusement plain in his voice.

"You're not getting it, Patrick. You're part of her master plan. I've lost my skipper's ticket, and she doesn't have one. But you do."

"Only for six passengers," he said. "And only coastal waters."

"Then you'd better put your leg up on a pillow and start studying," said Gillian triumphantly. "You're going to have a high-seas ticket by September, and *Glory*'s going to winter in the Caribbean."

"You do mean it," Patrick said, more to himself than her. "You really do mean it."

"I've got to get back to the store." Emerald's chair rasped back abruptly. Gillian slid out and embraced her. "Stay in touch, kid," Emerald said, and to Barr: "Take care of my investment, you hear?" Her mouth was smiling, but her eyes were bleak. At the foot of the companionway ladder she turned to Patrick, who had hobbled after her. "Good luck, Irish," she said, her voice low. "You're out of your league, you know."

As she vanished up the ladder, Patrick glanced around to see if Gillian had heard. But Barr had a piece of paper spread on the table and was sketching with quick, sure strokes, while Gillian watched him, her heart in her eyes.

ABOUT THE AUTHOR

TONY GIBBS is Wolcott Gibbs, Jr., son of the famous *New Yorker* writer, Wolcott Gibbs. He himself has written extensively for *The New Yorker*, has covered the Americas cup three times, was editor of *Yachting* magazine and is the author of ten nonfiction books about boating. He lives in Santa Barbara, California with his wife, Elaine St. James, and a sixteen-foot pulling boat which he takes to sea whenever he can.